Stuart Jones is a championship-winning race driver and a qualified international race driver coach. Whilst still at school, he was singled out for his writing. A number of his young scribblings found writing competition success. All assumed that his writing would continue after he left school. At 52 years of age, he picked up the pen again. A life of traveling the world, driving racecar exotica, and mixing with the fascinating people that populate the glamorous motorsport industry has provided him with fertile material that demanded that he should recommence his long-dormant writing.

To my dad for creating my dreams and to my mom for giving me the skills to make those dreams come true.

Stuart Jones

THE BROKEN TRUST

STIRLING SPEED, RETIRED RACING DRIVER

AUSTIN MACAULEY PUBLISHERS™

LONDON • CAMBRIDGE • NEW YORK • SHARJAH

Ordering Information:
Quantity sales: special discounts are available on quantity purchases by corporations, associations, and others. For details, contact the publisher at the address below.

Publisher's Cataloging-in-Publication data
Jones, Stuart
The Broken Trust: Stirling Speed, Retired Racing Driver

ISBN 9781641828000 (Paperback)
ISBN 9781641828017 (Hardback)
ISBN 9781641828024 (Kindle e-book)
ISBN 9781645366133 (ePub e-book)

Library of Congress Control Number: 2019935956

The main category of the book — Fiction / Crime

www.austinmacauley.com/us

First Published (2019)
Austin Macauley Publishers LLC
40 Wall Street, 28th Floor
New York, NY 10005
USA

mail-usa@austinmacauley.com
+1 (646) 5125767

To Lisa, my wife, for helping me to keep all the plates spinning and to Josh, my son, for always believing in me.

Prologue

The small but high revving engine noise spiked as the overworked rear tires broke traction for a split second; Roger Speed was starting to push hard. Despite the promise to his wife, Suzanne, that he would be taking it easy on the test, Roger knew that this was his chance to prove that he had what it took to rise to the very top of professional motorsport. For too long he had been known as a club racer, a journey man. Now, with the chance to test for a top team in a prototype Formula 3 car in front of the team owner, Lawrence Troutman, Roger had his chance, and he was going to grasp it with both hands.

Lawrence Troutman stood on the outside banking of the long, difficult climbing right-hander, aptly named 'school' corner, his back to the chopping sea, facing the small but tricky Anglesey race circuit as one of his own prototype Formula Three cars buzzed around the circuit. The lively F3 car appeared to carry a little too much speed into a combination corner that started with 'Douglas In' the understeering car resulting in a poor entry position for the important exit of the corner, 'Douglas Out.' Roger cursed his mistake and knew that he would now be delayed getting the power on through the mount view kink and out onto the fast downhill start / finish straight.

Roger gave himself a talking-to as he hurled down the straight, quickly responding to the requests from the engine for more gears.

"Come on, Roger, you can do better than this. Come on, boy, slower in, faster out. Come on, Roger, get a grip."

The School corner rushed up without delay. The lone figure of Mr. Troutman clearly defined against the blue sky backdrop on top of the banking that rimmed the high speed, high grip corner.

Roger knew the start of the corner was the difficult bit, as the neutral camber offered no assistance to the wayward cornering racecar. Roger breezed across the brake pedal whilst blipping the throttle pedal at the same time to allow for a quick change from 5th gear to 4th. Happy that the car was settling, Roger loaded the throttle pedal up before the car could get too comfortable. The normally aspirated F3 Novamotor engine instantly responded. The car seemed to almost hunker down as the weight transfer and modicum of down force pressed the small F3-sized slick tires hard into the polished tarmac. Roger knew he had judged it just right. Mr. Troutman was witnessing one of his F3 cars on the limit.

The left front suspension failure was felt through the steering wheel before Roger actually saw, with his widening eyes, his left front wheel slam back into the aluminum tub he sat in. With a quarter of its grip gone, the F3 car got its way and abandoned the direction of the corner, heading straight for the banking at 120 mph. Roger tried to minimize the angle of impact, but his toolbox was empty. He let go of his steering wheel, crossed his arms, and gripped his safety harness. The huge impact had the mercy to take away Rogers consciousness so as to spare him the horror of the inferno as his fuel tank irrupted!

Chapter 1

Peter Smith felt out of proportion in the huge dimensions of the room in which he waited, almost like an 'OO' gauge character on a model railway that had mistakenly been placed on a much larger 'O' gauge model railway. A single immaculate plush, and, no doubt, heavy, gold-armed, purple-cushioned chair had been placed within the palatial waiting room on which Peter Smith now perched and awaited to be summoned. The pure white floor-to-ceiling oversized double doors swung open together, controlled by the opening arms of an immaculate usher. No words were spoken, but permission to enter was communicated by the standing position of the usher at the edge of the open door.

"Sir."

"Thank you for coming, Peter. Please sit. You have had time to study the file?"

Peter Smith sat down at the ornate, old leather-clad desk and placed the file in question on the aged leather.

"Yes, sir, I have."

"And you agree this Troutman chap needs our treatment?"

"Yes, sir, indeed. Lawrence Troutman has become…"

"One of our cases, Peter. He is a powerful public figure. You have a plan?

Peter Smith reached into his file and removed and slid across an A4-sized photo of a face, knowing his boss would instantly recognize that face. A raised eyebrow was the only giveaway.

"Stirling Speed, he once attempted to show me how to drive my Aston around Brands Hatch. Since his sudden retirement, he seems to have dropped completely out of the limelight, your reasoning?"

"Mr. Speed, or Stirling, as he prefers to be called, has a connection with Troutman, and not the obvious one." Peter

Smith hesitated, knowing his audience time was limited and information had to be kept concise.

"His uncle, Roger Speed, was killed in a race car a number of years ago when Stirling was still a child, and he was killed in one of Troutman's race cars. Our investigations show that Stirling has been asking questions about the accident for quite some time, and we strongly feel, sir, that Troutman was involved in Stirling's Monza accident. We strongly feel that Troutman wants Stirling dispatched. Stirling Speed is the perfect bait to draw Troutman out."

"Be sure to keep this clean, Peter. If we cannot cleanly bring Troutman down, then we need to let him go. We can never compromise our arrangement, Peter."

"I know, sir, Stirling's involvement would be critical. If we cannot get him involved, then we will have to postpone any action against Troutman."

As the large doors closed behind him, Peter Smith knew this was going to be a difficult case, and a sense of guilt pricked from deep inside. By all accounts, Stirling Speed was happily retired. Peter Smith knew that he was about to shatter that happy retirement.

Chapter 2

The bee's striking colors seemed fluorescent in the bright English sunlight. The permanent knowledge that a bee is black and yellow seemed somehow distant now with the actual visualization of the vibrant colors of this industrious insect as it purposely visited each crisp, scented flower. To be lost in the moment, just watching, listening, and feeling the surroundings. Noticing that a bee is indeed black and yellow, instead of being told that was the case, were moments that Stirling never now took for granted. Taking an inquisitive interest in all things ensured that each moment of each day made life so much richer.

Relaxing on a beautiful summer afternoon, tucked away in the corner of the beer garden of his favorite country pub, situated in an idyllic country village, five minutes' walk from his cottage, was the perfect Sunday afternoon for Stirling. The bee continued on its pollinating mission as its observer, Stirling Speed, retired race driver, took another considered sip of his pint and savored the chestnut undertones that complemented the creaminess of his chosen ale for today.

For so many years, from such a young age, Stirling knew only of things that fell within his focus. A focus so intense that, at times, Stirling would appear hard, ignorant, arrogant, with no knowledge of life that surrounded him, no interest in the day-to-day humdrum. For so many years, Stirling's tunnel vision focused on his driving, focused on one day becoming a world champion racing driver, a quest that was initiated by his, now long-gone, innocent uncle.

Stirling's uncle raced cars—not professionally, but for fun. Although Stirling was never taken to any race meetings, as a child of ten years old, his uncle could hold Stirling's avid attention by explaining why a racecar would backfire and sometimes belch flames out of its rourty exhaust as its driver wrestled the errant racecar on the brakes into a corner. Stirling never really understood what his uncle was saying but loved being able to repeat the explanation to his beaming dad and falsely smiling mother. What really set the seed, the itch that had to be scratched, the quest that finally cost so much was the Friday night 'pint'. Every Friday night Dad and his brother Roger would go out for a pint together, Roger and his apparently beautiful wife Suzanne, staying over to be willing recipients of a hearty Saturday morning breakfast from Mum. Whilst Dad and Roger visited the local public house Stirling was allowed to sit in Rogers's sports car and dream. The day dreaming Friday evenings sat in the black leather clad interior of a fiery red Triumph TR4A set the obsession in place. Holding onto the hard, cold, Moto Lita wood steering wheel, engulfed in the scent of old car leather, bolstered with a hint of petrol no doubt from leaky twin SU carburetor's, Stirling would dream of taking the checkered flag.

Then suddenly, Roger never came anymore; the dream machine that he would rumble up the road never came anymore. Roger was dead, and Suzanne, with her long auburn hair, just disappeared from our lives. In later years, Stirling was informed, 'Killed in one of those wrong-place-wrong-time accidents on a race circuit', and various vague stories surrounded Suzanne's absence Mum had all race pictures removed, all race talk banned. Friday night dreams were to remain dreams, but dreams can become fuel for reality.

"Can I get you anything else Mr. Speed?"

"Stirling please, I know both names sound ridiculous but just Stirling and no thank you, just the bill as they say."

The friendly and respectful waiter brought Stirling back into the now, and a very nice now it was, Stirling thought. From the day he had suddenly walked away from the transparent world of Formula One, he had managed to satisfy his driving addiction by testing racecars and coaching drivers whilst still keeping out of the limelight, even though his successes on the racetrack had made him a world-famous commodity.

Stirling looked across towards the door of the country pub and considered going to settle his bill inside, but his gaze halted at the car park. There it was again, a quite distinctive off-white

Alpha Romeo GTA Junior with French plates. Stirling first noticed it when it was parked in the lower paddock in the Spa-Francorchamps circuit in Belgium. Stirling had been there testing brake duct designs for Bentley. The Alpha, maybe from the 1969 era, looked at home in the paddock, and Stirling had thought what a good picture it would have made.

On the way back from the circuit to home a stop off in Brussels was in the diary. A team was evaluating two drivers, one young, inexperienced. One older, experienced, but hard work to manage. They wanted Stirling's wise input. Walking out from a top drive at the peak of your career does mean that your shelf life is longer. The perception is that you are still as fast, still as keen, still know what you are talking about. In reality, Stirling always felt a slight fraud as they threw money at him to consult. As Stirling walked out of the unofficial meeting, which was held at a humble but privately hired pizza restaurant not far from the Charlemagne building, Stirling's eyes had fallen onto the pretty little Alfa again.

And now, here he was, deep in the English Cheshire countryside, at a pub chosen for its quietness, and there sat the very same Alfa, cooling its heals.

"Thanks, you take cash, I presume? And do keep the change."

"Yes, and thank you, M... errm, Mr. Stirling."

"Just Stirling. The white Alpha in the car park with the French plates, you didn't happen to see who was driving it?"

"No, sorry, I didn't. I'll just get your change."

Realizing the mistake he had made, the waiter hesitated to be bailed out.

"No, please, keep the change."

Stirling was used to people getting flustered around him. It wasn't every day that you served a pint and Ploughman's lunch to an ex-Formula One triple world champion!

Entering the pub and heading for the loo, Stirling tried to seem interested in the pub's décor whilst trying to spot who looked like a white Alfa Romeo driver. A difficult task whilst trying not to be obvious, and just calling everyone to attention and popping the question, 'Excuse me, but could I ask who drives the Alfa?' would be a tad too obvious!

Chapter 3

It had been a long but steady drive. The '69 Alfa had, as always, purred along, but the Alfa's unreliability stigma always lurked in the background when covering miles away from home.

The research had proved right. Pulling outside the gates of Drayton House, the slender, distinctive battleship-gray bonnet of a shapely E type could just be seen resting on the gravel drive, confirming this was indeed the residence of one Stirling Speed.

Now, sitting in the local pub, it was time to plan the next move. It was going to be difficult, and the timing needed to be right, as it was not a moment to look forward to. Unexpectedly seeing Stirling Speed actually walk into the pub, looking around at the décor, had caused a quickening of the pulse. To see him so close, in the flesh, so to speak, not from a distance, not from a place of concealment. Maybe five-feet-nine, dark hair now starting to lose some of its blackness, tailored jeans, crisp white casual shirt, structured, handcrafted shoes, and a man who clearly looked after himself, Stirling Speed certainly had a presence that was hard to define. Maybe a presence that could only be achieved by reaching the very top of one's chosen profession, then choosing to walk away from it.

At one point, this followed man looked right across, but then his eyes settled on the vague painting behind and above of some long-lost farming scene of a bygone era. It was then pure luck that Stirling was stopped on his way out and invited to stay for a drink with a well-wisher not wanting to be too forward but still keen to be associated with Stirling's presence.

Stirling politely replied, "Thank you for the offer, but I need to still get some gear sorted out and then grab an early night. I have an early call tomorrow, as I have to be in Manchester City Centre for a breakfast meeting, which means a 6:30 start, then it is off to Monte Carlo for the Grand Prix."

The well-wisher made the obligatory answer, "It's a tough life, Stirling."

Who then replied with the standard follow on, "I know. But, hey, someone has to do it."

At that, Stirling bid a pleasant farewell and made his way out of the pub door. So there it was, a plan had been formed. Up early, wait, and then follow Stirling Speed into the city. Just maybe the right situation would develop for the confrontation, and then there would be no turning back!

Chapter 4

Waiting for his alarm to go off, Stirling was well-rested and ready for his strange breakfast meeting. A workout in his exquisitely restored Victorian-styled gym, a light meal, a good read, and then melting into freshly laundered, white linen sheets had ensured a good night's sleep.

His housekeeper had a relentless fine eye for detail yet managed to go about her housework without any fuss or inconvenience to Stirling. He ensured she wanted for nothing, and there was a fierce loyalty between them, but Stirling still got pangs of guilt for being the only beneficiary of her cosseting.

Savoring the start of a new day, he smiled to himself. A sharp shower awoke all the extremities up and prepared his face for a clean, close shave. A hot towel opened his pores, and a good lather, agitated with his solid silver badger hair shaving brush, prepped the overnight growth for obliteration. Stirling had various shaving implements, and today, he chose a twin-edged, reassuringly heavy matching silver razor that he carefully, almost surgically, maneuvered around the contours of his face. Removing a fluffy white towel from the neatly stacked pile, Stirling looked around 'his' bathroom. It was 'his' bath room, as he had gone to such lengths to research and restore the derelict Drayton House and had enjoyed the whole project that he had immersed himself in.

Looking across and out of his arched, plain glass bathroom window, which stretched to the floor, he could see his rolling meadow, edged by a tall, impenetrable hedge, hiding a single-track lane. A plain glass that allowed Stirling to look out but also allowed any one to look in! Stirling's days of the paparazzi were long over. If anyone did choose to trespass, then what would they see? Maybe someone would appreciate that he worked hard to keep his body sharp. Maybe they would see the well-documented scars of his Monza crash? Either ways, Stirling liked the view and did not want it hiding away for the sake of a peeping tom!

As Stirling dried himself off, another early riser in a white Alfa waited patiently in the single-track lane, its occupant unaware of the view into Stirling's private world just over the other side of the thick, impenetrable hedge.

Chapter 5

"Mr. what was it again?" Lawrence Troutman, head of the WMSO, World Motor Sport Organization, had not forgotten the name, but he wanted this little man to fully realize that he bore no importance in his multibillion-pound world. He was a mere irritant, to be flicked away.

"Smith, plain, simple Mr. Smith. Mr. Peter Smith, actually, from Special Investigations. I am part of a team that looks for answers when questions have been asked. We operate…"

"I asked for your name, not your life story. Yes, I can confirm that I have been involved with the prototype racecars that you have stated. And, yes, it is a sad fact that there have been some unforeseen circumstances that have led to failures, resulting in fatal crashes. Motorsport can be so cruel." Troutman looked towards the floor and then out of his vast office window, into the skies of London. Is that not what anyone would do whilst contemplating tragic crashes?

Peter Smith could play the game as well, and so he paused to look at his notes, giving weight to his next statement.

"You bankrolled the development of these prototypes and supplied the fuel tanks for them, manufactured at one of your subsidiaries. And the 'some circumstances' actually amount to five sets of circumstances that have resulted in five drivers losing their lives."

"My world is a tough world, not like yours, Mr. Smith. You make a mistake and you press delete on your Apple laptop and start again. In the world of motorsport, risks are always risks. You make a mistake, and you pay the ultimate price. As ugly as that might seem to you, Mr. Smith, it is a fact of life. These guys chose to get into their cars, they were not forced at gunpoint. They died doing what they loved. I salute them for…"

It was Peter Smith who interrupted this time, carefully placing five faces captured in photographs in front of Troutman. "Steve Fields, Tony Flune, Mario Gostino, Louise Hopper, and Roger Speed. Do you remember them, Mr. Troutman? Do you remember their thinly concealed joy when you offered them a fully sponsored drive in one of your prototypes? In fact, Louise Hopper was just pregnant, did you know that?"

"Why should I know that? I do remember, I see all their faces and I grieve for them, and that is why I spent time with their wives and girlfriends. That is why I financially looked after them after the tragic events."

This time, Troutman looked right into the eyes of Smith. "Your point, Mr. Smith, for opening up these painful wounds?"

"Questions have been asked, Mr. Troutman. I and my organization find answers no matter who is involved in finding those answers. We are usually called in when money is doing a lot of talking, or should I say when money is stopping a lot of talking."

"I have invested in many race cars over the years that did not kill anyone!"

"But you invested in five that all had suspension failures and their fuels tanks exploded on impact. In each case, you were to become very close to the drivers' wives and girlfriends after the tragic events. With Louise Hopper, you had taken personal interest in her race career."

"I cannot be held responsible for the angle a race car hits a barrier or bank! And yes, I did offer support after the tragedies. Louise, for a while, fooled me that she was talented, but…"

Peter Smith decided to score another point and interrupted Troutman. "Of course, Mr. Troutman you are right, I am sorry to have, well, should we say, bothered you."

Peter Smith had rattled the most powerful man in world motorsport, probably the most powerful man in world sport. Peter Smith had achieved his goal; he had confirmed to himself that the Troutman investigation needed to go up another gear.

Lawrence Troutman's back now faced Peter Smith.

"Mr. Troutman, one more question?" Without turning around, Troutman replied,

"Yes, young Peter?" a weak attempt to regain the high ground and score a point back.

"Louise Hopper, you never supported her boyfriend after the accident, yet you spent a lot of time helping Louise before the accident…"

"That sounds like a statement, Mr. Smith, not a question."

"Okay, Mr. Troutman, I do have one more question left. Do you know what happened to Roger Speed's wife after the accident? She seems to have just disappeared. When I say disappeared, I mean her whole identity disappeared. She is listed as a missing person, simply gone. Gone after, investigations show, receiving a lot of your 'personal' help after the tragic accident of her husband. Can you be of any help with this matter, Mr. Troutman?"

Troutman rounded on Peter Smith and leaned forward on his vast leather-clad desk with clenched knuckles supporting him.

"I will take that as a rhetorical question. Now, if you do not mind, I have some important matters to attend to, and I can assure you, Mr. Peter Smith that you are not an important matter."

As Peter Smith left Lawrence Troutman's office, he was confident that, at some point in the future, he would become Troutman's most important matter!

Chapter 6

Stirling, when fully focused, had the ability to see and hear everything in slow motion, so he could absorb and assimilate every detail. This was a state Stirling was used to, and he would be at this heightened state of awareness whenever he was strapped into a racecar. As he became more experienced, he realized that he was able to reduce his inefficient emotions whilst at the same time increasing his awareness. When asked during interviews where his speed and success came from, Stirling often tried, perhaps naively, to describe this ability that he seemed not to have cultivated but inherited.

"By the time I strap into a race car, it is as though this tight ball of pressure, brought on by the world of top level sport, has deflated. My emotions have flat lined, so as I can pool all my energy, observation, and concentration to assimilate the information that is bombarding my body via all my senses. At 170 mph, I can see the tire movement of the car in front, hear the split-second hesitation as the driver delays addressing the throttle pedal as he waits for the his tires to find the elusive grip. I recognize faces in the crowd, spot disturbances in the crowd."

Often, interviewers would smile and quickly jump to their next scripted question, not really getting the state of mind and alertness that Stirling had just tried to explain. In day-to-day life, Stirling seemed to see things more intently, more clearly than many around him. Small details seemed bigger to him.

As Stirling guided the long, bulging bonnet of his E-Type along the damp country lanes, it was not long before a rearward glance in the chrome-rimmed mirrors picked up yellowish-white headlights, following at a distance. Headlights of another era, possibly the same era as his E-Type, and certainly not the crisp white or even glowing blue-white lights of the vehicles that presently graced the roads in their millions!

Allowing his hungry Jaguar to breath in more of its addictive fuel air mixture, Stirling pressed the accelerator. The E-Type leaped forward, eagerly relishing the unraveling early morning empty roads. The yellow, aging headlamps initially diminished but then soon regained their following distance. Stirling knew this mysterious little Alfa was clinging onto his Jaguar's tail. A race driver needs to be able to focus. The persistent Alfa was a concern. But for now, the concern needed to be shelved; Stirling needed to focus on his imminent meeting.

The call Stirling had received made it clear that the meeting was of great importance and the accepting invitation to attend, although politely dressed up, was obligatory. No further details could be provided, other than the necessary location and time. When Stirling had asked who he should look out for, the very polite lady chuckled respectfully.

"Don't worry, Mr. Speed, our contact will recognize you!"

Now seated in the grand foyer of the Midland Hotel, Manchester, Stirling sipped and savored the aroma and smoky tones of the rich coffee he'd ordered. An approaching man caught Stirling's attention.

"Mr. Speed, may I first thank you for being so trusting and attending this meeting. I thought it less threatening if you came to me rather than I approaching you on your territory, so to speak. My name is Mr. Smith, Mr. Peter Smith, from Special Investigations, and we need your help!"

Stirling's senses were on full alert, this meeting was definitely different to all the other meetings he'd had—and as a professional race driver, he'd had many! Stirling carefully observed this plain little man as he politely and patiently answered the attentive waitress' enquiries.

"No, thank you, no specialist teas for me, no lemon. Just plain tea, thank you."

He was dressed in a gray suit, a white shirt with faint gray pinstripes, and a gray tie. Clearly all well-made, clearly immaculate, but just gray! Peter Smith was not a man you would spot in a crowd; he would be, without doubt, just part of the crowd. Yet, this man had a self confidence that put one slightly on edge, like a great white shark cruising through the waters, minding its own business, but all the time you are aware that you do not want to attract its attention. Stirling decided that it was

24

time to show this shark who was boss, having wasted many an hour with potential sponsors who offered the earth and liked the glamor of Formula One but lacked the means to be part of it.

"Mr. Smith, you should know that, since retiring, I lead a very private and fulfilled life. I appreciate all that has come my way, but I am not interested in getting involved in any investments, promotions, comebacks, and I am not interested in anyone who wastes my time. So, unless you have some life or death situation, I am afraid you might fall into one of those categories."

Peter Smith allowed a pregnant pause to show respect for what Stirling had said and a pause that also said, 'Are you finished, well then I'll begin!'

"We know that you like to be called Stirling and not Mr. Speed, so if I may, Stirling. I am glad that you have brought up the subject."

Stirling wondered which subject, and Peter Smith read it straight away. "The subject of life and death!" Peter Smith continued, "In my job, sadly, I have to deal with life and death more than I would like to. And before you ask, no, I am not a doctor."

Stirling looked on blankly. "Sorry, a failed, mistimed little joke. Let me take you back in time. Your Monza testing crash, no doubt, is still clear in your mind, despite the period of time since it happened."

The resulting scars and constant dull ache from Stirling's extensively repaired shoulder ensured that it was always fresh in his mind.

"Can you tell me what happened?" Peter Smith put his hand up apologetically with a facial expression that clearly said, 'Just bear with me.'

He continued, "I know it is well-documented, but please, what happened?"

Stirling somehow knew this was a picture that he had to appreciate for him to take onboard what Peter Smith was about to say and so patiently relayed the story of his bone shattering crash.

"The team had asked me to try some new reactive suspension parts that had been designed by a third-party design company. On the sixth lap, I exited the Parabolica with the car fully loaded up and responding well. Telemetry showed that we hit 186mph on the approach to the first Variante Del Rettifilo chicane. I braked 1 meter later than usual for the 60 mph chicane, and as a result, entered the chicane 5 mph quicker. As usual, I took some of the right curb, but then the car slid mid-chicane, resulting in me hitting the left outer curb as I exited the chicane. I accelerated hard, pulling through all the gears, and entered the Curve a Grande flat, in fifth, at a 152 mph, slightly slower than normal, as I'd botched the exit of the chicane."

"Then, it happened, a front pull rod on the left suspension totally failed. I somehow managed to lessen the angle of impact. The barrier impact was hard, but not as bad as it could have been. Unfortunately, my teammate, Jaap, came around the corner unsighted and hit me square on, at 158 mph. The car was split open and I was thrown out, still attached to my seat. My shoulder had taken the worst of the impact. The failure was put down to damage that I had done on the exit of the chicane."

"I woke up two weeks later, feeling quite content with life in my hospital room and a shoulder that had extensive scaffolding protruding out of it and two broken legs. It took another week for me to remember who I was and that I had not always lived in a hospital; that I once had a complete and functioning shoulder."

"Jaap's burns healed to the point that he is now quite proud of them, and I went on to stage a crazy, obsessive comeback and win another championship." Stirling then seemed lost in space for the moment.

Peter Smith was genuine in his sympathy,

"It was a terrible thing that happened, to all, you seemed to have the Midas touch, then life hits you hard. I am so sorry!"

"Stirling I must warn you that, with what I am going to tell you, your life is going to get more complicated than you could ever imagine. But if you value justice, then you will come on this journey with me. Can we focus on how Jaap received his burns?"

Stirling knew that his life was about change forever. But somehow, he felt fine with that. Stirling, somehow, felt that all he had done up until now had been leading up to this point, and he felt comfortable, even slightly excited, about it. Yet, he had no idea what this seemingly boring gray man who had just appeared in his life was going to say.

Stirling continued, "He was really unlucky, but it was lucky for me. This is only what I have been told, because after being ejected out of my ex race car and hitting the tarmac—still in my seat—I was not feeling totally chipper, and so my body decided the best course of action would be to pop into a coma for two weeks. Jaap's car was not too badly damaged, and he leapt out of the car practically before it had stopped. He sprinted over to me and as he got between me and the remains of my car, it exploded. He took the full force of it but he shielded me!"

Mr. Smith paused before speaking; he clearly did not want to overload Stirling but let him absorb the whole impact of where he was going. "Are you okay, Stirling, you don't mind talking about it?"

Admittedly, Stirling had gotten fed up of the repeated, same questions during his comeback. Everyone asked about the accident whereas Stirling really wanted to talk about his most recent results and car development. As for the 'traumatic effect', Stirling said, "I watched and read about the accident, like everyone else. 'Stirling Speed had been involved in a career-threatening accident'. I have no memory of it. The last thing I remember was having an early morning espresso and fruit salad breakfast sat on the hotel's terrace, overlooking the slowly waking village square. I then left for the circuit. In fact, one of the first things that came back to me after I woke from my two week 'lie in' was the memory of a wonderful smell wafting from a nearby bakery in that square that morning. That is my only memory. So, despite the press' obsession of wondering if I could beat the accident demons in my head, I am afraid to say that I never had any."

Stirling realized that Mr. Smith could have coped with a simple yes or no answer and he had probably rambled on too much.

"So, basically, yes, I am okay."

"You remember, Stirling, that the cars were confiscated by the WMSO, the World Motor Sport Organization?"

"Yes, I remember, standard procedure really. Italian law being as it is, the WMSO wanted to protect the team from any litigation for the accident, something that drivers and teams had fallen foul off in the past. As you may know, for many years, both the double world champion Jim Clark and prolific car builder Colin Chapman had to avoid the long designer-clad arm of Italian law after serious accidents in the theater of speed, Monza."

"What you might not know, Stirling, is that when the cars were eventually returned to the team with a full report of the accident, the car you were driving was missing certain crucial parts,"

Stirling had not known this. A race driver staging a 'comeback' concentrated on what was in front of him, not on the past. He had naturally accepted that he had made a small mistake entering the Variante Del Rettifilo chicane and paid the price, time to move on. His focus was then switched onto convincing himself that contrary to what the doctors were telling him and all the press was certain of, his demolished shoulder would one day find the strength and movement to guide a Formula One racecar again.

For the next twelve months, every moment, awake or asleep, was utilized towards achieving that goal. Days would be full of excruciating pain as Stirling called again and again for medical procedures and physio routines to be recommenced. Nights would be spent in high oxygen chambers, providing his fractured body with the perfect environment for it to repair itself. All around, observers wondered how Stirling was able to summon this superhuman determination.

For Stirling, he knew how to make things happen. His tunnel vision narrowed, and he focused on only what was needed to achieve his goal. During his immobile days, imprisoned in his hospital bed, he had wondered how the mistake he had made at Monza had been caused. Because, for the first time during his pilgrimage to be the best driver ever, he'd allowed his mind to wander onto another subject; he had lost focus. He had been, for the first time, looking back, casually at first, then more intensely. Not back at his life's journey, but that of his TR4-owning uncle, the unknowing motivator behind the future triple world Formula One champion, Stirling Speed. Roger Speed had perished in a violent, fiery racing accident, a wrong-place-wrong-time accident, so Stirling had often been told. Then, there was the mystery of the disappearance of his much younger and beautiful wife.

He had not set out to look back; it had started with his ever-efficient PA. Loopy Lisa, he always joked. But Loopy Lisa ensured that Stirling could focus, her organizational skills and ability to say 'no' ensured that Stirling was always where he needed to be, when he needed to be, and always with what he would be needing.

"Stirling, we will pick you up via helicopter at 9.00 am from Drayton House, so please have some clothes on if you happen to be in your bathroom when we land in your meadow."

"Loopy, you know that you dream of that day happening. Maybe one day, for a treat,"

"Mr. Speed," knowing the irritation this caused Stirling, "if that day does ever arrive, please ensure that I haven't eaten first. I do hate it when something hideous puts me off my breakfast!"

Helicopters were an evil necessity for Stirling's demanding diary, and although the trip over Snowdonia mountains to the little-known but excellent race circuit on the Isle of Anglesey had been eased by the stunning views, he still disliked the noise and the feeling that he was suspended inside of a brick. The crowds that had gathered to catch a glimpse of the current world champion and his sponsors pleased Stirling. Maybe more would take notice of this gem of a circuit. The fact that that they had named a section of the track after his late uncle was the only excuse Stirling needed for him to get Loopy to make time for this in his diary. Lisa then took on the task of convincing his sponsors that this would be good time spent!

Stirling took to the circuit in the appropriate manufacturer's car, and after exploring its limits of adhesion to the delights of the crowd but dismay of his green-faced press passengers he pulled up on Speed Rise for the photo call. It was at this point, as he smiled and was being angled this way and that with various dignitaries that his focus widened. The newly named Speed Rise was actually all that remained of the old circuit before its massive redevelopment.

It was at this point, on what would have been School corner, where his uncle had perished. He understood that his uncle, an occasional club racer, had been remembered because of his links with Stirling, but suddenly a question loomed in front of Stirling, a question that had never appeared before. Why was a mediocre club driver, past the age of motorsport career thoughts, no serious money or sponsorship, no major successes would be driving a state-of-the-art Formula Three car, provided by a young, ambitious man who was to become head of the WMSO, a man who was said to be the most powerful man in world sport? Why had a young Lawrence Troutman provided the car and test for a man whose only fame was to come many years after his death? Stirling felt an unease deep inside him and knew that he needed to look further into this.

And look into it he did. Numerous requests to speak with Mr. Troutman about the past incident had clearly been ignored. Sadly, Stirling could no longer ask his late father, and his mother quite rightly chose to blank out that dark period and so had little information to provide. Even trying to find out what had happened to the crashed car ended in numerous dead ends. Stirling had employed a private investigator to find out what had happened to Suzanne Speed. The investigator had been helpful and keen to continue the investigations, at first. Until one day, sending an email to Stirling saying politely but with no explanation that he was dropping the investigation. Stirling received no invoice for his services.

Stirling had spent a week staying near the circuit, spending time asking questions. The world's press, as usual, was getting the wrong end of the stick and putting out stories that two time world champion Stirling Speed was about to buy the Anglesey race circuit in memory of his late uncle! Although Stirling could not put any reasoning behind it, he knew that he needed to find out why his uncle had ended up in that race car, on that day, on that race track. Stirling knew how to get results—focus! Stirling would focus until he got the answers that satisfied him.

Stirling paused again to allow for the returned waiter to fuss. "For you, sir."

"I think another tea," Peter Smith said.

"And for Mr. Speed?" the waiter clearly showing signs that he was pleased with himself for recognizing the ex-world champion.

"Just Stirling, please. A lemon and ginger tea would be perfect, thank you."

"Before your…" Peter Smith seemed to hesitate as though struggling to form the word, "…accident, at Monza, you had started to ask many questions about why your uncle was driving that car on that fateful day."

"How do you know that?" Stirling was definitely starting to feel a slight sense of irritation.

"We were contacted by a…" Again, Peter Smith appeared to be choosing his words carefully, "…an interested party that was worried for your safety when you started to make enquiries. The interested party brought to our attention that your uncle's accident had three aspects of it that linked it to four other fatal accidents."

"Okay, you have my attention. Please, Mr. Smith, less of the hesitations."

"Steve Fields, Tony Flune, Mario Gostino, Louise Hopper, and Roger Speed all, sadly, lost their lives testing race cars."

"Many drivers have piled in whilst testing, Mr. Smith!"

"With respect, Stirling, I will stop my hesitations if you stop your interruptions!" A slight smile crept across the serious conversation.

Peter Smith continued, "All crashed fatally whilst testing race cars, but the way they crashed and perished is the first link, they all had suspension failures and all died when their cars then exploded!"

Peter Smith stared at Stirling and unapologetically hesitated. Stirling instantly picked up on the reason for the genuine hesitation.

"So, my Monza shunt was sort of similar test, suspension failure, explosion… But I'm still here to listen to you! Okay, coincidence, I think, you said there were three links."

"Four of the five cars were confiscated for investigation. When the cars were returned, they all had the same parts missing, the failed suspension part and the fuel tanks!"

Stirling knew what was coming, "And I presume the same parts were missing from the car I demolished."

Peter Smith did not need to answer that and continued, "I mentioned four of the cars, the fifth car was actually the first car to have an accident, this was your uncle's car. It disappeared straight after the accident. Despite many efforts, it was never found and so never confiscated! When the interested party came forward with this story, we needed to be convinced that something was not right, that this was just not an ugly string of coincidences. The interested party was able to tell us the location of the remains of your uncle's racecar, a crashed, damaged, burned-out but complete racecar. When we retrieved it and examined it, we found very disturbing evidence of foul play.

"The failed suspension member had clearly been manufactured to look the same as the other parts but had the remains of an explosive device built into it. In the remains of the fuel tank, although none of the internal tank bag was left, what was left was a remotely controlled incendiary device that had been activated. Stirling, I can only say it as it is, your uncle, Roger Speed, was murdered."

A hesitation was now needed. Stirling, for the first time in his life, was struggling to slow down the input into his mind.

"Murdered?" Stirling's eye blinking rate had now slowed as he peered at the gray little man in front of him.

"We strongly suspect the same with the other drivers. We strongly suspect that an attempt was made on your life. When we heard of your imminent Monza test, we tried to make contact with you, but Formula One race drivers can be difficult to contact, thanks to the protective teams, PAs, and managers around them."

"Sorry," was all Stirling could mutter.

"Close-circuit cameras in the Curve Grande where your accident occurred show the grainy image of a man with a mobile phone in his hand. He can be seen pressing his phone as you make contact with the barrier. We think the signal fails, and he is seen pressing the phone again as Jaap runs towards you, and then the remains of your car explode. Instead of watching the horrific scene in front of him, or even filming what would have been a YouTube hit, 'Stirling Speed's Monza Crash', he instead bolts from the scene, never to be heard of again."

"Well, that's the last time I'll ever complain when my phone loses signal!" Stirling was now starting to be able to slow the freight train of information being hurtled at him.

"Stirling we need to…"

"Three links, you said there were three links, what's the third?"

Peter Smith got to the whole point of the meeting. "The suspension parts, Stirling, the fuel tanks, and the money behind the tests were provided by…"

Stirling almost whispered the name, "Lawrence Troutman."

"We believe, Stirling, that Troutman positioned these drivers and you into these cars in order to murder them. We do not know why, and we cannot prove he did, but," Peter Smith changed from team player to a man on a personal mission, "but I know he did!"

"Troutman? How can he be involved in something like this? He is Formula One, he is known throughout the world, and he is always banging on about his wonderful family. Can he really be involved?"

"Stirling, he will come for you again, but this time we will be waiting, this man is a murderer and needs to be stopped! He clearly sees you as a threat because of your terrier-like persistence investigating your uncle's crash. He knows you will not stop until you have an answer. He knows he is vulnerable but we can use that situation to draw him out."

Stirling skimmed back through the information that had just been hurled at him. "What about the interested party that came forward with the information and the crashed race car?"

Peter Smith continued, patiently, "The person was clearly very scared and under, we would say, some sort of threat, but they clearly had a concern for you. The racecar should have been scrapped, but the scrap merchant employed by the young Troutman had an eye for his future retirement and an interest in racecars, so he never actually scrapped the car! Our interested party stumbled across this information. Clearly, someone has gotten to him, someone he feared!"

"What about Suzanne, my uncle's wife? Did they find anything at all there?"

"I am sorry to say it, Stirling, but I am afraid no. We have also looked into all avenues but have found nothing. She just disappeared and when someone disappears around Lawrence Troutman—given what we now know about him—I feel the prospects for Suzanne still being alive are sadly not good. I am sorry."

"And who was this person, can we see them again?"

"We know of his location, Stirling, but let's just say he is not needed and that it is safer for him if we stay clear of him."

"Him? So it's a *him*, so who?" Stirling persisted.

"Let's say he is a decent, brave man who decided not to invoice you!"

Chapter 7

"Well, er, I've never driven an E-Type Jag before. But, hey, I'll give it a prod, my mate. I don't suppose I could get a picture, you and me." Before Stirling could reply, the taxi driver continued, "My wife will rip me apart when I tell her this one, just won't believe me, see, especially as I fish a lot.

Stirling assumed the fish reference was alluding to some previously told tall stories. This one, though, was going to be of skyscraper proportions.

Stirling had decided to get control of the situation with the mysterious Alfa. He'd never liked a racecar that drove him, and he applied that philosophy to his life. Never be a passenger, you never know where you might end up. The meeting had been disturbing, and as warned, life-changing, but he was ready for the ride. Next on the agenda was the unveiling of the Alfa driver, who had patiently waited for him across the road from the hotel meeting. No mean feat, as the Manchester City Centre traffic wardens were a tenacious group.

The summoned taxi driver was irritated that, instead of his usual hotel entrance pickup, he had to drive down into the basement car park to locate a 1968 battleship-gray E-Type Jaguar. The clock was running from the entrance, though, and he was prepared to argue his point with his clearly awkward fare. The elegant, low-slung lines of the E-Type were easy to spot amongst the faceless and somewhat bulkier modern car designs. As the taxi rolled to a stop in front of the bulging E-Type bonnet, the driver was already emerging from behind the wood-rimmed steering wheel.

"Oh, my sod of grass, it's Stirling Speed. I got a poster of you up in me bedroom. Yeah, sat in your racecar, helmet off, looking all cool like, great picture, mate. Sort of weird that my wife allowed me to keep it up." The bubbling driver was on a roll.

"Couldn't work out why, at first. Then one night, during a bit of, well, you know, giggle time, she muttered your name! Turns out she's got the hots for you, can you believe it? Tell you, it puts you right off the job at hand."

Stirling was wide-eyed and jumped in with a sincere, "Sorry!"

"Nah, don't be, sort of did me a favor. I soon realized that it, well, keeps things moving with her, if you know what I mean. Wow, when I tell her I've met you today," he paused thoughtfully,

"Might be worth stopping off for a bottle of her favorite tipple, Asti Spumanti, always a sure bet to get things moving." The now-beaming taxi driver finished his grand plan off with a definite wink in the direction of Stirling.

Stirling desperately cleared the romantic image from his mind and focused. "So, are you willing to swap things around a bit?" The taxi driver shifted uneasily, clearly not comfortable with Stirling's request.

"Oh nah, mate, not really into that sort thing. I know her indoors is not much to look at. But, you know, after a couple of beers, a plying of a bottle of Asti, and a dimming of the lights, I still do love her. Really couldn't do the sharing thing. I mean, would like to…"

Stirling managed to control his shout, "No, no, no! I mean, can we swap the cars, I'll drive the taxi and you my E-Type."

Chapter 8

Stirling's plan was to get the Alfa to follow the Jaguar whilst he followed the Alfa at a distance in the taxi, and then, when the Alfa stopped, all would hopefully be revealed. The taxi driver would pilot Stirling's trusty set of wheels to the car park of his local pub in the village. Then, well, Stirling had not quite planned what would happen next; but no matter what, he was going to confront the driver, who hopefully had not noticed the stand-in Jaguar driver. This, Stirling reasoned, would give him the chance to observe the Alfa's driver during the journey and give him the edge. Well, that was the reasoning.

After the agreed photo and a promise to keep the framed photo on the bedside cabinet, a complaint about how long the E-Type's bonnet was, and a suggestion that parking sensors on it would not go amiss, the stealthy Jaguar edged shakily into the bright daylight to take its place amongst Manchester's traffic crawl.

Stirling's plan commenced as the taxi-driver-driven E-Type headed out onto Chester Road with a white Alfa Romeo and racing-driver-driven taxi on its tail.

Stirling closed in on the Alfa as casually as he could, his eagerness to view the driver getting the better of him for a moment. He did not want to spook the driver at this point but was desperate to see the face of this mysterious driver who had stealthily eased into Stirling's life. He could now clearly see the oxblood-colored leather seats. The low back and front seats left a clear view of the back of the driver's head. He appeared quite short and slim, had possibly black hair, but it was hard to be sure, due to the perched baseball cap. Stirling could just about, rather tantalizingly, get glimpses of the driver's forehead through the rearview mirror, but nothing more. The driver seemed more focused on what was going on ahead than behind. The driver appeared competent and seemed very good at following, which was no surprise, given the practice of following Stirling around Europe!

The taxi driver seemed more comfortable with his Jaguar after a stumbling start through the city's central traffic and seemed happy to keep the cat trundling along. Judging by the occasional whiffs of faint blue smoke emitting from the Jaguar's two polished, stainless steel exhaust, he was enjoying releasing some of its pent up performance as well.

As the assorted trio pulled off the main road to start the final approach along the lanes to the pub car park, Stirling dropped back even further, not wanting detection at this point, but the Alfa seemed totally fixated on the shapely behind of the E-Type. Stirling was now completely devoid of emotion, he was reacting and ready to react to any occurrence.

The Jaguar eased onto the well-kept pub car park but seemed hesitant about where to park and rest the big cat. The Alfa drove past, U-turned, headed back, and parked on the opposite side of the lane, now facing Stirling's parked taxi. Certain his master plan would now be revealed, Stirling considered blocking the road but thought better of the idea. That would somehow take this surreal moment to being real! Stirling found himself striding towards the Alfa, feeling just as he had many times before— confident, calm, and prepared—towards his waiting racecar on the grids of the world.

Being a left-hand drive, the Alfa had parked on the wrong side of the lane to get a better view of the strangely out-of character, indecisive Stirling as he struggled to find a suitable resting place for his Jaguar. The taxi driver's indecisiveness was playing into Stirling's hands and keeping the Alfa's attention, allowing Stirling to arrive at the end of the Alfa's stubby bonnet. The Alfa driver suddenly flicked their attention to the approaching Stirling. In an instant, the burbling, little but eager Alfa engine rose to a meaningful bark. And with an audible crunch of gear engagement, the Alfa leapt forward. The usually exquisitely balanced Alfa GTA, now unable to cope with the suddenness of everything, let out an agonizing screech from its overloaded rear tires. Stirling momentarily became an uncomfortable car sandwich as his E type pulled on one side of him and the Alfa lost no time departing on the other. Ignoring the taxi driver's mouth movements, Stirling calmly but very firmly issued orders to the now-very-wide-eyed taxi driver.

"Passenger seat, now!" Stirling, now at the very height of his abilities, had already assessed and predicted that an extra pair of hands might come in useful.

In the caressing hands of Stirling, the Jaguar eagerly responded exactly as told. With a measured and controlled amount of initial wheel spin, the hungry Jaguar sprung after its white prey, which was now bolting for cover via a right-hand fork in the road. As the long, straight six engine busied itself in first gear, Stirling timed the change into second perfectly with hardly an audible change to the engine note.

Despite the blur his life had now suddenly become, the passenger taxi driver did wonder how on earth Stirling had managed such a smooth, speedy gear change, as he had spent most of the trip from Manchester to Tarporley avoiding using first to second gear changes, because they were, well, challenging.

Third gear followed swiftly; the silky race-bred engine was breathing deeply, thanks to its rather modified cams. As Stirling approached the right fork, a timely lift on the throttle ensured the long nose of the Jaguar responded readily, swinging right and now able to chase the in-flight Alfa.

Stirling realized the Alfa's mistake straight away. By heading out onto the open, straight roads and not sticking to the tight, twisting lanes, the Alfa had played into the Jaguar's long legs. Growling from its exhaust and snorting from its machine-polished intakes, the big cat easily began to close in on its vulnerable Alfa prey.

Stirling left it to the last moment before jinking out onto the wrong side of the road to pass the Alfa. His taxi driver passenger now chose this moment to closely examine the footwell of the Jaguar, which was getting very hot, thanks to the glowing exhaust passing just underneath the thin layer of carpet and metal on which his nervous feet rested. The Alfa driver noticed the sudden movement in its mirror just too late. Stirling was aware of this, and although the Alfa was trying to squeeze him, he knew that he had positioned and held onto the throttle until a car turned into his path from the fast approaching T-junction. Stirling lifted and dropped back in behind, having to compensate for the now-heavily braking Alfa as it approached the T-junction.

With scant regard, the Alfa flicked left in front of the traffic, to a cacophony of horns, just managing to avoid the jaws of the Jaguar. Stirling had no choice but to squeeze the brakes, bringing the hot Jaguar to a skipping stop. A small gap in the traffic appeared, and Stirling accurately slotted the Jaguar into it.

Keeping the straight six on song, Stirling prepared to swat away the crawling traffic in front; his Jaguar was now hungry for its prey and was not going to lose interest easily. Just as Stirling was about to execute the big overtake, his up-to-now-dumbstruck passenger found his voice. "He's turned, he's turned!"

Stirling hesitated on the throttle, "A direction would be handy?"

"Right, no, left. I mean left, left." The Alfa had realized its error and was darting for cover in the twisty lanes but had failed to cover its tracks. Stirling braked hard for the tight left, knowing that the big Jaguar would not be hustled around the corner. The slow entry ensured the big cat was sure-footed and enabled Stirling to nail the throttle hard and early. A slight right-hand skip from the back of the hard-accelerating Jaguar was corrected intuitively.

Now, the Alfa could just be seen disappearing over the brow in front. The Jaguar leapt forward; the scent of fuel vapors and hot oil strong in its nostrils. The chase was back on. Stirling kept the throttle pinned as he crested the hill. The revs winced as the back wheels broke traction, the Jaguar literally leaping through the air. Concentrating on keeping the steering straight, the Jaguar made a perfect landing, but more importantly, it gained a monstrous amount of ground on the scampering Alfa. Realizing that a sudden change in direction was the only way of staying out of the grasp of the pursuing beast, the driver of the Alfa stamped on its brakes and threw the car right with the vehicle struggling for grip as it managed to make the sudden turn with armfuls of opposite lock.

"Got him." Stirling watched the Alfa dive into one of his old hunting grounds, Oulton Park Race Circuit. Braking the Jaguar firmly, its engine barking as he blipped the throttle, dropping down through the gearbox, Stirling wasted no time throttling the

Jaguar over the Bailey bridge entrance. The view over the bridge was not a welcomed one. The inner plains of the circuit were full of grazing, resting road cars, all there for a clearly very popular track day event. The Alfa was lost somewhere deep within the pack.

Thinking out loud, Stirling said, "Two entrances to the paddock, the far main entrance is the one to hit." Stirling was banking on the fact that the Alfa driver was not familiar with the circuit and would not notice the second entrance.

"Oh, my sod of grass, when we took off, I farted. And, well, I think it may have been more than a fart, it certainly does not feel too good down there!"

"Stay with the car, look out for the Alfa, do not let it out, do not draw attention to us. I'm going in on foot."

Stirling, still in his emotional desert, grabbed his hat with the large, disguising peak and ventured forward into the paddock, leaving his hot, ticking Jaguar with the unsteady taxi driver standing by its side. Within a few strides, a commotion was building, with Stirling Speed's name appearing to be the hot topic. Stirling rounded to see a large group of enthusiastic track-day drivers and associates heading his way under the guidance of a proud taxi driver, only too pleased to show off his new best friend.

Stirling suddenly walking away from the world of motorsport and the associated public limelight ensured his obscurity with non-motorsport fans but had only heightened the furor when recognized by diehard fans. Within moments, Stirling was surrounded by well-wishing but demanding fans. As Stirling tried to make his excuses and his escape, he managed to catch a glimpse of his prey as it slipped quietly over the distant Bailey bridge, to live and run another day. The Jaguar would go hungry today.

Chapter 9

Reflections of leaping flames bounced around within the rather large glass of white Viognier. Stirling sat in his high-back, rich burgundy leather chair as if hypnotized by the display. The slowly charcoaling logs gave out their rich aroma, almost complementing the would-be-hanging smoke from the battlefields of Tchaikovsky's 1812 overture that reverberated around Stirling's classically styled room. Assimilating the vast volume of new information that had been heaped upon him that day, he needed to be sure that his next course of action was indeed the right one. He also needed to get to the bottom of the mysterious, persistent, and still elusive white Alfa Romeo.

Upon standing to leave his meeting with Peter Smith, Stirling had in an almost throwaway, joking sort of way asked for the Alfa 'terrier' to be called off now. A final prick of surprise to add to the stabs he had already endured when Peter Smith clearly stated that the trailing white Alfa Romeo had nothing to do with his organization. They were, of course, aware of it and were making enquiries, but the owner had been recently registered as dead. "Excellent," was Stirling's reply, although he was really meaning that this was actually far from excellent!

Tomorrow was to be a day of packing and a quick check over of the Jaguar, readying it for another continental road trip, this time heading south, through France, to the jewel of Monte Carlo. Peter Smith had already got it all worked out.

"You are booked to demonstrate a 1977 Tyrell P34 Formula One race car that, I believe, is owned by Mr. Troutman, around the principality during the historic Grand Prix week."

Stirling had again exclaimed, "How did you know that one?"

Only to then feel slightly stupid when Peter Smith replied that he had read it the week before in the 'Autosport' magazine.

Peter Smith continued, "During the week between the historic and main Grand Prix, Lawrence Troutman is throwing a party on his yacht, you are now on the guest list. Not an easy thing to do since your sudden dropout from the public scene."

Stirling remembered the steely, serious look that Peter Smith had given him at this point. "Stirling, we need you. You can get close to Troutman, we need you asking questions, we need you to hook Troutman and drag him out into the exposing open."

Stirling knew the direction to go. Unlike the retreating armies of the now-booming 1812 Overture that filled Stirling's room, he knew the only way now was forward! The jigsaw had been started, the corner pieces were in place—and he had even started to join them up—but the big central picture was still to reveal itself! If only he had the box with the completed picture on it, so he could see if he liked the end scene.

"Stirling, I am sorry, but I am afraid that we have a rather persistent visitor at the front door who is refusing to go away. I have threatened the police, but they said to show you these before calling them."

Stirling's clearly rattled housekeeper held out her open hand. In it were an aging set of car keys looking very similar to Stirling's Jaguar keys. The difference with these keys was that the badge on the attached key fob did not have Jaguar written on it; instead the Italian name, Alfa Romeo, shouted back at Stirling's eyes.

Walking up the hallway to the firmly closed, solid wood front door, Stirling wondered who or what would greet him on the other side. Opening the door slowly, Stirling positioned his body weight against the door to prevent a sudden rush and to make the target area for his possible, would-be assassin smaller. Peering around the now-slightly-ajar door, what met Stirling's desperately inquisitive eyes was not in his wildest dreams what he was expecting.

Stirling stumbled out a greeting.

"How do I know you are not an axe murderer?"

The strong French accent replied, "Because I am your daughter, and generally daughters do not murder their long-lost fathers!"

Chapter 10

Some unexplained sense whispered into Stirling's inner ear and urged him not to pick up the phone to his solicitor. Something urged him to listen to what this petite, pretty, French, falsely smiling, perhaps 22-year-old girl had to say.

What did unnerve Stirling was that, even though he had never set eyes on this girl before, there was a similarity that was unmistakable, a familiarity that he could not place but was certainly searching for a place in his mind. So, Stirling did what any perfect English gent would do and offered a cup of tea. An offer that was politely accepted.

"I know this must be a huge shock for you, me just turning up like this."

The girl spoke good English, but this was clearly her second language, as her speech was not rushed but considered, even though she was clearly uncomfortable and nervous.

"I have followed you since I found out that you were testing for Bentley at Spa-Francorchamps. So many times I've built up the courage to approach you, but it was just so hard to do. I just kept thinking that the right opportunity would arise and it would suddenly become easy."

Stirling listened intently as the young girl struggled to convey her sentiments in what wasn't her mother tongue. It was certainly better to listen than to comment at this point.

"For so many years, I have asked my mother who my father was, but she always denied me the knowledge. Always in a loving way but never giving the answer I wanted. Now, she is dead, taken before her years by cancer. I am sorry I rush this news to you. I realize you once knew her, yet here I am, telling this news in such a way. I am sorry. I am not thinking or saying well."

Stirling knew that he could not be the father of this child in front of him. He did not like complications in his life that would remove his focus from his driving. He had, despite press speculation, been faithful to his first and only wife. They had met not long after his F1 debut, and in a whirlwind, he had found himself married. Maybe the Monza shunt had subconsciously made him realize that there was more to life than driving, but the whole thing turned sour soon after his track return. As Stirling simplified his life, his limelight-seeking wife had found excitement in a celebrity gym instructor and she walked away a few million pounds better off for her troubles! Stirling had walked away slightly poorer and a lot wiser. He was sure there were plenty of 'nice girls' in the sea and that the right girl was out there, but he certainly had not been testing the water! Hence, he could be confident that this girl was not his daughter and so was happy to be patient and maintain his listening ear.

"Please, do not worry about me, I am fine. You have not even told me your name yet," Stirling said.

"It is Sian."

"Sheaarn? How do you spell it?" Stirling exaggerated an inclined ear.

"S. I. A. N. Sian, it's Welsh." The pretty French girl smiled back.

"Okay. Please go on, I am quite interested to know why you think you are my daughter, as you believe."

"When Mamie died, I was left in our house in France, near the border with Italy and Monte Carlo. I was also left a small income from careful investments Mamie had made, her beloved Alfa, and an envelope to be opened after her death. This was left inside of it."

Sian rummaged inside of her rustic, well-worn leather satchel that sat on the tall kitchen stool next to her. Stirling had taken the stranger into his kitchen, a sort of half-way house, whilst she unraveled this story. He somehow reasoned his study to be too formal, his living rooms too personal. So, there they sat, pseudo father and daughter in the homely kitchen, the stoked fireplace enthusing a friendly warmth, Stirling with a fresh lemon and ginger tea, Sian clasping a civil cup of tea, and Stirling's housekeeper busily preparing Stirling's travel hamper for the following day's road trip.

Sian finally produced a sealed, clear plastic wallet, inside of which was an envelope. From inside the envelope, Sian produced a picture and handed it over. Although Stirling had never seen it before, he recognized it instantly. It had been taken by Stirling's dad in the field behind where his Uncle Roger and Auntie Suzanne lived in Anglesey, in Wales. Stirling clearly remembered the photo being taken. He was a smiling ten, may be eleven-year-old, stood in front of a laughing Roger and Suzanne, who was wearing one of those, 'You have gone too far' looks, no doubt responding to one of Dad's comments.

"Why would you have this picture? How can it have come into your procession?"

Sian responded sincerely and honestly, "I had never seen it myself before opening the envelope for the first time. Look at the back of it. There is writing in English, not French."

Stirling studied the scrawled writing on the back of the photo. "Your mother's writing?" he enquired.

"I think so. I think she wrote it when she was ill!"

Stirling read out loud, slowly and carefully,

"Dear Sian
In life, there had to be a lie to keep you safe, my dearest. Now in death, there should be truth, but in the truth lies danger. From your land your name came from."

Stirling hesitated, "So, your name, Sian, you said is Welsh?"

"Yes, Stirling, I never knew, but I checked when I read this."

Stirling continued,

"Who you seek has the treachery of King David with him, so from him you must be protected. I pray only that your quest leads you to the young David who slayed the giant Goliath, for he will protect you in your quest for truth.

Stay safe, as we have kept you safe, and may you both forgive me for breaking my silence.

Your departed, loving Mother, Jane.
Thank you both for letting me be part of your lives."

"She was trying to tell me where I came from and who my real father was. Stirling, you were once called the 'King David

46

of Formula One', the slayer of the sports' goliaths, when you first made Formula One! I have the magazine headlines here!"

Sian pushed the cutout copies of some of the early magazines with examples of this slightly corny headline, the type of which were so popular then, that accompanied a grainy picture of a very young and innocent looking Stirling Speed.

"I simply googled 'King David, the slayer of goliath' and one of the things it picked up was this old headline about you. Then, I discovered you originally lived in Wales! It all fitted." Sian was trying but failing to keep the tears back now.

"I miss my mother so much. She always followed your career and watched all your races, so I know it is true. I know it is, and I have tried to be strong, but I…"

Stirling's housekeeper stepped up to the mark and wrapped her comforting arms around the now-sobbing Sian. Stirling decided now was the time to stop this, this, whatever was going on here, and break the news to Sian that he was not her father or King David, for that matter. As the words formed in his mouth, he met the glaring but kindly eyes of his housekeeper.

"I think this young, brave girl needs a good sleep and a big, hearty breakfast tomorrow morning. Don't you think so, Stirling? Then, all of this can be ironed out in the fresh daylight tomorrow will bring."

Stirling rose early the next morning from an unusually but understandably troubled sleep. A good, bracing run through the leafy forest tracks that surrounded Dayton House would ensure that he could settle into a serious stretch of motoring as he pointed his E-Type in the direction of Dover, then onto Monte. As he walked back into the kitchen, he was met with the wonderful aroma of a cooked breakfast in preparation and his housekeeper enjoying her first cup of tea whilst skimming through the early morning's delivered newspaper. Her eyes were half shielded by the magnified lenses of her golden half-moon spectacles and peeped over the top of them.

"Good morning, Stirling, breakfast in 30 minutes, if that is okay with you?"

"Perfect, ma'am." As he always teasingly called her.

She returned to the comfort of her magnified lenses, began leafing through the pages again, and without looking up continued, "Dare I bring up the subject of a certain young girl we presently have as guest?"

"Where is she now?" Stirling looked towards the doorway that led to the hallway.

"She is awake and showering now. I presume you are not her father?"

"No, and before you ask, I am certain. But, I cannot walk away from the fact that she has the picture, that she followed me, and that she approached me. I think the King David stuff is a shot in the dark, but there is something about all of this that seems to make me want to help her."

Stirling did not tell his housekeeper everything and had certainly not mentioned anything about the meeting with Peter Smith, but he knew that she knew he was holding something back. They had been together a long time, and their relationship was now more of a natural bond!

"Be careful, Stirling, life can sometimes be a lot more challenging than one of those silly race circuits that you use to waste your time driving around and around!"

Stirling picked a small slice of the freshly baked bread and gestured towards his wise life coach. "You just concentrate on getting my breakfast done on time. Otherwise, there will be an advert for a new housekeeper required in the post office!" He popped the warm, crusty bread into his mouth and exited.

"Yes, and you'd still have to get me to write the advert for you!" She popped her golden half-eye glasses carefully into the metal, cloth-covered spectacle case that reassuringly shut with a spring-assisted light clunk and returned to the task of getting breakfast ready… on time!

Upon Stirling's return to the kitchen, 30 minutes later, Sian was already seated at the very solid-looking farmhouse table and devouring a full English breakfast. It was going to be a nice day, and the top of the stable-type door had been left open to let the morning light come flooding in. Stirling sat down opposite where a place had been laid. Not his usual place, Stirling noted, but clearly positioned there for enhanced communication by his housekeeper.

"Beats a croissant and a pot of yogurt, I think," Stirling said.

Sian beamed back with a smile. "Yes, and good morning, Mr. Speed."

"Stirling, please. In fact, I insist, if we are not going to fall out."

"Okay, Stirling. Why the downer on Mr. Speed?" Sian reached for the toast, having demolished her once-full breakfast plate.

"My irritation with it started at school." Stirling's eye caught the exasperated look and outstretched arms of his housekeeper in the background. She had heard the story many times before and felt that Stirling had more pressing matters to discuss.

"But that's a long, long story. Sian, I do have to tell you something that will be painful…"

Sian interrupted, "I know, Stirling, you do not have to tell me. I am happy that we have met and maybe some other time as well—by arrangement, of course. No more stalking. I will be packed and gone in 30 minutes. Deal?"

"No, Sian, that's not what I want to say. There is no easy way to say this to you, but I am afraid I know for certain that I am not your father. I am certain of it. I am happy for you to have checks done, but trust me."

"No, Mr. Speed, you must be."

"I am not, but I want to help you find out who is, and I would like for you to come with me on my trip to Monte Carlo. Leave your car here, we can sort that later. Who knows what adventure we will have?"

"But the photo, the note?"

Stirling's housekeeper stopped further comments and took hold of Sian's hand in both of hers.

"Your journey has not ended here, Sian. It has just begun, and now you have someone to help you along it, someone you can trust with all your heart. Stirling is a very honest and honorable gentleman. Take his word and trust it. What you seek is not here!"

Sian looked out of the half-open kitchen door into the flower meadow beyond. She was saddened that the truth was being spoken but, somehow, felt a comfort in knowing that now she was among friends who cared!

"I understand, thank you, both. I understand, honest." The tears battled to be released.

Stirling was next to speak, "But that's the point, Sian, none of us in this room understand. But I am determined for us to work together to solve this puzzle. We clearly do have some sort of connection, we just need to find the socket for the plug to go into, then we will both be…"

"Electrocuted?" interrupted a falsely, but trying, smiling Sian.

"Well, that might be the 'shocking' truth of it all," Stirling bounced back.

"Sian, you get packed up. And, Stirling, with comments like that, I think it's time to go… Please!" Stirling's housekeeper hustled them both out of her kitchen but then discreetly held onto Stirling's shirt to delay his journey and put distance between him and Sian. Stirling turned back to his housekeeper.

"What, ma'am?"

"Are you sure about taking Sian with you? Are you sure that you can control this situation?"

Stirling paused, not for effect but to pluck the right words, "Sometimes, when you have a wayward race car, you have to just forget the theory, forget the finesse, and just chuck it into the corner and sort it out. You have to have the confidence that, one way or another, you will come out on the other side. Trust me, I will sort this, but I get a feeling that it will get a bit messy first!" Stirling turned back to leave, then felt that more reassurance was required.

"Hey, what doesn't kill you can only make you stronger."

"Coming from a man who once ended up more dead than alive, I don't really find that reassuring, Stirling. Please take care!"

Chapter 11

Stirling walked towards the warming Jaguar, its polished, stainless twin exhausts gently belching out the night's condensation. He placed the prepared travel hamper next to the well-worn leather bag that had traveled for many years around the world with him. Sitting into the Jaguar's semi-bucket seats, Stirling closed the door with a clunk that only old cars have and looked out along the bulge of the gray bonnet. By keeping Sian close, he could work on the mystery she had brought to him whilst going fishing for Laurence Troutman at the same time. Having survived many years of thrashing racecars around the circuits of the world, Stirling knew that he was going to need all of his self-preservation skills! This road trip was certainly a trip into new territory for him.

"You wear driving gloves?" Sian's French accent filling the very English car.

"Very observant, young Sian."

"It's just that you don't see them a lot these days, is what I mean. You use them because you raced for many years with your race gloves?" Sian's English was getting more confident

"No."

Stirling massaged the Jaguar out into the busy M6 motorway traffic and settled the big cat into its stride.

"Why then? Why the gloves?" Sian persisted.

"Can I just drive? I really enjoy hitting the road and driving—quietly!"

"Do you get a rash from holding the wheel?"

Stirling flashed Sian a quick look. "People dress to go out, if you're going to the theatre, going out for a meal, going to the gym. People dress when they go to do something they like."

"Okay, but why do you wear driving gloves?"

Stirling checked his off-side mirror and squeezed the throttle, which resulted in a guttural roar from the straight six engine and the Jaguar leapt into the outside lane of the motorway.

"I like to dress to drive."

It was Sian's turn to flash a smiling look at Stirling. "No, you don't… really, even to go to the shops?"

"No, but I do if I am on a road trip or long journey."

"Why?"

"It's all part of the enjoyment. Look, some people will sit in front of the TV for hours, some will go to the pictures to watch a film, some to the ballet or theatre. Well, I like to go for a long drive and, over the years, I have found that I will always dress for the drive, just like some will have an outfit for flying in. I have my driving shoes especially made by Bottega Venetia, my gloves are by Dents', my sunglasses are either Driving Wires or Birkins. The polka dot material encased within the sides of my Birkin sunglasses is known as the Birkin polka dot, named after one the Bentley boys, Tim Birkin, who always wore a blue and white polka dot cravat when he was racing. My white polo shirt is tailor-made for me with a slightly thicker collar, so as I can put it up to keep the draught out of my neck when I have the Webasto roof open during a long, draughty driving stint. Details, my dear Sian. I love driving, and to be honest, it has served me well, and I am a world champion, so I can do as I like, even if that is wearing leather driving gloves!"

"You are a crazy Englishman, I think, who is a bit of a fanatic!"

"Oh, I used to be, but not anymore, though. I have learned to enjoy the here and now; I take time to notice things around me. A fanatic will have one focal point that gets all the attention whilst missing the world that they are passing by."

Sian sank deeper into her seat and slid slightly lower into the car, a sign that she was settling into this journey. After a week of uncertainty and following, Stirling she definitely preferred accompanying him instead.

"A French girl with a Welsh name? Suppose that could be a coincidence, given that your mother was English?" Stirling pondered. "Or was she trying to tell you something? Trying to tell you where your roots are?"

"Yes, I know. Obviously, I could not check on my father's history, but my mother was born and bred in London. She qualified as a nurse and a midwife. I was able to discover that, before she moved to France, she was registered as working for a very exclusive private clinic in Elstree, just north of London. Looking at this time period, she must have been pregnant with me and I think I must have been born just as she moved to France. So, I am a French citizen. Nowhere have I found any connection with Wales, other than on the note on the back of the picture. 'From your land your name came forth.'"

"How about your mother's family?"

"She was an only child. My grandparents would visit when I was younger. Then, as they stopped traveling, we would visit them. Now, only my grandmother survives, she is poorly and is cared for in a home just outside Luton, in England."

Stirling chose the toll road past Birmingham, as he always did. 1968 Jaguars and snarled Birmingham M6 traffic do not go together well.

"And you found no Welsh connection with your grandparents?"

"No, although how good my checking is, I do not know."

"Any other family, friends that might link you with me, Wales, or the picture?"

"Not really. We had good friends in our village, and I had good friends at school. My best friend was—well, is—well, are, even, Aimee and Hannah."

"So, you knew these both from school?"

"Aimee, yes, but Hannah was really my mother's very close friend but wonderful to me when she came. She lived in Italy and would come to visit often, and she helped nurse my mother when she was so ill."

Stirling began to slow the Jag's progress and slipped down the gears as they approached the tollbooths for the M6 toll road.

"Can you pass me my wallet in the glove compartment, seeing as you are closest?"

Sian reached in and found a well-worn but immaculately kept diary-like burgundy leather wallet. "This feels like it has history to it!"

"It does, a good history, and a few sad memories as well."

Sian had hardly noticed that Stirling had brought the galloping Jaguar to a smooth, seamless stop and watched as he slipped an unfolded, crisp note out to pay the toll keeper.

"Do please keep the change."

Unable to resist the urge that all get when leaving a toll booth or peage upon seeing an open, straight road ahead, Stirling took a big slice of throttle and the Jaguar barked away from the booths. Each gear change instantly killed the bark of the Jaguar's engine which soon returned with another stab on the throttle. Stirling was holding onto the higher gears and saw the speedo start to play with higher numbers.

"We have competition," Sian said.

Stirling's glance in his mirror revealed that the drivers of a silver Mercedes and a blue BMW had also fallen for the temptation and were speeding away from the tollbooth in the outside lane.

Sian, looking back over her seat could see that the BMW M5 had the legs on the Mercedes and pulled out from behind it to start an overtake maneuver.

"Come on, Stirling, don't let them have us!"

The Jaguar, with its hot XK engine, howled with all its mechanical might as Stirling guided it into the inside lane to give the two computer-managed German machines space to do battle.

"We got the jump on them, but I'm afraid 40 odd years of development might beat us here, Sian."

At an indicated 135 mph, the battle was over and the young bucks backed down, the proud Jaguar just keeping ahead by a nose.

"Yes, we had them." Sian leaned forward and patted the black dash of the E-Type.

Having allowed the pouncing cat off its leash, Stirling eased the speed back to the vicinity of a legal one and re-established his right-foot-controlled cruise mode.

"She goes well. Now, I know how you could catch me on the straights when you were hunting me down," Sian said.

"She does go well for an old girl, in fact, she can be quite indecent at times. You drove well that day I followed you, clearly you have had some practice."

"Karting. I have always loved cars and racing, and Mother eventually gave into me and took me to the local kart track, where I actually ended up winning a kart championship. So, don't talk to me about Formula One championships! Did you kart, Stirling?"

"Yes, but in absolute secrecy. My dad took me to the local indoor tracks but kept it all from my mother. My uncle, my dad's brother, in fact the one on your picture, was killed in a racecar, so the whole subject was taboo. Even after three world championships, she never acknowledged that I raced. She obviously knew but never acknowledged. When I retired, I went to see her, and only at that point did she recognize it. When I told her, she turned to me and said, 'Well, you are best out of it all, and that was that!'"

"That is sad."

"No, not really."

"No, it is. Hannah hated racing and Mother insisted that I did not mention my karting to her, which was sad because I always wanted to ring her and tell her if I'd won."

Stirling reached across to the Jag's radio and turned the knurled silver nob that started off with a click then progressed in volume as *Handles Messiah* clearly became audible and then filled the car.

"I am sure we are missing something obvious here, Sian. We are missing the signs…"

"You are missing the signs. You are missing the signs that I am hungry!"

Stirling smiled, he was surprised but pleased that he felt comfortable with this new addition to his life."

"Ok then. I think a hamper break at Newport Pagnel service station, home of the Aston Martin I might add and then destination Dover and some first class dinning on the ferry over to Calais is the plan for the day."

Sian screwed her face. "Can we not have a burger stop and then a quick Channel Tunnel plan instead?"

"Clearly you have not experienced one of my housekeeper's hampers, so for that faux pas I will forgive you but to travel through the Tunnel would just not do at all."

"And why would that be, Mr. Stirling?"

"Well, traveling in the tunnel does not allow you to salute the white cliffs of Dover as we leave the great shores of Great Britain."

Sian twisted around in her supportive seat. "Please, tell me that you are joking."

Stirling returned the Jaguar to a tram lined 1st lane on the M6 motorway, having blown past a line of choked, speed-limited trucks. He smiled and increased the volume on the radio to do justice to Vivaldi's *Four Seasons* now bouncing from the silver speakers.

About to begin the same maneuver, a plain blue BMW approached the same line of trucks. Its driver glanced in his mirror to pull out from behind them. His backseat passenger, a small man dressed in an immaculate gray suit, sat doing what he did best; blending into everyday life whilst watching, carefully, the classical outlines of an E-Type Jaguar in front. Having set Stirling up as live bait to hook Laurence Troutman, he felt responsible for his safety and was not about to let him out of his sight.

Chapter 12

Laurence Troutman peered out of his window, hands clasped behind his back, awaiting a reply.

"Mr. Troutman, there have been complications; we had to pull the hit again. He is very high profile, it needs to be very clean or questions will be asked."

Troutman's voice came back in a deep tone, almost whispering.

"I respect what you do. I respect that you are noted as the top of your game." His voice began to rise, "I think I show that respect with the stratospheric money that I pay you and the services that I provide for your organization. This 'target', as you call him, is still around, still asking questions."

Troutman swung around and stared at the thickly set man in front of him, his controlled fury now exploding with desk-thumping savagery. "And he is still a threat to my very existence! Has the muscle between your ears absorbed that one?"

Troutman walked from behind his desk, lowered his tone and then began pacing his grand office. "For four years you have been 'hitting the target'. One of those years he spent recovering from your first botched attempt, then another year winning another world championship, then two years of retirement, yet your 'target' is still paying king and country his taxes!

"All you had to do was turn up on time and press a button, on a cell phone, at the right time, then. Then boom, all this would have been solved."

"Mr. Troutman, you know what happened that day, our man was delayed."

"He planned to be delayed, then he blabbed his plan to all and sundry!" Troutman interjected.

"I know, then it was all just unfortunate circumstances. As you know, the bad signal, the car breaking up, then his teammate getting in the way, it just turned into a bad situation."

"'A bad situation?' Well, let's see how many more bad situations we have had. 'Leave it to us, we will deliver, we will use our methods you said but…!"

"He is not a man to walk into the usual traps, Mr. Troutman. He… well, lives a simple life, and despite many situations we have set up, he does not fall for the usual traps that everyone else does. Sex, drink, drugs, or money… We have had to change our approach. Mr. Troutman, we are professional when we take on a hit like this."

Troutman now closed in on the powerful and controlled man standing in his office. The man looked straight ahead whilst Troutman shouted at his temple.

"You failed at Monza, then you failed again and again and now I see on my guest list for my private party, on my private yacht, the very man that you should have dispatched and you say, 'Leave it to me, I am a professional'?"

"Mr. Troutman…"

"Have I finished? Have I finished? Are you trying to interrupt me?" Troutman uncontrollably screamed back. "Still, I see no world headlines or a world that is mourning the tragic passing of a three-time world champion and you tell me you are a professional? So, what happened this morning, Mr. Professional?"

"He has not fallen for any of our honeypots, so we had to try a more direct line of hit. We followed him this morning, down the M6. We know that he always uses the toll road which is usually quite quiet. We were to hit him as he left the tollbooths. One shot, then chaos whilst we made our escape. One dead world champion and a cold trail!"

Troutman fell back into his high-back leather chair. "And you missed. Professional, you say?"

"The target accelerated hard from the booths, which did catch us out but we would have had time to get alongside. But then, another car came from nowhere and got between us."

"Bad luck or bad planning, either way, you are useless."

"But that's the point, Mr. Troutman, it was neither. The BMW was there to protect the target. It purposely got between us and the target."

"I think you will find that was a bored bathroom fittings salesman spicing up his day."

"No it was not, Mr. Troutman."

"How can you be sure, why?"

"Yes, Mr. Troutman, we can, because the backseat passenger pulled a gun on us and we had to take evasive action! We had no choice but to abort. There is someone else involved, Mr. Troutman, we need to tread carefully and find out who this other party is."

Troutman slowly swung round in his chair and looked out through the wall, which was actually a ceiling-to-floor glass window, and looked over the roofs of London. Then slowly, he rose and walked round to his waiting employee. He raised his arm and out stretched his index finger.

"I will tread where and how I want. You and your bumbling organization will now dispose of this irritation my way. Do you hear me, my way!"

The man stood and took the onslaught of Troutman. He could smell Troutman's coffee and cigar breath in his nostrils.

"Now, get out of my building." Troutman resumed his stance, looking out of the window.

The man, usually a man to be feared, usually a man you would not want to meet in your worst nightmare, hesitated, bristled then bent low and picked up his brown, slim leather bag from the chair opposite Troutman's desk. He knew that he could finish Troutman off here and now and could be rid of his irritation. He could finish him with his bare hands or with any of the three weapons he had concealed about his body. Troutman was clearly a man out of control; his usefulness for the organization was now being compromised by his reckless behavior. He also knew that if he spoke out of turn or even decided to finish Troutman, here and now, with no permission, then he would be the next one to be finished.

"Okay, Mr. Troutman, we will await your instruction." The man turned and left.

Troutman poured himself a whiskey. He had known Stirling Speed since his karting days when the boy clearly showed he had talent. But Troutman had always felt uncomfortable with the closeness, the connection with his uncle, Roger Speed, a man that he had dispatched or, to make it clear, murdered! Troutman had covertly tried to prevent Stirling's meteoric rise to motorsport stardom. But, he had not counted on Stirling's unnerving determination and focus. Troutman always knew what the uncomfortable feeling deep inside him was. He knew that, one day, Stirling would start to ask questions about how his uncle died. He knew that he had left loose ends and he needed to make sure that those ends stayed loose.

Then, out of the blue, some pathetic little Welsh circuit had a bit of a makeover and decided to name one of the corners after a driver who had once perished there. Speed Rise… in memory of Roger Speed. Suddenly, Stirling was asking questions, started requesting meetings, wanting to know why Roger was in the car and where the car had ended up. He had even hired a private investigator to discover the whereabouts of his auntie! Troutman was in shallow water and felt vulnerable. He had to remove Stirling Speed, he had to remove the threat that could take away his life, his money and his world!

Chapter 13

"Yes," Troutman responded to the knock on his office door and in walked his shapely PA, his lustful eyes falling instantly upon her figure.

"You look ready to be ravished my dear."

His PA, chosen for her looks and discreetness, knew exactly what role she had to play if she was to keep her lavish lifestyle that she had become so used to. She had also seen and experienced the private, violent and ruthless side of Lawrence Troutman. A side that the public, and particularly his wife and family, never saw. Although many would view her as a glorified prostitute, she just saw it as part of her job to satisfy Troutman's animalistic sexual drive. Also, deep inside, she feared him. She knew she was on a ride that was hard to get off until Troutman had finished with her. She played his game and pretended to unbutton her blouse.

"You can ravish me here and now, or you could deal with the documentary team sitting just outside that door, waiting to make a film about you over the next few days!"

Troutman grabbed her and smothered his lips over hers and ran one of his hands through her long, silky, dark auburn hair, his whole body taken over by his unquenchable erotic passion.

"Mr. Troutman, is this sexual harassment?" his PA playfully muttered.

Troutman wrapped the hair he had played with tight around his hand and yanked his PA's head back hard with it. Rage had re-entered his eyes.

"You never joke like that, my dear. Do you understand; never even think of crossing me, not even in a joke. Your loss of the lifestyle that I have given you would be the least of your worries. I own you and always will, well, at least whilst you are still alive that is."

"It was a thoughtless joke, Mr. Troutman, thoughtless. I am here for you to do what you want. I am sorry, I was just playing."

Troutman relaxed and let his hand fall.

"My dear, when I have finished with you, and that time will come, you can be assured that you will be looked after for life. You have a good deal, so do be careful never to cross me, I would hate to obliterate your beauty. You are still very acceptable to my eyes, for the time being."

Troutman pulled away, ran his eyes over his possession straightened his tie and re-tensioned his shirt over his bulging stomach by tucking it deeper into his trousers. His PA straightened his naturally wavy and slightly-too-long hair. She knew that he liked to be fussed over, and she focused on her long soak in her bath, in her expensive marble bath room, in her apartment that overlooked the River Thames, all paid for by Troutman. It was a small price to pay. She knew that at some point, Troutman would get bored of her. She would be replaced and given an allowance for the rest of her life. *More fool him*, she thought.

"Now, let the show begin. Please bring them into my office."

Troutman's PA opened the leather-covered and studded office door.

"Mr. Troutman will be only too pleased to see you now. Please step this way."

Troutman's eyes glinted with delight as a tall, slim lady with long blonde hair led the camera crew into his office.

"May I thank you all so much for your patience. My time, sadly, is always squeezed when I am not with my family."

Troutman walked from behind his desk wearing a perfected nice-to-see-you smile and walked straight up to the tall blonde lady, who was wearing the same smile, and took her hand.

"Now, let's start with your, I am sure, beautiful name, then you can introduce me to your friends."

The tall blonde lady flicked her shining hair and spoke through a smile, "Well, my name is Michelle. I'll be the pain in the butt that will be following you around, asking you annoying questions and producing the documentary about you over the next few days, leading up to the Monte Carlo Grand Prix."

She turned, hand outstretched, to her crew. "Here, we have Pete on camera and 'Si' on sound. We kept the team very small so as to be less intrusive. We really appreciate you allowing access to your… well… multimillionaire lifestyle that is so remote to… well… ours."

Troutman's eyes never left the eyes of his new blonde best friend. "You never know Michelle may be in the future you will end up having your very own multimillionaire life style, you never know."

Troutman flicked a glance over to his waiting PA. "That will be all, my dear, and thank you for your assistance."

Turning back to his interviewer Troutman smiled again. "My PA is such a wonderful girl, so loyal, so hard working. I try to give her anything she wants. I reward loyalty, Michelle."

"She is a very lucky girl." Michelle looked back at Troutman's PA but realized that she had left the room.

Troutman's PA returned to her lavish desk and looked out over her dramatic view of London. Just maybe this girl would be her replacement, allowing her to be free to start building her own life. A prick of conscience ate inside of her and a small voice called out, *'Warn her, warn her!'*

But why should I warn her? Nobody warned me.

Troutman was now completely ignoring the sound person and cameraman, focusing his whole attention on Michelle.

"So, what is it that you want from me, Michelle? I am at your personal disposal."

Michelle responded, pleased that she had got off to clearly a good start with the world famous, most powerful man in world motorsport. "Mr. Troutman."

"Oh, we can get personal I am sure, let's keep it to Lawrence."

This man really knew how to break down barriers, Michelle thought whilst feeling slightly flushed. "Lawrence, you are known to be the wealthiest and most powerful man in world motorsport. You are known for your very generous charity work but the thing that really impresses is that your family life and marriage are so solid. You always take time to highlight the importance of family life and how every man needs to have a strong woman behind him. It seems that despite the glamorous world that you live in, with all of its temptations, you seem to have the perfect marriage, the perfect life. I really want to turn you inside out and discover what really makes you tick."

"Well Michelle, I think if anyone is going to turn me inside out, then I am sure you are the perfect person for it. Now, how about we head back to my house in Buckinghamshire and we can get down to you turning me inside out as soon as possible. We have a busy few days coming up. How long did you say that you will be with me?" Troutman knew exactly what his meticulously planned schedule was but played the easily pleased man well.

"Our last night of filming is next Wednesday in Monte Carlo, when you have your yacht party." Michelle looked at her watch and continued, "Well, that is great. Thank you for seeing us in your office, we will head off down towards your house and catch up with you later, if that is okay."

Troutman clicked shut his slim black leather brief case, slipped his platinum Mont Blanc pen into his pocket, and picked up his gold Vertu phone.

"Why don't we let the boys head down to the van whilst you can go upstairs with me?"

"Upstairs, Mr. Troutman?" Michelle feeling slightly wrong-footed by Troutman's suggestion. Troutman liked playing his games.

"Yes, Michelle, why don't you head upstairs with me to my helipad, where my pilot is waiting to fly me, and now you, to my home. Then, you can meet my wife and family."

Turning to her crew, Michelle felt distinctly out-positioned.

"Yes, okay, lads, is that ok? I'm okay with it if you two are." Not really waiting for a reply, Michelle picked up her bag.

"Right, then, I will see you both at Lawrence's house. May be a good idea to get a shot of the helicopter and it taking off. If that is okay with Lawrence?"

"That is fine with me, Michelle," Troutman buzzed his PA. She responded immediately and entered the office.

"Could you please escort Michelle to the helipad, I will be along shortly."

"Of course, Mr. Troutman, would you like me to take your case up?"

"No, thank you. I'll be along shortly, I just have a quick call to make."

Troutman's PA and Michelle entered the mirrored lift. Both felt a distinct uneasiness in the air. The closing of the lift door signaling time to talk and both started talking at the same time.

"Mr. Troutman seems…" Michelle started.

"Be careful," Troutman's PA blurted out.

Michelle looked away from their reflection in one of the full-length mirrors and looked directly at this suddenly flustered woman.

"Sorry, what do you mean by that?"

The lift had already arrived at its destination and the door was beginning to open.

"Just be careful, please, Lawrence is…" she stopped suddenly and smiled as the pilot standing outside of the opening doors appeared ready to greet his passenger and was clearly slightly surprised not to be greeting Mr. Troutman.

Troutman had speed-dialed the number he required, and the recipient had immediately answered the phone whilst his PA was still leaving his office. He delayed for a moment, not saying anything until his soundproofed door had closed shut.

"I want you to keep a close eye on my PA. I feel a change of loyalty in her heart."

Troutman listened to the response.

"No, is that what I said? I said, keep an eye on her. If the heart change becomes more apparent, then perhaps it will be time to find a new tenant for her apartment."

Troutman headed up to his helicopter to the waiting Michelle inside.

"Michelle, thank you again for waiting, I hope you are comfortable. I seem to spend more time sorting charity problems these days than managing world motorsport!"

The pilot stood in the cabin waiting for the right moment to greet his employer. Troutman flashed an irritated but controlled look at him.

"So what are we waiting for, I pay millions of pounds for this helicopter to save time and here we are, going nowhere!"

Chapter 14

Stirling guided the long nose of the Jaguar through the familiar leafy lanes that led to the French chateau he always stayed at when traversing France. Run by an elderly couple that treated Stirling as the son they never had, he always found the location a relaxing escape from the hectic world that was Formula One. The chateau, with its rustic balconies that caught the fresh aromatic evening breeze that blew across the vista of nearby vineyards, was the perfect place for Stirling to sit, glass of wine in hand and to simply reflect.

"Stirling, why have you not been eating? Every time you come, you have wasted away more!"

"Rosa, you say that every time the boy turns up. Don't worry, I will carry the weight for him."

The short, well-weathered, well-rounded man slapped his belly unapologetically whilst his wife Rosa looked on ashamedly.

"Your body is too far gone to worry about, it is a lost cause."

Sian giggled alongside Stirling's smile.

"Sian, this is Madame Rosa and Monsieur Thomas. If left to Madame Rosa, I would never have fitted into a Formula One race car!"

Rosa held open her arms and hugged Sian, then still holding onto her, she took a step back, arms outstretched and looked Sian over.

"Sian, we have to say we were hoping for someone a little older, more mature maybe to look after Stirling, but I understand the boy has needs and you no doubt, will fulfill those needs for him."

Thomas nodded enthusiastically at Rosa's statement, maybe a little too enthusiastically and as result got a disapproving Rosa's eye!

Stirling jumped in.

"Rosa, there is no romantic connection here, we are just traveling together on a bit of a mystery tour. It's a long story, but we are just good friends."

"Oh, but Stirling you need to find a good woman for yourself soon." Rosa gestured between herself and Thomas by waving her hand back and forth.

"We are getting old, Stirling, we may be not around for many more years. In fact, looking at Thomas, time is running out fast, it may be a matter of weeks!"

Sian giggled again whilst Thomas rolled his eyes at them both. For all their bickering, Stirling felt it heart-warming that Rosa and Thomas had been together so long they were as one and that, even in her joking, Rosa realized that once Thomas was gone, her life would be at its end too.

"Rosa, leave the boy alone. Sian, let me have your bags," Thomas said.

"No, sir, it is really okay," a widely smiling Sian replied.

"Sir, sir? We'll have none of that. It's Thomas, or you can go pack your bags back into that excuse of an English sportscar."

Rosa reached across and took the bags off Sian and past them to Thomas.

"Please, Sian, do let Thomas take your bags. It will make his day to carry the bags for a pretty young girl and to be honest, he is useless at everything else. And I do mean everything else. When it comes to his performance in the bedroom..."

Stirling jumped in again, "Rosa, I think it would be good to get Sian settled in. It's been a long journey, and I need to nip down to the village!"

Sian, indeed tired from the long journey and the stresses of the previous day, did not question Stirling's village expedition and was only too pleased to be taken by her new friends to her inviting room. Rosa led the way whilst telling Thomas to, "Get a move on!" Thomas followed behind secretly, forcing his chest out and doing a very good job of silently mimicking Rosa, much to the amusement of the now-silently-giggling Sian.

Stirling briskly walked to the village. He knew exactly the destination he was heading for the village's only hotel car park. He knew exactly what he would find in the car park but deep inside, he wished he would not. He instinctively hesitated in the entrance and peered around the corner and scanned the cars parked. Yes, there it was, quietly cooling in the corner, sitting next to a very French-looking black and burgundy Citroen 2 CV.

Stirling had first noticed the dark blue BMW back in the UK whilst accelerating away from the tollbooth on the M6 motorway. He noticed that it had joined in with the impromptu race with a silver Mercedes. He noticed it again in the ferry terminal car park, which, okay, could have been a coincidence but then he noticed that it always kept a very discreet distance behind even after a couple of loo and coffee breaks. On the winding road up to the chateau, he could again occasionally make out its roofline through the camouflaging hedgerows. He was being followed… again!

Okay, time to grasp this particular nettle. Stirling was met with a pleasant, 'Bonjour' upon entering the hotel reception that, which was decorated rather macabrely with hunting pictures, various weapons of death, and a few stuffed heads of unlucky victims.

"Hello, do you speak English?"

"Why, Mr. Speed, yes, of course. Do we have the pleasure of your company this evening?"

"Thank you, and no, but I do need to ask you a delicate question. Would you know who the driver of the blue BMW M5 that you have parked in your car park?"

"Yes, Mr. Speed, I do."

"Could you tell me who they are or point them out to me?"

"No, I am sorry, Mr. Speed, but I am not able to provide that sort of information. I am sure you understand. Is there any other way that I could be of assistance?"

"Call me Stirling, please. Well, it is quite embarrassing, but whilst turning around in my car, can you believe that I have backed into it? Could you get a message to them? I really did not want to just drive off."

"I see. World champions are not very good at three-point turns, I think?"

"Nope, we're not, just good at going forward. I am afraid going backwards is not one of my strengths."

"Maybe Mr. Stirling, if you could leave some contact details, then I can pass them on?"

Stirling reached inside his jacket and took out his worn, burgundy leather wallet. From within, he took his equally well-worn sterling silver cardholder on which the simple words, 'Race Driver' were engraved. It had been given to him by a family he viewed as 'good' friends. Over the years, Stirling had accumulated many 'friends'. The more success he had as a race driver, the more 'friends' he accumulated. It came with the territory. Some friends were there because they liked the scene, some because they were hoping to receive some of the action, some because they wanted to use the Stirling Speed's machine to help build their own success.

Occasionally, though, Stirling came across 'good' friends. The ones he was there for, and they were there for him. When the world's press pried for gossip, they found none with them. When sensational columns needed filling after Stirling's Monza shunt, the 'good' friends were too busy looking after him to give quotes for the sensational, thirsty columns.

Presents like the genuine and simple silver cardholder reminded Stirling of the real world that surrounded the veneer world in which he was engulfed. Stirling took out one of his cards. They were simple, quality white cards with just his name, 'Stirling', scripted in 'Baskerville Old Face' font, and his mobile number, printed in a crisp, clear 'Arial' font—both in jet black ink. He then did what everyone does for some reason and placed the card between his curled index and second finger, then straightened them in a sort of soft flicking motion.

"My card, and thank you for your help."

The receptionist, seeing the lack of 'Mr.' or 'Speed' on the card, was now more confident to be less formal. "Thank you, Stirling. I will ensure that he…" There was slight hesitation for the receptionist to check himself. "I will see that the driver receives it."

Stirling walked purposefully and briskly out of the reception, out of the car park gates, around the outside of the car park, and then back through the hedges, near to where the BMW was parked. Within minutes, a powerful-looking character walked across to the BMW and began a quizzical inspection of it. Stirling seized the moment, and at the same time, unexpectedly seized a cricket-bat-sized fallen stick off the floor.

Okay, track position is everything. Let's go in all guns blazing, Stirling thought

"Excuse me, you will not find any damage on the car, but damage might occur to the car or person if you refuse to tell me why you have followed me from the UK."

The startled man swung around to see a man silhouetted against the hotel lights, brandishing a large stick and clearly in the mood for a fight. Instinctively, he reached into his jacket. Stirling quickly realized that he had applied too much power, lit up his wheels, and most definitely lost his track position! His stick, no matter how big, was going to be no match to what was coming out from the inside of this well-filled jacket.

'Drop the stick, Stirling!' screamed a voice in his head, but in this split-second of delayed time, Stirling's muscles and nerves seemed deaf to the plea and began a swinging motion, as if preparing to bat away the ballistic bullet that was preparing to be released down the barrel of the gun that this stranger had now pulled.

"Stirling!" A very loud, real voice shouted out from the steps of the hotel. It was now a startled Stirling who swung around. In an instant, the stranger accelerated Stirling's swing, removed the stick, and put Stirling's hand up his back in one swift movement.

"Let him go. Let him GO."

The stranger let him go but kept his hand firmly in his jacket, on his now-holstered firearm.

Peter Smith stood in the light of the hotel reception and looked around to ensure no one had witnessed the moment.

"Seeing that our car is not damaged and both you and my colleague are not damaged or dead, perhaps it would be good to step inside."

"Sorry, my mate!" Stirling smiled an apology to the now-composed stranger whom he had just threatened with his large stick.

Inside, comfortably seated, Peter Smith ordered two large brandies.

Stirling broke the silence, "What is it these days? Everyone seems to want to follow me. If we could just communicate with each other, then, maybe we could split the cost of a mini bus and all travel together."

Stirling stared at Peter Smith, his sidekick having been dispatched to the bar without any protest.

"Your observation skills are good, Stirling. We are good at blending into the scenery. We spend a lot of time following people. I am slightly embarrassed but at the same time slightly impressed that you spotted us. In fact, where did you spot us?"

"To be honest, I spotted your erratic driver in my mirrors when we left the M6 toll booth near Birmingham, in the UK. I have been keeping an eye on you ever since."

"That is impressive, Stirling. With the right training, you could do well working within our organization. You are alert, have natural good observation, are intelligent, and have access to all areas, thanks to your name."

Peter Smith's concentration seemed to wander for a moment as he sipped his brandy.

"Can we focus here? I thought you were going to make contact with me in Monte?"

"Stirling, you do have a lot to learn. You are my responsibility, and there is no doubt that you are being targeted. Troutman wants you dead."

"Well, trust me, when he tries, I will be waiting for him."

Peter Smith took another swig of his brandy and held its burning taste in his mouth before allowing the expensive liquid to ease down his throat.

"Stirling, I have to tell you that an attempt was made on your life this morning."

Stirling chose to put his swirling brandy down. "When, where?"

"As we left the toll booths, a silver Mercedes was waiting on the other side of the booths in the safety lane, lying in wait for you. When it saw you, it accelerated hard, but so did you. We were then in position to see a hitman raise a gun to get you in his sights. We were able to get alongside it and spoil his view whilst showing off some of our own firepower at the same time. We managed to muddy the waters of his clean target! Stirling, you are vulnerable, so never underestimate the cushion of backup. We are here for you just in case Troutman makes a desperate attempt to have you removed, just like this morning."

"Ah, the race… which we won, I might add. Well, you should have come forward sooner, then you could have shared some first-class dinning with us on the ferry!"

"Who says we didn't enjoy the first-class delights, Stirling?"

"Well, I didn't see you."

"So we did some of our job well, then." Peter Smith smiled but did not sit back in his seat.

Stirling noticed this. "I get the feeling there is more you want to tell me."

"Your feelings do not betray you. Yes, there is. Your young passenger, Sian, we have been doing a little digging. We are not sure where or if she fits in, but you clearly have your reasons for keeping her close to you, Stirling."

"She is a mystery, but I, well, I have a feeling that I can trust her. She came to me claiming to be my daughter, which I know is not the case."

"We know that, Stirling, we have checked her medical records. She could not be your daughter, but the general feeling is that there is a link somewhere, but there is more than that. Despite our resources, we are unable to establish who her real father is and…"

Peter Smith took another slow, considered sip of his brandy.

"You like your pauses, don't you?"

"I just need to make sure you are taking everything in, Stirling."

"I am use to taking things in at close on 200mph, so please fire away."

"Sian's mother, who recently passed away, was not her biological mother. In fact, we think that the mother Sian thought she had had been actually paid to look after her from birth."

"And you think that Sian had no knowledge of this?"

"We are certain. So, the search for her real father will now become the search for her real mother as well."

"She has a picture with her that she showed me. It is a picture taken by my dad. I just about remember it being taken. I am stood alongside my Uncle Roger and my Auntie Suzanne. I think behind their cottage in Anglesey, in Wales."

Peter Smith listened intently.

"There was a message written on the back of the photo," Stirling added.

Stirling reached for his phone on the round wooden table in front of them and flicked open the leather case, exposing the face of it.

"I took a photo of it. It's all a bit weird. This is what it said."

"Dear Sian,

In life, there had to be a lie to keep you safe, my dearest. Now in death, there should be truth but in the truth lies danger.

From your land your name came from.

Who you seek has the treachery of King David with him, so from him you must be protected. I pray only that your quest leads you to the young David who slayed the giant Goliath, for he will protect you in your quest for truth.

Stay safe, as we have kept you safe, and may you both forgive me for breaking my silence.

Your departed, loving mother, Jane.

Thank you both for letting me be part of your lives."

"How did she come by the photo and what does it mean? It is amazing that I've gone from a quiet life as an ex-F1 driver to suddenly being a target, trying to bring a murderer to justice, and trying to solve the mystery of my new travel buddy. Clearly, someone somewhere thought I was getting bored."

Peter Smith pondered, "My gut tells me we are dealing with a hidden link here."

"A link between Sian and Troutman? No, we are talking different universes here, never mind worlds. No, the two happening at the same time is just a coincidence."

"Stirling, in my line of work, usually coincidences are never coincidences. Troutman murders your uncle, Roger Speed, then attempts to take you out when you start looking into it, and then a girl turns up at your house with you in a picture she has. I think we can safely say that the plot is thickening."

Stirling swirled the last dregs of his now-pleasantly-warmed brandy and finished it off. "Point taken. Sometimes, you know, with a car, an irritating rattle needs to be allowed to progress and get louder before its source can be found. But for now, the only further development I want this evening is in the direction of my bedroom."

Stirling stood and grabbed his black Belstaff jacket from the back of the chair.

"Stirling, just a word of caution, a big stick is no protection against a gun."

"Yeah, but hey, I think I had him worried. When in doubt, come out swinging, I think is the phrase. But, I have to say that I am glad he turned out to be friend rather than foe! See you in Monte, unless we bump into each other on the road." Stirling reached inside the sleeve of his jacket and turned to leave.

"Stirling, the man you approached in the car park is ex-SAS and a highly trained killer. He is trained to kill and to protect himself at all costs when threatened. A man coming at him out of the dark whilst swinging a big stick would be classed as a threat. When he reached inside of his jacket, he was not reaching for his wallet to give you a tip. You have now entered a different world that is ugly and brutal and operates just under the surface of the day-to-day life we are so familiar with. In a racecar, you were always one step in front of what was happening, that is how you stayed alive. You now need to apply that same technique to all that you do, now that you are involved in my world. "

There was seriousness in Peter Smith's voice. He always felt uncomfortable when untrained, ordinary people became involved in one of his operations. Although sometimes, this was absolutely necessary, he still always felt responsible for bringing them into such a dangerous, complex environment.

"Good night, Stirling, and do sleep well."

Stirling sort of half-smiled a reply and left the hotel a slightly different man than when he went in. He was realizing that he had unwittingly stumbled onto a steep learning curve.

As he climbed into bed, he looked at the open French-window-type doors that led out onto the veranda and overlooked the sweeps of vineyards that lay beyond. The fresh aroma of the night breeze that blew through the open windows would normally assist in the gentle journey into a restful sleep, but tonight the breeze brought with it only a feeling of vulnerability. Stirling got up, walked over to the windows and looked out onto the dark, shadowed landscape and decided tonight it would be better to shut and lock them.

Chapter 15

"It's an Augusta Westland AW101 VVIP, or to be precise, it cost 20 million in real money. They ordered one for the president of America, but it was deemed too expensive and they canceled the order. You are a beautiful girl, Michelle, you must go to any lengths to get your story."

Troutman smiled at the wide-eyed, young journalist. They sat, the only occupants, in the sumptuous beige leather surroundings of this flying fortress of a helicopters.

Michelle flicked her long hair and flicked an answer back to Troutman, "Every journalist has their methods and mine seem to reap results." Michelle knew how to play the game.

"Well, this is my world, Michelle. Do you like it?"

"Well, I know this helicopter is big enough to have fitted my crew, their cameras, and even their van into here as well."

"But Michelle, not all are comfortable with this world, but you, on the other hand, I believe would fit in very nicely. And I would certainly be happy to go to any lengths with you, Michelle, for you to get not only your answers, but maybe the lifestyle that you have always craved for."

Michelle had been thinking how much it must cost just to keep this flying building floating in the air but suddenly caught a whiff of a real story here. She was used to men flirting with her, sadly, it went with the looks, but it had opened doors for her in the past, and she knew exactly how to control it, but this was different. This was the richest man in world motorsport, squeaky-clean at that, making a play, or was she just imagining it? Was it just playful banter, a case of Troutman knowing what she was used to hearing, so he was just playing along with it to make her feel comfortable?

There were a few moments of silence when both parties looked at each other as the flying palace continued to chop its way through the London air. Then, Troutman stood up, removed his jacket, and turned to hang it on one of the gold coat hooks on the leather-clad forward bulkhead. Michelle focused on the dark sweat patch in the middle of Troutman's shirt where his overweight body had pressed against the chair he had just risen from. Troutman was a fast mover, and she wondered what was going to happen next.

Troutman was known worldwide for being the perfect example of how a hugely successful business life could be combined with a wonderful family life. There had been many articles and documentaries about Troutman that had all gone along the same theme, hence the reason why it had been easy to get another documentary commissioned. They were always a surefire hit. Yet now, alone in Troutman's world, she had the feeling that Troutman wanted more than just an interview.

Troutman turned back towards Michelle, his hands fighting a losing battle to squeeze his taut shirt deeper into trousers that had found their level under Troutman's bulging stomach. He walked across to the still-seated Michelle, his eyes flicking between looking at Michelle's eyes and her bare, slender, long legs that angled away from him. Michelle now wished she had worn jeans or at least a longer skirt. He bent low over Michelle and caught the aroma of the shampoo she had recently used on her silky hair and then steadied himself by placing his hand on Michelle's naked knee. Michelle tried to focus on Troutman's expensive cologne and not on his body odor. She now knew where Troutman wanted go.

"Now, what is that drink going to be, Michelle?"

Michelle had experience on how to handle these situations, but she also realized that, in this case, her next response could actually change her life forever. A life of opulence and being a plaything for Troutman or of a bona-fide journalist who would break the real story behind Lawrence Troutman. Troutman remained motionless except for his hand that slowly but surely began to creep up Michelle's smooth, firm leg. Michelle made no attempt to stop his wayward hand and decided on the power of words.

"Just water, Mr. Troutman, and then perhaps you can tell me about the fantastic relationship that you have with your lovely wife."

Troutman stood and battled to hide his anger. He did not like the rebuff from Michelle. When Troutman had decided that he wanted something, he did not like not getting it!

"Okay, Michelle. Water seems like a good idea, then perhaps you can sit back and enjoy the flight. I have a few emails to answer in my forward office. I am sure my beautiful wife will indeed give you all the answers you want when we arrive home."

Troutman handed Michelle an unopened bottle of water and then left the main cabin to answer his emails.

As he left the cabin Michelle silently punched the air.

Yes, I have a story here. Trust me, Troutman, you little pervert, I will get the answers I want, not the ones you want to give me. Like the quick flash of the silver underbody of a trout battling up a river, Michelle had just seen the exposed underbody of Troutman and not the wonderful rainbow color of his public image. Michelle sat back in her high-back leather chair and cracked open her bottle of water as the rotors clattered above, satisfied with the direction all was heading.

Troutman has met his match with me, Michelle thought. *Yes, I could get used to the helicopter and the lifestyle very easily, but those sweat patches and that belly to circumnavigate, I don't think so.* She smiled to herself. Michelle knew that she was on a scent trail that needed to be tracked until her prey was tired and relaxed, then she would pounce. She looked down at her knee and could still feel the clammy hand on it. That one final action had changed the way this Troutman interview was going to go; in fact, Michelle thought that maybe that one action had indeed changed her life. *Mr. Troutman, I am coming after you, and you can keep your 20-million-pound flying brick and your pathetic advances, for that matter, to yourself.*

Chapter 16

A warm, refreshing breeze drifted lazily across the brilliant white silk bed sheets, causing Michelle to stir from her deep sleep. From her back, she could look up at the high, ornate ceilings. She rolled her head and looked towards the source of the breeze—a slightly ajar large window framed by ghost-like, swaying curtains. Anyone staying at Lawrence Troutman's 22-bedroom Buckingham mansion was certainly up to their necks in five-star luxury living. Michelle's room that she had been escorted to the night before looked as though it had leapt from the pages of a glossy dream house magazine. Parquet floors, stunning decorations, and a smattering of regency bedroom furniture.

Michelle's press intrusion on Lawrence Troutman's private life had begun the evening before with a warm welcome from his loving family. Their two perfectly mannered children had indeed seemed very excited to welcome their returning father. Troutman's almost regal and beautiful wife, Kristianna, had been the perfect welcoming host.

A lovely meal, bedtime stories for the children, and an evening spent chatting and drinking fine wine had succeeded in dulling Michelle's journalistic appetite. In summary, a satisfying evening, bolstered with a few glasses of a vintage, had ensured that all was idyllic within the Troutman household. It was clear that Troutman paid great attention to his wife's every word. Kristianna, the only child and heir to one of the largest cosmetic companies in the world, also knew that Lawrence hung on her every word. When Kristianna Troutman spoke, Lawrence Troutman listened! It seemed as though Michelle was working with pieces from two different jigsaws that somehow had to fit together. Admittedly, the wine may have helped them click together.

Now, though in the bright morning light of a new day, Michelle's journalistic instincts were beginning to surface again, above the alcohol-induced mist. She had not imagined Troutman's approach in the helicopter. She knew that with a twitch of lips, a flash of her blue eyes and a hint of the right reply she could have been in the arms of Troutman. His family life was a veneer but apparently a veneer that his family did not seem part of manufacturing. Kristianna clearly was a genuine lady. Back to the two separate jigsaw pieces again. The problem with veneer surfaces, though, was that they tended to be hard, difficult, and required caution to penetrate. Michelle would need to dig deep to see into Troutman's underworld.

"Dave? It's Michelle. Listen, I do not have a lot of time but I am staying at Lawrence Troutman's place in Buckinghamshire and I need you to do some serious digging for me." Michelle cut short the reply coming back to her on the phone.

"Let's just say that I am onto a scent trail and this perfect family might have some dirty little habits that need some fresh air applied to them. Now, I really need you to listen, because I haven't got much time. Start with Lawrence Troutman's PA in his London office. Where did she come from, is she in a relationship, where does she live, does she want to talk? After what I have experienced over the last twenty four hours, I get the feeling she was trying to tell me, even warn me, about something." Again, Michelle interrupted the reply.

"No, Dave, not tomorrow, not tonight, now. I need you to get onto this now. Trust me, we are onto a 'biggy' here. I have a feeling that we are going to blow a hole the size of the Channel Tunnel in the side of Troutman's family cruiser that will leave his dirty little secret world exposed to the public world. And we will be in the big time, my friend. Now, get that inquisitive nose of yours into every nook and cranny of Troutman's life."

Clicking her phone off, Michelle walked through the windows out onto the veranda and into a beautiful summer's morning.

"Michelle, good morning." A smiling Kristianna beckoned Michelle down to join them. Looking down, Kristianna and Troutman were sat taking breakfast together on the terrace.

"Good morning. I am afraid that I slept a little too well," Michelle grinned back.

Troutman went on to acknowledge Michelle but then was distracted by his buzzing phone. "I am sorry but business calls. Kristianna, please excuse me. I must take this pressing call."

After his polite excuses, Troutman made for the expansive gardens with his phone to his ear.

"What is it?" irritation clearly detectible in his voice.

"I am sorry, Mr. Troutman, to disturb you during breakfast with your wife, but your journalist friend has just made a call from her room."

"And? Get to the point and stop…"

The very fact that the caller dared to interrupt Troutman whilst he was in mid-sentence made him stop and listen to what the caller had to say.

"Sir, I think you need to come to the control room and listen to the contents of the call. I believe we have a problem to deal with."

With breakfast cleared away, Michelle and her crew set up the cameras and awaited the reappearance of Kristianna and Troutman for the first of their official interviews. Michelle pondered her approach. She knew in her heart that she was onto the biggest story of her life. Troutman had made one slip with the wrong girl. Maybe a moment's lapse after a long day in the office, but he had shown his vulnerable underbelly. Yes, there would be threats of litigation and slander, but she had stumbled on a story that the entire world would want to hear about. A story that she could live on for the rest of her life. As with all big fish, though, they need to be able to run a little then be eased back towards their capture, almost without knowing. She was not going to let this fish off the hook.

Kristianna was indeed beautiful, serene, in control, and clearly in a different class. Unlike Lawrence Troutman, she wore her considerable wealth with dignity. She appeared to be a lady with strong traditional values. A lady with an inner strength of character that all who met her were aware of. Michelle could not help but admire her. She had presence.

Troutman entered stage from the right and caught Michelle by surprise, as she had become lost in her thoughts. "Michelle, Kristianna will be but a few minutes. I am afraid cameras are more foe than friend in her mind."

Troutman's eyes suddenly darted to the discarded newspaper that lay discarded by Michelle's side, yet his head and smile remained fixed on his journalist guest. Noticing his weak attempt to disguise his eye's interest, Michelle ventured, "I see Stirling Speed is to demonstrate a race car at Monte Carlo."

"Yes, one of my P34 Tyrrells, actually."

"One of yours? You have more than one then?"

"I have a large collection of race cars, and I am pleased to say that I own a brace of the six-wheeler P34s."

"Nice. I will be sure to see that, as I have been a big fan of Stirling Speed since I was a small girl. In fact, I had quite a crush on him. Probably still do, if the truth be known. He's one of the world's good guys, I think. His focus and determination have always been an inspiration to me. When he had his Monza crash, would you believe I actually prayed for him, which I can assure you was a first for me. He seems to me to be the perfect gentleman. I would love to get an interview with him but he does seem to lead a private life these days, since his retirement."

Michelle stopped herself; she had clearly lost the attention of Troutman, who hesitated long enough to show his disapproval of not being the center of attention in his own home, or anywhere else for that matter.

"I see your crew…"

"Have gone to the van, not happy with the backlighting or something."

"I am glad we have a few minutes alone, Michelle. I do hope that there was no misunderstanding on our flight over here yesterday. You can see how happy my family is, and I would hate for it to be troubled in any way. I am sure you can understand my concern for the protection of my family and for you, for that matter. I would hate for anyone to be harmed just for the sake of a misunderstanding."

"Mr. Troutman, you made your intentions very clear yesterday, and I will decide who will be harmed with the message that you sent out. I certainly respect you and your family and the privileged position I am in but I am sure you can see, Mr. Troutman, I am just doing my job."

"Of course you are, my dear. If there was a misunderstanding, then please do accept my apologies. I do have a very interesting collection of cars. Perhaps later, Michelle, I could arrange to show some of them to you. I am sure it will add color to your documentary."

Let him run Michelle, don't fight him too hard, or he'll break the line and dive for cover.

"That would really be interesting, Mr. Troutman. I would love that. You keep them in your grounds?"

"No, down at my test track, not too far from here actually. I had it renovated for my own amusement, really. It is a rather fast pre-war track. It has old hangers that now house most of my race collection. I like to take them out every so often and give them an airing. I also keep some of my prototypes there as well."

"I had heard that you had your own private track."

"It is a fun place to relax, Michelle. I will take you there."

"Where are you taking this young girl, Lawrence?" Kristianna had entered the room.

"Ah, Kristianna, my love, I thought it would be interesting for Michelle and her crew to see some of my toys down at the track."

"Men and their toys, please, Michelle do not indulge him. It is time he grew up."

Chapter 17

Stirling had pushed hard on his early morning run to clear his carburetors, as he liked to tell people. In reality, Stirling liked to maintain his private philosophy, 'No gain without pain.' The harder you push, the more you enjoy the little rewards you give yourself. His reward this morning was a crisp, clean shave; a sharp, refreshing shower; then dressing in a freshly pressed white polo shirt, blue chinos; then a breakfast of porridge and fruit whilst sitting on the veranda of his favorite French villa guesthouse. Strange to some, but these simple routines seemed more satisfying to Stirling after a hard run at first light.

Stripping his gray sweats off, Stirling walked naked across his room. He paused in front of the full-length mirror and fingered his shoulder scars. *Well, at least I am still around to see them,* he mused to himself. He always felt a small pang of guilt for the damage he had done to the body he had been entrusted with.

Tony Brooks, a late 1950s Formula One driver of considerable repute, would never race in a race car he felt was unsafe, even sacrificing a world championship once by bringing his car in to be checked over after an incident out on the track. He valued his body and his life more than a race or even a championship win, which is probably why he was one of the few drivers from that perilous period of racing to actually see and enjoy his retirement.

Stirling turned to walk into the old-fashioned but immaculately cleaned en suite just as his phone let out a squawk reminiscent of an old vintage car horn. Stirling read the message.

Meet in the village square before you leave for Monte. Come alone. Peter.

Sian was very happy to spend more time with her new best friends and so put up no argument when Stirling suggested that he should head down to the village for supplies before setting off. Supplies of what, she was not quite sure, because the villa seemed to have an abundance of all things essential and non-essential to life. As Stirling's immaculate figure disappeared out of the door, she helped herself to some more of the fresh, warm bread that was cooling in front of her.

Stirling sat savoring the aromas from his chestnut-rich coffee and surveyed the slowly waking village square in front of him. His eyes soon settled on a neat gray man making his way across the square, heading right for Stirling. Peter Smith was straight to the point.

"We have just found out that Lawrence Troutman has a journalist in tow the next few days. Michelle Lark, she is called. She is spending time with his family as well, yet another documentary about the idyllic Troutman family. We have checked her out. By all accounts, she is a career girl looking to make her mark."

"I can't say that I have heard of her, should I have?" Stirling enquired.

"No, but what has been flagged up is that she has mobilized a private investigator she sometimes uses to dig around for her. This investigator just happens to be one that we sometimes are allowed to use when, well, let's just say some of his information and services suits us. It allows us to keep our ear to the ground. She has asked him to get into Troutman's London secretary. The inference is that Troutman has a less then savory side when it comes to women than he would have the world believe."

Stirling shook his head. "Obviously, I have known Troutman for a long time and I will agree that there is something not right about him hence my own digging around and the fact that, according to you, he wants me dead. But a womanizer or whatever, I really can't see that. He's a big family man and dotes on his wife, Kristianna. Plus, she strikes me as not a woman you'd want to cross. Remember, Peter, Lawrence Troutman would be nothing without her. It was her money that bankrolled everything in the early days. Surely, he would not risk all that for a bit of 'knee trembling'."

Peter Smith allowed himself a slight smile. "Knee trembling? Now that is a new expression to me. I think this journalist has smelt something that has got her twitching, and I think it would be good to make contact with her. We will ask if she would like an interview with you. Let's draw her in and see what she thinks about Mr. Troutman. She might be the inside eyes and ears that we need."

Stirling chose this moment to finish off his coffee and to use the time for a moment of consideration. He decided that he could see no downside to this suggestion. "Okay, sounds good. Let's do it."

Peter Smith slid a picture over to Stirling of Michelle Lark. "You just need to wait for the call."

Stirling lifted the picture. "That is one good-looking journalist. I feel this might be one of my more enjoyable interviews."

"Focus, Stirling, your life is at stake here."

"Think I'd better keep the picture, Peter, just in case I don't recognize her."

He slid the picture away from a not amused Peter Smith, gave him a cheeky wink, and walked over to his gleaming grey E-Type that sat waiting to stretch its legs on the run down to the jewel that was Monte Carlo.

Chapter 18

"So, Mrs. Troutman,"

"No, please, it is Kristianna."

"Thank you. Okay, Kristianna, we cannot dismiss the fact that you privately own the largest cosmetic company in the world?"

"Yes, Michelle, but these days I am but a figurehead. The business is run by very professional and, more importantly, trustworthy, honest people. My grandmother put a great deal of emphasis on building a trustworthy team. Trust was a subject that my grandmother was passionate about."

"Your grandmother set up Arias Cosmetics?"

"No, this is a common misconception. My grandfather set up Arias. Those were difficult financial times and my grandfather enjoyed his drink. The positive side to his drinking was that he drank with people who could open doors for him, the right doors. He saw an open door that required a supply of cosmetics and he stepped through that door. It was a means to an end for him, it funded his drinking binges and gambling."

"But this business grew well and was successful?"

"So it appeared but unknown to my grandmother that, to start the business up and to expand it, my grandfather had mortgaged everything they had. And what they had was passed down to my grandmother by her parents who had died before their years in an accident. He even stole jewelry that my grandmother held in great affection. It was all that she had left of her mother. For a while, he maintained a story that thieves had broken into their house and stolen the jewelry. Eventually, the truth came out that he had sold it to raise money."

"All turned out okay in the end, though, Kristianna?"

Kristianna delayed her reply and looked out along the long lawn that lay outside the windows. A gardener could be seen attending to minuscule details within the perfect-looking garden. She turned and looked straight into Michelle's eyes. Her stock response to this common statement was, 'Yes, we are fortunate to be in the position we are in.' This time though, Kristianna spotted trust in the eyes of young Michelle.

"Michelle, I would like to say, 'Yes, all turned out well' but it was not as simple as that."

Michelle had researched well before and instantly picked up that Kristianna was, for some reason, going off-script here. Little was known about the early days of Arias Cosmetics.

"As the money came in, the drinking and gambling became more expensive. Then, one day, he emptied the bank account of money that was set aside to pay staff wages and ran off with his mistress that he had met in one of his drinking holes. My grandmother was left with a three-month-old daughter, my mother, a failed cosmetic company with staff waiting to be paid, no home, and owing the bank a fortune. So, to answer your question properly, no, it did not turn out all right."

Michelle turned to her camera crew to make sure they were getting everything then turned and blinked her eyes at Kristianna in a moment of silence that really said, 'I respect the insight you are giving me here.'

"Wow, Kristianna, you have my attention. What a horrible little man, if you do not mind me saying."

Kristianna had indeed commanded Michelle's attention, this lady certainly had presence. Lawrence Troutman sat with a slightly glazed look in his eyes in either a heard-it-all -before' state or a 'captivated-by-the-story' state. It was hard to tell which.

"Sorry, Mr. Troutman, you must have heard all this before, but it is just great to get the background."

Troutman looked on vaguely and Michelle realized that the glazed look was actually an I'm-busy-thinking-about-something-else look—probably about how to make his next million.

"Errm no, I mean, yes, my wife comes from a line of strong women."

Kristianna sipped her freshly delivered lemon and ginger tea.

"Thank you, Mary. May we have lunch at, say, 12:30?"

The question was accompanied with a warm smile from Kristianna and the maid responded with an admiring, "Of course, ma'am."

"Now, where was I?"

Michelle eagerly responded, "You were left with nothing."

"Yes, my family was left with nothing."

"I am sure Michelle is not interested in the history of Arias, my dear. I think they are here to talk about the here and now, actually."

Michelle looked at Troutman then back to Kristianna to await her response. Kristianna said, "My family was left destitute due to a weak man who could not control himself. My grandmother sought a meeting with the bank manager. She attended with no accounts, no business plan, but with just one question."

Michelle sat forward, resting her chin on her hand, and rested her arm on her now-crossed legs that caused her long, flowing khaki summer dress to fall open slightly at the split, unintentionally exposing more of her long, smooth, slender legs. Troutman adjusted his gaze and focused on the still busy gardener outside. Michelle adjusted her dress so now only her naked ankles were left exposed.

Kristianna continued, "She told the bank manager that she could bring nothing to him but the one thing she had held close to her all her life, something she had never failed in. She had never broken a trust and would never break a trust whilst she still could draw a breath. She asked the bank manager to trust her to turn the company around and to pay off the debts. Somehow, he knew that he could trust the word of this desperate lady in front of him."

"From that day on, she never did break a trust and insisted that all around her were trustworthy. Eventually, it was written into everyone's contract. That one act of trust by that bank manager saved my grandmother's life and her daughter's future. It was the best financial decision that manager ever made for his bank. Both my grandmother and the bank went on to prosper, and it started with a solid foundation of trust. My family, Michelle, and the company that I am privileged to be the head of are totally based on trust. Anyone breaking that trust is discarded like refuse."

Kristianna, glanced over to her husband, who was busy silently tapping away on his phone. Troutman instantly picked up on the glance. "Kristianna, how rude of me."

He turned to Michelle. "I employ so many people to make decisions, yet constantly they want my input."

He turned back to Kristianna. "My dear, I feel I must excuse myself to leave you two alone. Michelle is with us, of course, at Monte Carlo, so I am sure I can fill in the boring bits if required then. Oh, and of course we will be catching up later, Michelle."

Michelle had become engrossed in Kristianna's story telling and so looked blankly for a moment at Troutman.

"You wanted to see some of my collection?"

"Of course, Mr. Troutman, I will, I am, looking forward to it. Thank you."

Troutman got up and exited the room via one of the doors behind Kristianna, gently stroking his hand across her hair as he left.

Trying not to seem too eager this time, Michelle continued on her voyage into this unchartered territory.

"Kristianna, may I ask you about your mother?"

"She died when I was just seven. Old enough for me to remember her touch, the smell of her perfume, and her wonderful smile when I did something well. Old enough for it to hurt so much. She died of a broken heart."

Michelle looked down, as though desperately searching on the floor for the right words for her next question. Kristianna ended the search for her.

"Before I am sure you eloquently ask, yes, she committed suicide."

"Arias Cosmetics was doing well?"

"Oh, yes, by this time, my mother was leading a privileged life. But then a man came into her life, a man who was to become my father. He was a charming, good-looking, carefree builder. Well, a carpenter, to be precise. My mother completely fell for him, as many women would have. He could charm the birds from the trees."

"It all turned sour as soon as he got access to our money. Like my grandfather, he gambled and drank. It soon became clear that he was having many affairs. He left my mother when he was confronted about them but not before infecting my sweet mother with a sexually transmitted disease. My grandmother worked so hard to support my mother during this period but she had been stabbed to the heart and the pain was just too much."

"Then, one morning, she breezed into my room and woke me by bouncing on my bed. I opened my eyes to my mother laughing and looking radiant. We rushed our breakfast down and went out on a wonderful girly day. We had our hair done, our nails too, and she allowed me to buy some makeup, for the first time. She smiled so much that day, after months of me watching her cry. I now know that this is how she wanted me to remember her, a beautiful, fun mum. It must have been so hard for her to give me that day. It was the best gift I have ever received. That night, she read me a story and tucked me in, her last words to me were, 'Trust me, Kristianna, today I have been truly happy'.

The following morning, Grandma and I left early to holiday on the family yacht that was down in the south of France. The next day, I was sat dangling my feet off the side of the moored yacht when my grandma eased down onto the deck next to me and dangled her feet off the side as well. I cuddled into her protective arms and felt warm and secure. She squeezed me tighter then told me that Mother had gone to sleep with a beautiful smile on her face and had not woken up the following morning. We sat there for so long in silence, just looking at the calm, glinting sea."

"Many years later, when Grandma handed the reins of Arias over to me, she asked me to remember that calm, glinting, beautiful sea that we had gazed upon that day. I remembered it well. She then went on to tell me that the same sea could be whipped up into huge, disturbed waves that could wreak devastation. Then, she went on to tell me the full story about what my mother had endured. She told me that, after tucking me into bed that night, my mother had retired to her room and took an overdose of sleeping pills. The storms within her had just become too great for her to control."

Kristianna reached into her handbag and brought out a small silver box, no bigger than a matchbox, and handed it over to Michelle. Michelle, desperately hanging onto her emotions, took the box and opened it. Inside was an aged, faded lipstick.

"This was the lipstick your mother allowed you to buy that day?"

"Yes, I keep it with me at all times."

Michelle looked out of the window to hide her filling eyes. A smooth, well-manicured hand appeared in front of them, offering a soft white tissue. Michelle turned back, anger in her eyes.

"And that scum… I am so sorry, Kristianna, the man; sorry, I mean your father, what happened to him?"

"My father? Funny, I never think of him as my father." Kristianna seemed to be lost in thought for a brief moment as she tried to imagine this hideous man as 'her father'.

"He sued my grandmother for his share of the estate and was awarded a huge settlement. He died many years later whilst sleeping off a night of drink. There was an unexplained gas explosion on his yacht that the Arias money had bought for him."

"Kristianna, I am so, so sorry, I never realized that you had gone through so much."

Kristianna smiled back. "Michelle, you are young and have so much in front of you. Remember, what does not kill you makes you stronger. I am a strong lady. My grandmother vowed that her family would never again be gouged with the hurt caused by a broken trust. Anyone benefitting from what my grandmother had built up would be punished mercilessly if they ever came close to hurting her family ever again."

A silence then followed, in which both knew that something of huge gravity was about to follow. Kristianna turned to the crew. "I think it is time for you guys to head into the kitchen and demand a well-earned brew from the cook."

As the door closed behind them, Kristianna turned to Michelle. "Michelle, when I put my trust in someone, they take on a huge responsibility."

Time seemed to cease as Kristianna peered intently at Michelle. "Should I put my trust in you, Michelle?"

Michelle scrambled desperately to see which direction this freight train was going. Did Kristianna want Troutman's dirt hidden or exposed in all its filth?

"Michelle, you wanted the story behind Lawrence Troutman, and this is my story. I am the power, the force, and the money behind him. I, like my mother and my grandmother, fell for a charming, good-looking man. I was in a position to fund his wildest dreams and create the world empire that he is the head of. I trusted him, Michelle. If my trust has been broken, then I cannot allow my family to be harmed. I once allowed a broken trust to be overlooked and I still feel the pain of that in my side. But now, I am older, wiser, and stronger. Can I trust you, Michelle?"

Michelle was not sure whether to press Kristianna or not further on the overlooked trust. But one thing she was now certain of was which direction the freight train was going in.

Michelle leant forward and took hold of Kristianna's hand in an effort to add weight to what she was about to say. "Kristianna, you can trust me, leave it to me. Whilst I am able to draw breath, I will not let you down."

This time, Kristianna reached over to squeeze Michelle's hands. "Do what you have to do, Michelle, but please be careful."

Michelle squeezed an acknowledgment back.

"Now, Michelle." Kristianna had resumed a warm, sincere smile again. "My two children are going to provide us with a guided tour around our house, and they have even made an itinerary for us."

Kristianna passed a hand-written itinerary, and on the front it neatly read, *'You are invited to a giyded tore around the Troutman residue!'*

"My youngest has a little more work to do on her spelling, I think."

Kristianna smiled as the children appeared, right on cue. Michelle laughed. Inside, she knew her life would never be the same again. As corny as it seemed to think, never mind say, she really felt a connection with this fine, strong, loving mother. Michelle always was somehow certain that, one day, if she worked hard enough, she would get the break she deserved.

Kristianna's two children stood patiently, beaming at Michelle. "Well, Kristianna, we'd better let your beautiful children show us around your 'residue'. Lead the way, guys."

A discreet maid chose this moment to pass a message to Kristianna. "Ah, yes, the cars are never far away. Michelle, after your exhausting tour, Lawrence has sent a message saying that he will pick you up at six to take you to his playground, or should I say his test track. I will arrange an early lunch for you. Now, children, take us on your tour and enlighten me to the secrets of our house."

Michelle found that she could only feel admiration building for this lioness of a woman in front of her as she played with her cubs—a role model she was going to try her all to support.

Chapter 19

"Stirling Speed allowing his bags to be carried for him. I think secretly Stirling Speed does like the high life." Sian's teasing comment was a sure sign that she was now feeling quite comfortable in Stirling's company.

Road trips seem to either break relationships or make them. Sian had spent the whole trip down from Stirling's Cheshire home to the glittering Monte Carlo revealing her life story. It was a one-way conversation, as she reasoned that she knew Stirling's, as his had been written about so many times over the years. Whether all that had been written about Stirling was actually true was another conversation for another time.

Every time Sian mentioned her mother, Stirling's mind rallied. He felt slightly guilty that he already knew more about this young girl than she did. The mystery of Sian's mother's identity was still a bubble that remained inflated, waiting to be burst. Stirling had allowed one ear to listen to the silky straight six stretched out under the long bonnet of his E-Type as it strode across France. He allowed his other ear to listen to Sian's light ramblings. He allowed his mind to dance around the Sian-Stirling-Troutman conundrum, the resolution of which still was proving evasive.

"For your information, Miss Cheek, I allow my bags to be carried so that the usher does not miss out on the tip and the autograph that he will probably flaunt later. Remember, young Sian, a good driver drives by what he cannot see, not by what he can see at the end of his nose! I believe that is your room. I have got to go down to the pit garages for a seat fitting in the P34 that I am to drive. If you are coming with me, you need to be at the reception in 30 minutes. If you snooze, you lose!"

The smiling young French girl mocked a salute with a straight back. "Yes, Captain Speed... Sorry, yes, Captain Stirling."

The 1976 Tyrell P34 six-wheeled Formula One car sat naked in the garage. Its clothing, the bodywork, carefully placed by its side. In its naked state, it was clear to see just how vulnerable the F1 race driver of yesteryear really was.

Stirling stepped into the low-slung, six-wheeled oddity and, straight legged, guided his race-boot-clad feet down onto the pedals they would dance on in two days' time. He carefully eased his way onto the gentle, warming seat bag that had just been filled with expanding foam. Stirling rested his elbows on the fuel tanks on either side of him and pulled on the leather and nickel-plated steering wheel in an attempt to mimic his driving position as the gurgling, warming expanding foam crept around his back and in-between his legs. In front of him were four almost-go-cart-looking tire-clad wheels, behind were two huge tire-clad wheels.

"What are you doing?" Sian asked.

"We are forming a seat to my size and seating position by using expanding foam in a bin-liner-type bag. Normally, a cast would be taken from the mold we are forming and a proper seat would be made, but because this is just a one-off demo drive, I will use the actual molding as my seat. When the foam has hardened off, the mechanics will trim it then cover it with tank tape to maintain its integrity.

"Luxurious, then!"

"F1 is about function, not form. If it functions well, then it becomes a thing of beauty."

"Why four wheels at the front, six in total? Is this the only car like it?"

"This was the most successful of the six-wheel designs. March tried a six-wheeler with four wheels at the back, and although it was tested, it was never actually raced in, period."

"So this was a good design, yet no one copied it?"

"The configuration initially provided some significant advantages. The lower tires offered a smaller frontal area and so the airflow over them was less disruptive, making the car, for its time, more aero-effective. The car changed direction well, by that I mean it turned into corners well because there was a bigger combined contact patch on the road. And once they had gotten over the brake temperature issues, the tires' temperatures were more stable. In the end, though, rapid tire compound developments meant the specially sized and made tires fell behind in the development race, with conventional tires for the four-wheeled cars—and so performance suffered. Then, a new regulation came in that banned six wheelers. And so, in the end, the whole concept was canned."

A smiling Stirling looked up into Sian's wide eyes. "Ah, now I feel enlightened... Not!"

Sian shrugged but continued with her childlike-but-fun 20 questions. "So, is this your car?"

"No, no," Stirling replied. "I am just the nut that holds the steering wheel. No, this car belongs to Lawrence Troutman."

"Wow, be careful with it then."

"You will have the pleasure of meeting him shortly; he is apparently coming down to meet me here."

The two mechanics looked at each other, then both looked at Stirling, and one spoke, "I am sorry, Mr. Speed."

Stirling held his hand up. "Please, just Stirling, we can definitely drop the Mr. Speed."

"Sorry, Stirling, we thought you knew, Mr. Troutman will not be along. He changed his plans last minute to go to his private test track with some guests, so he delayed his travel arrangements."

Stirling levered himself out of the car, "Well, I would like to say that missing Mr. Troutman has ruined my day, but I can't, because, guess what, it hasn't. Thank you both for your help. I will see you Thursday. I will be down in plenty of time. Oh, and given that I don't have that much time out on track, I presume we will be running scrubbed rubber and bedded pads."

"Yes, Stirling. The brake pads are already fitted, and that stack of tires there are the actual ones that you will be using."

"Excellent. Come on, Sian, you can buy me a coffee."

Sian followed Stirling out of the garage, but not before, discreetly, behind Stirling's back, turning out her pockets to the smiling mechanics to show that she had no money.

Without looking back Stirling called out, "You can owe me!"

Chapter 20

A tart grapefruit, a raisin, and coconut bran followed by a sinful, butter-enriched scrambled egg on granary toast, washed down by a coffee that took no prisoners and offered no compromise, were Stirling's treat this morning. Stirling had engaged the services of a good friend to take Sian on a shopping cruise around the opulent Monte Carlo.

Despite sitting at the same breakfast table on the hotel outcrop that sliced into the crystal sparkling Mediterranean for all the years that Stirling graced the Formula One circus, only now, on this morning, did he really notice his surroundings, see the buzz of life around the breakfast tables, see the boats that sat like pearls on a blue, undulating cushion.

For years, breakfast was a carefully managed, vitamin, calorie, and fluid intake. Various PAs would flit around, confirming and tweaking schedules for the day. And somewhere between press conferences, TV interviews, sponsor events, and product launches they expertly managed to schedule time when Stirling could actually drive a racecar. Did he miss Formula One now? No. Did he regret how focused and blinkered he was? The answer was probably yes. He now wished that he had enjoyed the journey more. One goal achieved was only the trigger to set another goal. But then the question would have to be asked, would the end destination have been the same?

Monte Carlo was Stirling's favorite place to race. He had so many memories as a child being brought on holiday there. He even still had a childhood scar on his right leg that originated in Monte Carlo. Having fallen down a grid where the cover had been left off, he ended up having a small operation on his leg that necessitated an overnight stop in the Princess Grace Hospital, a place where many a race driver had previously ended up and where some had even finished their days on earth.

The handsome but, sadly, tragic Ferrari driver, Lorenzo Bandini, having made a minute misjudgment at the chicane, careered into concrete barriers that were protected by straw bales. His fuel tanks erupted, ignited the straw, and the trapped Bandini suffered horrific burns that he later succumbed to in the Princess Grace Hospital.

Monte Carlo had seen its share of great joy but also had experienced great sadness. The sadness brought about by the death of the much-loved Princess Grace in a road accident in the hills above the principality could still be sensed even today. Stirling felt privileged to be part of the principality's history.

"*Café, Monsieur?*"

"*Oui, merci.*"

No hectic schedule for Stirling today, though. No free practice or qualifying to prepare for, just one appointment in the diary for today. The invitation read:

> **Mr. Lawrence Troutman personally invites**
> **you and your partner aboard the Serene Lady for drinks at**
> **8.00 pm.**
> **Black tie to be the order.**

Despite the light schedule, Stirling was in no mood to enjoy it. The situation that Stirling now found himself in was developing fast and he needed to stay ahead of the curve. Peter Smith had hit Stirling with a lot more new information and news the night before. News and information that he wished he'd never heard but now that he had, he knew there was definitely no going back.

"Troutman appears to be struggling to keep all his plates spinning, and you can rest assured that he can see them starting to slow down. When just one of them stops, his empire and all his nasty little secrets will come crashing down. And boy will that be a noise when it happens."

Peter Smith had expanded on more information that his organization's ongoing investigation had brought to light. They had found a deeply entrenched, far-reaching financial link between Troutman's empire and a Mafia-like criminal organization known as Luna. This twilight organization had developed into one of the underworld's big-league players.

Troutman's vast and complicated financial empire made for the perfect model to 'money launder' Luna's ill-gotten gains. This link led to the further discovery that a good many of Troutman's employees were, 'reformed characters', ex-criminals who had connections with Luna. Troutman apparently showed great charity by using these 'reformed characters' in key positions within his vast world-wide organization.

The present chief engineer to Lawrence Troutman's race collection and racecar development company, one John Beechy, had indeed been such a character. Investigations had highlighted that John Beechy was a feared man in the underworld. The sort of man who we know, deep inside of us, shares the world we live in but hope in our worst nightmares that we never meet. He was a man whose barbaric services were clearly valued by Luna. Yet, now here he was, holding down a respectful, well-paid job that he hardly seemed qualified for. He appeared to work closely with Troutman. Wherever Troutman was in the world, John Beechy seemed to be lurking. What a charitable heart Troutman seemed to have.

"Stirling, keep a close eye out for this character, Beechy. We are certain that he is a triggerman for Troutman. Why he needs a trigger man, we are not yet certain."

That next piece of news from Peter Smith hit Stirling like a train. "Stirling, I am afraid the situation is getting uglier by the day. Stirling, we know for certain that John Beechy was at Lawrence Troutman's private test track last night when the young journalist got killed driving one of Troutman's cars!"

"No, not the pretty little thing who wanted to interview me?" Stirling instinctively reached into his bag and brought out the picture of the young, smiling journalist that he had jokily taken from Peter Smith.

"An accident?"

"Information is still scarce, but it appears there was a failure in the car and it burst into flames when it impacted with the banking. We know that Kristianna Troutman is devastated and has canceled her plans to travel to Monte Carlo. She had apparently spent time with her during the making of the documentary."

To Stirling, this latest news had seemed surreal. It was as though he was in some dramatic film or book. How could this be happening around him?

"Sadly, Stirling, this sort of thing goes on every day around the world. But thankfully, the common people who go about their day-to-day life never have to deal with it."

Stirling had looked around the quiet bar in which they were sitting, within the Fairmont Hotel. A small bowl of assorted nuts had been placed in the middle of their table by a young waiter dressed in a crisp black and white uniform. A gently played piano blended carefree background music into the low hum of polite chatter that came from little huddles of well-dressed people. Ordinary people just going about their day-to-day life whilst just under the surface of their daily life, a young, innocent girl was murdered.

"I am afraid that I have more news to give you. The private investigator I told you about this morning has been found dead this afternoon along with Lawrence Troutman's London PA, in her apartment. The police are saying that early investigation has shown it was a night of sex and drugs gone wrong. But we think it has a Luna hit all over it. Troutman is becoming erratic and careless. He will slip up. We are now looking to set up a pincer movement on him to force him into the shallows. We have you on one side but we are also looking to see what Luna's position is in all of this, especially after these latest tragic events. They will not want their dirty washing to get mixed up with Troutman's. The more we squeeze though, the more Troutman will thrash around. We are now seeing what he is capable of and anyone prepared to get involved with Luna is well down the line of being bad to the core."

Stirling had gone on to ask, "Have you any development on why he wants an ex-Stirling Speed?"

"We have a team studying and watching Troutman's every move. He is fiercely protecting or hiding something. We believe that his involvement with Luna is enabling him to maintain whatever it is that he is up to. Regarding you, we think he has allowed a chink in his armor at some point in the past, which certainly leads us back to your Uncle Roger. Yes, he has let his guard down at some point and is vulnerable. We need to find that soft spot. His actions toward you must mean that he thinks you have dangerous knowledge."

"But I don't."

"I know, but we are missing something. We need to keep him thinking that you have something on him."

"And, Sian, any news about her?"

"Well, that is a no and a yes. No, in so much that we have drawn a number of blanks. We do know that whom she thought was her mother was actually not. We can find no connection with you. It's the next blank that actually tells us something. We have drawn an absolute blank trying to trace Sian's real mother and father."

"And that tells us something?"

"Yes, Stirling, it does. Try looking past the obvious, or as you race drivers would say, try looking through the corner towards the exit. Don't look at what is right in front of you. The organization I work for has eyes everywhere in the world. We can find, get, investigate, and instigate, anything to further our investigations, yet we have drawn a blank trying to find Sian's real parents. It tells us, Stirling, that there has been a cover up. Sian's mother and father have been made to disappear or they themselves have worked hard to hide their identity."

"Do you think Luna or do think there is any link with Troutman?"

"We do not think so. First, we do not think Troutman's involvement with Luna goes that far back, and also, this disappearance is too elegant. If Luna wants someone to disappear, they send them a concrete pair of slippers."

"Or pump them with dodgy drugs. And the young journalist?"

"She was definitely onto something. Telephone records show that she was in contact with the private investigator in the morning, hence his contact with us. I think we can safely assume that there was an involvement between Troutman and his secretary that was not strictly professional."

Peter Smith finished where he had started, "Stirling, Troutman is struggling to keep all his plates spinning, when one stops…"

Stirling drained his morning coffee and looked out at the awakening Mediterranean. Whether it was years of ingrained competitive race driving or an ingrained characteristic, Stirling always turned and faced a challenge head-on, be that a flat chat corner, a difficult car, or stiff opposition. Stirling was now ready to face Troutman and look him straight in the eye—ready to beat this guy physically and mentally.

Stirling tipped his discreet but attentive waiter and headed up to his sea-view apartment. It was time to change into his running gear and hit the foothills of Monte Carlo in the climbing temperature of the day. He wanted his body and mind well prepped for this latest challenge.

Chapter 21

The large reception of the Fairmont Hotel was busy—Monte Carlo was busy. A number of gala dinners, sponsors' receptions, and parties ensured a sprinkling of well-known faces mixed in amongst the swelling numbers of people flying, shipping, and driving in readiness for the jewel of Grand Prix racing, the Monaco Grand Prix.

A smiling but uncertain family hovered in the reception, delaying their journey out of the hotel doors whilst desperately not wanting their delaying tactics to seem too obvious. Their observant and keen young son had tugged at his older sister's hair, who had then pulled on her mom's hand, who had then excitedly grabbed her husband's shoulder whilst commentating in an uncomfortably loud whisper that was actually at a normal talking volume, just with less mouth movement,

"Robert, Robert, there is that very nice racing driver you like, the one who smashed himself up… the Speed guy."

Robert had quickly taken control of the situation after a pregnant period of staring, then mimicked, unintentionally, his wife's limited mouth movement and whispered loudly

"Get me something to sign," without looking at his wife, his gaze firmly fixed on his celebrity prey.

"Not a napkin!"

Roberts's wife desperately dug deeper in her well-equipped holiday handbag.

"He'll be gone in a minute. He'll be a busy man, anything… No, not the car park ticket, come on, quick."

Stirling watched discreetly and with a smile the scene that he had seen so many times before in supermarkets, hotels, restaurants, and airports. He always wished people would just come up to him and say, 'Hi, just wanted to say hello, this is my family.' Stirling was still a big fan himself and would always feel excited when in the presence of some of the all-time greats of motorsport—Stewart, Lauda, Moss, Surtees, Prost.

Stirling looked down, then knelt down on one knee and took hold of the coloring book and purple crayon that the little girl had approached with. The distant Robert froze with a look of horror on his face, then took decisive action and abandoned his wife and son to be in the presence of his daughter.

"Hello, what is your name?" Stirling asked.

"Emily. You are famous."

"Well, you are beautiful. Is this your family?"

His wife had then abandoned son and set off in pursuit of husband whilst accidentally undoing the top button of her blouse and removing her hair bobble, setting her restrained ponytail free to flow. But all family members had now regrouped.

"This is Daddy, and Phillip."

Stirling signed his purple signature and finished with his little drawing. He'd always thought he had invented his little character, but many aficionados over the years said that the character had originated from within the offices of a certain Murray Walker when, as a young gent, he had worked at Fort Dunlop, in Birmingham.

Phillip took hold of his sister's now-valuable coloring book.

"What's the bug thing you have drawn?"

"It's what I call a groundhog! He has big fat tires for legs and speeds around the circuits of the world. Do you know what he eats?"

Phillip was now deeper into this conversation than he had initially intended but was happy to have a stab at the answer.

"Does he eat, errm…"

The whole family now focused and waited proudly for their fellow member to answer.

"Does he eat racing drivers?"

Robert put his hand over his eyes, he had needed his five-year-old to step up to the mark on this occasion.

"Well, I hope not, and I am still here, so I am sure he does not. No, he goes around the circuits at night after all the race cars have gone to bed and with his vacuum-like, wide mouth sucks up all the bits of rubber that have been left on the circuit from the race tires. That makes his own tires even stickier, so he can go faster and faster round the corners without skidding."

Robert now decided he needed to take control of this conversation.

"I admire your driving Mr. Speed and your Monza crash!"

Everyone mentioned the Monza shunt and never the three world championships he had battled for. *Maybe I should have taken the easy route and just had the shunt*, Stirling often thought but never said.

"Thank you. I had plenty of practice at the driving but not as much of the crashing, fortunately."

The next moment of silence was just long enough for Robert to realize that it was not his best opening line.

"I love your blue tux, Mr. Speed, different but very handsome," his wife said. Robert stared at his wife.

"Alas, the blue tux that looks black in the evening is not my idea; I stole it from a certain King Edward."

"Thank you," Roberts's wife strangely replied.

Stirling dropped to one knee again, the only movement that still resulted in a stab of pain from his once-shattered legs.

"And will you two be watching the race cars?" he asked the children.

"Yes, from the swimming pool, Daddy says."

"Ah, so you will be looking down on Loews hairpin from the hotel's pool area. Well, you look out for a blue racecar with six wheels on it and I think the driver of it might just give you a little wave on the first lap of a demonstration run. And remember, if you hear any snuffling tonight when you are in bed that might be Mr. Groundhog having his dinner."

The children looked at each other and giggled. Stirling looked up. "Sian, here at last." Stirling took hold of Sian's hand and showed no signs of discomfort, only concentration, as he stood up.

Robert and his family knew that it was time for them to retreat. Stirling was sure there was a slight dip in Robert's head as he backed away.

Still in earshot, the Robert family's conversation ignited. "Well, what a nice man," the wife said.

"And he'll be busy…" Robert said.

"Oh, and how handsome," she remarked.

"Well, if you can afford the right tailored clothes, dear, anyone can look handsome."

"And his girlfriend... so much younger."

"I noticed that, and very nice she was. In fact, she had very nice..."

"Robert!"

"Shoes dear, very nice shoes."

Sian did look beautiful in her very newly acquired flowing aqua evening dress that hung in the right places but fell in a carefree cascade. Her natural, free-spirited curls had now been brought into line and straightened, which highlighted the shine of her black, black hair.

"Sian, you look stunningly gorgeous, for a change!"

"Thank you, Stirling that was nearly a compliment. You look good as well, for an old man."

"Thank you, Sian."

Stirling started towards the hotel doors, stopped, then took hold of one of Sian's hands. "Sian, I really need you close to me tonight!"

"Oh, Stirling, I really didn't think there was anything like that between us..."

"There isn't!"

"Thanks for that compliment as well."

"Sian, listen to me now, because I am really not joking. This is as serious as it gets. We are linked somewhere, somehow, and we are going to meet someone tonight who is very, very dangerous."

"Troutman?"

"Yes, and I have to say that you being with me makes us vulnerable."

"Stirling, I can look after myself, honestly." Sian could not stop herself. "Except when it comes to Monte Carlo shopping, then I definitely need your help."

"SIAN!"

"Okay, okay, I'm sorry. What do you want me to do?"

"Stay close to me. Do not get separated. If anyone asks, you are my cousin, along for the ride. I do feel responsible for you, Sian, so please do not make this harder for me."

A switched-on usher then chose the moment to break the icy silence. "Stirling." Then, his confidence failed him, "You did say to use Stirling then, Mr. Speed... Mr. Speed, your car is waiting to take you to your engagement."

Stirling smiled at the usher. "Yes, honestly, Stirling is just fine. And really, we do not need a car, the walk to the harbor front will be nice."

"In these heels? I don't think so! Please, ignore Mr. Speed and lead me to our awaiting carriage. I am his cousin, you know."

Stirling stood and looked as Sian strode off, arm-in-arm, with a very proud young usher.

Well, Stirling old boy, it was you who allowed her into your house and allowed this story to begin, Stirling thought.

Stirling stepped outside into the Monte Carlo evening's warmth to see a metallic-dark-blue Rolls Royce Silver Ghost waiting with its driver looking straight, next to its open rear door. Sian was already making herself at home and was pouring herself a full-bodied port from the crystal decanter carefully shelved in the back of this four-wheeled palace.

Stirling allowed the chauffeur to press the door shut so it sealed without a click. "You'll need to get that down your neck a bit sharpish, because the journey down to the harbor is going to be about four minutes long, my dear."

"Don't worry yourself, Stirling, I can deal with it. Cheers!"

Chapter 22

The Serene Lady sat with poise on the harbor front of the billionaires' playground that was Monte Carlo. At 465-feet long and 60-feet high, the 200-million-pound yacht was easy to spot. And its 42-member crew ensured that it glistened from whatever angle one cared to direct the camera. Even the 24-carat gold letters that spelt the name of this sea lady were never allowed to show any form of weakness in the constant war against corrosive salted sea elements.

Like a floating magic carpet, the silky Rolls Royce conveyed Sian and Stirling the short distance down through the most famous racing tunnel in world motorsport, under the hotel and out alongside the glittering, star-filled, darkening harbor, gliding to a stop in a cordoned off VIP area behind the tethered Serene Lady.

Sian reached out to open her door, which from the inside looked more like an opulent crafted piece of furniture. She opened it a little too quickly for the arriving chauffeur, who managed to conceal his irritation admirably, then stretched her legs out, adjusted her twisted dress, and used the chrome-clad wing mirror to bare her teeth and check that no carefully applied lipstick had migrated onto them. It was at this point that she became aware of the barrage of flashing lights behind her. In reaction more than observation, Sian swung around to see the wall of photographers and interviewers crammed around the small area that had been protected by purple rope swinging between waist-height chrome posts. With blinking eyes, she watched Stirling appear from the other side of the Rolls and stride to the perimeter of their protected zone. Flailing arms stretched over the protective rope, some with hands that contained microphones, some with autograph books. A good many of the arms were backed with calls of Stirling's name, some with questions attached.

"Stirling, can you tell us who your new girl companion is?"

"Have you ever thought of making a comeback, Stirling?"

"Stirling, please, can you…?"

"What have you been up to, Stirling?"

Sian stood back against the Silver Ghost, clearly in retreat, only to be politely but firmly persuaded to Stirling's side by the under-pressure chauffeur, who was required to vacate his parking slot for the next star.

Stirling took time to smile, listen, sign, and be photographed without skillfully actually answering any of the questions that were being fired at him. Then, they were guided by a smiling earphone-wearing host into another zoned area where Sian was removed from Stirling's side whilst he was positioned next to Troutman's new, Monte-Carlo-launched, supercar, the Centar. Yet more photographs flashed away, before the same smiling host reunited Sian and Stirling and finally guided them up the glorified gangplank and into the bowels of the awaiting Serene Lady.

Stirling smiled at Sian. "I can never understand why people have parties on boats."

Sian gave Stirling an inquisitive look back in reply. Stirling continued, "No matter how big the boat, the numbers invited always seem slightly too many for the available space."

Stirling had once mentioned this observation to one of his team principals during his racing days. The reply was that it was good to rub shoulders with the rich—you never know when some of their money might rub off on you.

"A drink, sir, madam?"

"I think your finest champagne for the lady and a tonic water, with lemon and ice, for me, please."

Sian took the opportunity to slap Stirling across his arm.

"Stirling, you could have warned me. I really had no idea that it was going to be like this tonight. I am sure the press has gotten some wonderful pictures of me rearranging my dress and polishing my teeth!"

Stirling turned to Sian and raised his eyes. "I can arrange to have you taken back to the hotel, if you would prefer."

"No, I didn't say that I couldn't get used to it. I just said I would have liked a heads-up."

The ordered drinks arrived. Stirling passed the champagne and took a swig from his own glass whilst having a careful look round.

"I think, young Sian, considering that you were solely responsible for damaging my credit card to the tune of £5000 today, and the fact that I allowed it, should have been a hint as to the type of evening that was coming up."

"That, Stirling, is a very good point. Next time you allow me to exercise your bank card to the tune of 5K, I'll know that there is a good evening coming up. Time for another champers, I think."

Stirling gestured the waiter over. "You go easy tonight, Sian. And do not fall overboard."

"Yes, Dad, I mean, Mr. Speed."

A very straight-standing waiter smiled falsely at Stirling. "Mr. Speed, Mr. Troutman has kindly requested your company, if you please."

Stirling gestured to Sian with his eyes and they both followed the nifty waiter across the crowded, bustling deck and up some steps that were discreetly guarded by two well-dressed muscle men who stood with aging drinks in their hands and were engrossed in pseudo conversation. Stirling noticed that their eyes tracked his and Sian's every movement as they headed towards the stairs.

The stairs took the pair not only up to another deck, but up to another level, or perhaps it is better to say another class of guests, an altogether more exclusive club where the noisy laughter and music had been replaced with a quieter, civilized conversational hum. Up on this deck, there was clear space and distance surrounding the small huddles of very-VIPs. As they followed the waiter as closely as the closed-circuit camera that Stirling had noticed following them, a good few faces turned, recognized, and acknowledged Stirling with a smile and sometimes a simple nod whilst appearing to look through Sian. Stirling smiled and nodded back.

"Do you actually know everyone?" Sian enquired.

"The world of Formula One is an exclusive and small club that reaches out to a worldwide audience. Trust me, the inner sanctum of F1 is quite, well, you could say, incestuous!"

Deep inside the hull of the yacht, inside a secluded cabin, screen watchers studied the faces of their guests who had been granted an invitation to the exclusive deck. One screen watcher focused in on Sian's petite, cute face.

"I want a name and history quickly. I need it now! Do not dare let Mr. Troutman have to ask first! We need that information now."

John Beechy did not like to be kept waiting, especially when it meant running the risk of incurring Troutman's wrath due to information tardiness. The watcher increased his concentration and widened his search on the databases that he legally and illegally had at his disposal, yet still the stranger on Stirling Speed's arm proved elusive to his prying eyes.

The waiter halted, and with that so did Stirling and Sian. Troutman had just been handed a note that he glanced at, smiled at, folded, and then passed back to his messenger. Troutman repositioned himself with his hands clasped behind his back. This was a posturing technique Troutman often used. The greeter would offer their hand for shaking, only to find it in no-man's-land and then have to retract it and accept defeat in Troutman's petty game of one-upmanship. Stirling knew his games, so a mere verbal greeting ensued.

"Mr. Speed, or as you prefer, just plain Stirling."

"Lawrence, or as you prefer, Mr. Troutman."

Their eyes battled with each other for a fleeting moment. Grand Prix drivers relish a challenge and are eager to rise to it. Stirling's eyes shouted, 'Do you really want to take me on?' Troutman's eyes fiercely glared back, 'Who do you think you are?' The moment of the duel passed as Troutman's eyes relaxed onto the exquisite, albeit slightly wild, creature stood innocently smiling at Stirling's side.

Troutman stooped his head slightly, focused on Sian, and creased a smile. "And you are the mysterious…?"

Suddenly, Troutman hesitated and almost stumbled, his poker face crashed, but for a moment, and then quickly reset itself.

It was a 'tell', a moment of visual communication that a poker player's opponent is constantly on the watch for. A moment of pressure, a moment of weakness, and Stirling had not missed it. As a race driver subconsciously catches an unintentional slide with a quick flick of the steering wheel, so Troutman caught this careering moment.

"And you must be the mysterious… Sian."

Stirling stepped forward slightly in the way to ward off Troutman. "Sian is my long-lost young cousin!"

Sian couldn't quite remember whether she was supposed to be Stirling's niece or cousin but continued anyway, "Thank you for inviting us onto your ship, Lawrence."

Stirling controlled his smile whilst Troutman bristled.

"I believe in formalities, my young Sian, so Mr. Troutman is where we are at, for the time being, until we become more acquainted," said Troutman.

Sian gave Stirling a cheeky, sly grin. "Thank you for inviting us on your ship… Mr. Troutman."

Troutman smiled, pleased with his win. "It is a mere yacht, Sian, and beautiful people are always welcome on my yacht.

"There you go Stirling you are a beautiful person," said Sian.

Troutman continued, "Exquisite looks are only one qualification for invitation; sadly, I find I must expand my hospitality to other less-pleasing groups."

"So, Lawrence, please put me out of my misery, I know that I cannot compete with Sian's looks, so what less-desirable group do I find myself in?"

Stirling knew that he was now poking the tiger with a stick.

"Every zoo, Mr. Speed, has a star attraction that all want to come and stare at. Usually, a fearsome creature mortals can approach, confident that it is restrained by bars! The creature is able to wander about freely within its cage, go about its daily life freely. But the moment that creature becomes a danger…" Troutman turned and smiled at Sian and gently took hold of her hand. "Allow me to take you on a personally guided tour around my ship, Sian."

Stirling decided he had not finished with his stick. "And tell me, Lawrence, what happens to the dangerous creature?"

Troutman turned and fixed his stare on Stirling. "Then, Stirling, Mr. Troutman is called in to arrange to have the creature put down, exterminated, and life goes back to normal and everyone is safe again. Sian, let me show you the wheel house."

"I think I'll come along with Sian, if you don't mind, Mr. Troutman, I have always had an interest in steering wheels." Stirling threw his stick away.

Chapter 23

"Why do girls do that?" Stirling asked.

"Do what, kind sir?"

A slightly drunk and very tired Sian enquired, accompanied by forced blinks where most of the effort was clearly being put into the eyelid's opening mechanism.

"Pay a fortune for a pair of shoes, endure them for half the evening, then spend the rest of the evening padding around on now-sore feet, holding a glass in one hand and a pair of shoes in the other," Stirling fired back as they walked and padded through the now-relatively-quiet reception lobby of the Fairmont Hotel to the awaiting lifts.

"Well, technically speaking, Mr. Stirling, I did not spend a fortune on them, you did."

Stirling paused his walk and looked down towards his patent leather handmade Oliver Sweeney shoes. Sian's head followed with what seemed like relief, and after a moment's delay, was able to focus on Stirling's shoes.

Stirling then commented on the reason for his pause. "Yep, just checking, I do definitely still have on my feet the exact same pair of shoes I went out in. And, let me check with a quick wriggle of my toes, yep, I can still feel my toes and they are not sore, so all is good in my feet world."

Sian jacked her head back up as Stirling, rather accurately and expertly, Sian thought, pressed a blurred button on the lift panel.

"Well, Mr. Speedy Stirling, let me put you right, sir."

Sian held up two fingers, fortunately in victory salute mode and continued, "One... I didn't buy these oh-so-beautiful shoes, you did, have I already made that point?"

Sian looked at her hand holding two fingers in a confused and quizzical way, desperately trying to remember what she had forgotten.

"Three… Now listen carefully, sir. In the beginning, God created a shoe, and he saw it was good! So, He created another shoe to complement the first, and they became a pair of shoes, and he saw that this was very good. He then created Eve, so as the beautiful shoes had a habitat and he saw that this was good as well!"

Sian now lifted up one finger in an attempt to fortify her point. "People like you, young Stirling Speedy, have come up with the idea that shoes evolved because they were needed. That they evolved to make our lives better. But no, Speedy, we are here on this planet to be used by pretty, pretty shoes. Sometimes, our shoe slavery means we have to endure great pain, sometimes financial pain, by you, and sometimes physical pain, by me."

Stirling now stood holding Sian's room's door open; he'd had the presence of mind to get a spare lock card.

Sian passed through, physically shrinking as tiredness and one too many glasses started to win the battle against the awoken state. Sian clambered onto the bottom of her bed and crawled up in it. The beautiful shoes were carefully placed on the pillow next to the pillow where Sian finally rested her weighty head.

"No falling overboard for me tonight, Mr. Speedy. All back, safe and…"

Stirling went on to make a reply then realized that he would be talking to an expensive pair of shoes. Stirling carefully moved Sian's hair from her pretty face and covered Sian's spent body and crumpled expensive dress with a crisp, white sheet. Attempts to remove the beautiful shoes to their rightful place on the floor only resulted in a tightening of Sian's sleeping grip. Stirling left the room with a glance back. Upon shutting the door, he found himself hesitating as he analyzed a sudden feeling of foreboding and responsibility! He so needed to look after this girl and protect her from the sharks that circled.

Chapter 24

All in Monte Carlo had not yet retired. Stalwarts sat in bars, putting all the problems of the world right. Clubs continued to discreetly pulse, and casinos shifted into top gear as the high rollers rolled in, out to impress their latest hangers-on. All were having a good time, all but John Beechy. Deep inside a yacht moored in the prestigious Monte Carlo Harbor, John Beechy again took the full force of a blow from one of the biggest fish in the sea, never mind the harbor.

"I pay your organization millions. I allow your organization to use my business. I surround myself with the most up-to-date surveillance and security systems, and yet when Stirling Speed, who for some reason is not dead, turns up with a mystery girl on his arm, I am handed a note that says, 'Name—Sian, background—question mark'."

Beechy knew not to offer a reply and held his killer instincts tightly under control as Troutman closed his red, sweating face with Beechy's. Beechy concentrated on his instructions to tolerate Troutman at all costs as he felt and smelt this out-of-control man's coarse breath. In Beechy's view, this man was becoming a liability, but his view stood for nothing. He was just a tool used by higher, more powerful, and more dangerous forces.

"Well, I do wonder, Mr. Beechy, why I sully myself with your presence."

Troutman removed his face from the vicinity of Beechy's and turned away in a false show of arrogance to hide the very real fear that he would display the look of concern and panic that burned inside of him.

"I know who the girl is, Mr. Beechy. Now, listen carefully, I want this girl, Sian, removed from the scene immediately."

"Removed as in dispatched?"

"Do I really have to spell it out for you?"

Troutman reached for a notepad and pen from within one of the drawers of the highly polished cabinet unit that edged the sumptuous cabin they stood in. He then stooped to write, paused, and then commenced a quick, agitated scribble that he then handed to Beechy whilst looking out of the floor-to-ceiling plate glass window that sealed them from the glittering harbor. Beechy looked at the three words hurriedly written on the ripped page, a single name written in capitals, and then beneath, a first name and surname.

"I have given you the name of a London clinic. I am sure even you can get the address. I have also given you the name of a…" Troutman hesitated, seemingly and strangely, searching for the right word. "…the name of a person who attended the clinic a number of years ago. I would like you to obtain the medical records for treatments she had had there."

Beechy drew his head back on his neck in subdued wonderment, *Where was Troutman going with this one?*

"The medical records? Mr. Troutman, that could be difficult," Beechy muttered without first giving it much thought, but Troutman now seemed to be in a world of thought himself, as he remained looking out over the dark harbor, and subconsciously raised his right hand to his lower lip.

"What? Yes. Just do it, and when you have it, show to me, me, you hear? No one else. Now, leave me."

"I'll get on it, Mr. Troutman."

Beechy pushed thoughts of squashing this irritant out of his mind only to realize that he was not at the top of the food chain and that any squashing would only be actioned under instruction. Beechy was certain though, that it was time to report Troutman's increasingly erratic state to the big predators who sat on the top perch in Beechy's dark world.

Chapter 25

A chorus erupted!

"Mummy, Daddy, there is Mr. Speed."

Indeed, a very large Mr. Speed loomed over them on the huge screen that had been erected in the little park opposite the Fairmont Hotel, at Loews hairpin. The swimming pool area of the hotel looked down on the tight first gear hairpin. But hotel guests also had the added bonus of being able follow the progress around the circuit by watching the screen that was relaying live feed. Robert was clearly feeling slightly out of his comfort zone amongst the moneyed visiting Monte Carlo Grand Prix crowds and so quickly jumped on his children's outburst. "Emily, Phillip, quiet. I am sure everyone does not need a running commentary."

He forced a smile and glanced from side to side at the people lining the perimeter of the Fairmont's pool area as they enjoyed their bird's-eye view of one of the most famous and glamorous race circuits in the world. Soon, Stirling Speed would launch into his demonstration run in a 1976 Tyrell P34 Formula One racecar.

"Oh, Robert, the children are just excited."

Robert's wife was also excited. She turned to the young couple that had just filled a space for one at her side.

"We met Mr. Speed last night in the hotel foyer; he looked so wonderful in his tuxedo, so wonderful. He says that he will wave at me when he comes around." Robert's wife used her fingers as a crude comb and ran them through her carefully and laboriously straightened hair.

"At the children, my dear. Mr. Speed said that he was going to wave at the children, dear." Robert jumped in and then instantly continued the conversation with the young couple. "Yes, Stirling and I were chatting about his Monza shunt. I think he appreciated my informed comments. He must get so fed up of fans asking about his racing."

The young couple smiled back then looked at each other inquiringly. They had recognized the words 'Stirling Speed', but English was not a language they had yet mastered!

The large screen focused in on a microphone-holding presenter, then proceeded to follow him to where Stirling was sat helmetless, strapped into the readied Tyrell P34.

"Stirling Speed, it is just great to see you back in a Formula One car on the streets of Monte Carlo, penny for your thoughts?"

The microphone was thrust in front of Stirling and his head filled the screen. "I still have the same passion for driving that I have always had, and it is indeed a privilege to drive the P34. It's an F1 car that has been on my bucket list for a long time, and I have always have been fascinated by its design. I have to say that the cars I was used to driving around here had considerably more down force than this beast, so I am hoping it doesn't try to take a bite of my backside."

The commentator expertly judged the end of Stirling's comments and retracted the microphone at just the right point. "Stirling, the car is owned by Mr. Lawrence Troutman. I am presuming that he would like you to keep it out of the barriers?"

"Oh, I will try my best, but I do believe that he has a brace of them. If I break this one, I am sure he has another that we can roll out to play with. And rumor has it that he can afford it if I do end up… accidently breaking it."

"That is true, Stirling, I am told that you are indeed driving the spare one that was transported down just last night after an undisclosed problem occurred on the P34 that had actually been prepared for today."

"Well, I think we should thank Mr. Troutman for his generosity in ensuring that the show continues."

Stirling's head shrunk and the commentator's body came fully into view, which now swung around to the pulling back camera.

"Thank you, Stirling Speed, still an enthusiast at heart and, as always, raring to go. As Stirling gets helmeted up, I am going to step back and let you soak up the glorious noise, or should I say music, of the Cosworth DFV Formula One engine of yesteryear as it fires up. I do not think it will be long now before

Stirling will have it singing around the streets of Monte Carlo. As the saying goes, sit back and enjoy folks, I think we are in for a treat."

The screen followed in the footsteps of the cameraman as he walked around the back of the squat P34, sat on its almost-cartoon-like fat rear tires.

The screen became filled with the simple but effectively sculpted tray that served as the rear aero foil and then the air was suddenly filled with the sharp, fierce crescendo of engine sound as Stirling stabbed at the throttle to stop the hard spark plugs from fowling. Fearing the potential eardrum damage of his viewers, the producer cut away to another awaiting cameraman, and the longer shot now showed the full glory of this blue six-wheeled Formula One anomaly. A race engineer stooped low and unplugged a slave battery—used to boost the small, lightweight on-board battery—and then Stirling's red-gloved hand could be seen raised with a prominent thumbs-up sign. A 'thumbs up' from the battery-holding race engineer came back in reply. Another race engineer could be seen giving one of the huge rear tires a slight rock forward in an effort to assist Stirling in his selection of the first gear. Then, a crescendo of revs screamed out of the two exhausts, which were soon engulfed by smoke now pouring off the spinning overworked rear tires, and Stirling was hurriedly on his way, accelerating hard towards Sainte Devote corner.

All around the street circuit, a bristling could be sensed amongst the expectant spectators as the cacophony of one of the most successful Formula One engines reverberated around the ancient streets of this opulent principality.

"Now, watch for the wave, children."

Robert was confident that Stirling would be able to cope with a bucking 1970s Formula One car on cold tires negotiating one of the tightest corners on the F1 circuit and would honor his promised wave. The Cosworth screamed as the cartoon-like rear wheels broke traction exiting Casino Square.

"Here he comes kids, he's coming, watch."

Stirling lifted and braked early on the undulating run down from the Square. A ripple of applause broke out as the shining blue Tyrell broke cover and headed down to Loews hairpin. With another crackle of over-run from its hot exhausts, the Tyrell looked very sure-footed as Stirling rolled the steering lock onto its stops to negotiate the tight, left, first gear corner.

As the Cosworth started to cry out again, the rooftop vantage point allowed all to see Stirling lift his left hand off the returning leather-clad steering wheel and hold it up high for all and Emily's family to see. Robert, bursting in pride and admiration, joined his children in waving excitedly back whilst a slightly more subdued wife appeared to be in another place as her mind drifted into areas that she knew were best kept private.

Next lap, the Cosworth was now clearly on full song and could again be heard wailing as traction broke and the Tyrell slithered out of Casino Square. No elongated crackle of over-run this time as Stirling punched down the gears with a blip of the throttle. The Tyrell now sprung urgently into view, looking like it was refusing to take instructions and reluctantly turned into the corner but as the Cosworth barked, the back of the car became alive and seemed to pivot into the right-hand corner.

A short straight down to the hairpin saw the Cosworth gasping for air as it sucked with all its might to balance the amount of fuel that was being asked for by the flat throttle pedal. The Tyrell dipped heavily at the front as Stirling now more deliberately caught first gear. No wave this time as Stirling battled the front of the car into the corner, forcing it to obey his instructions. Before the now alive racecar could finish devouring the hairpin, the Cosworth was roaring again. Robert and his fellow viewers stared down into the spacious Tyrell cockpit, able to see the master at work in his office. Stirling flicked the tiny steering wheel right, away from the corner, almost appearing to catch the sliding oversteer before it had even started. A small flurry of flames escaped from the twin exhausts as Stirling braked hard for the next right-hand corner that led to the Monte Carlo sea front.

As the physical car disappeared from view, all eyes flicked to the large screen to see the now-broadcast race car briefly heading towards them all before it flicked right and accelerated hard away into the tunnel—the cameraman expert in his panning. Gasps of admiration now clawed at the air as the Cosworth, now in its territory, was allowed off its leash. Stirling gunned it without mercy onto the fastest part of this tight, outdated circuit and headed off into the false lights of the tunnel, formed by the overhead Fairmont Hotel.

The commentator relished the challenge of finding ways to describe the spectacle and skill that Stirling was now displaying. "Stirling Speed is not holding back, this is just how we want to see these iconic race cars being driven. He is so on it! Look at that car buck and kick. He has taken hold of the beast, slung it over his shoulder, and said, let's go play. Drink it in, people."

The Tyrell leapt into view again, and now it was tamed, eagerly responding to Stirling's inputs, no fighting back, totally in subjection to its master, Stirling Speed.

"Now that is a driver, kids," Robert shouted as Stirling squeezed the throttle whilst purposely holding onto a touch-too-much steering lock on the exit to induce a lurid slide, expertly controlled with counteracting lock. The crowd peered down the road at the disappearing race car to watch the predicted flash of flames from the exhausts as Stirling flicked the car out towards the seafront and set the car for a late turn onto the run to the tunnel, , so as he could hit the throttle early.

"Listen to this, kids."

Robert waited for the scream of the hungry Cosworth as it launched through the tunnel, but the scream did not come, nor did the erected screen give the broadcast image at all expected. The Tyrell seemed to take too much curb on the inside apex of the seafront's right-hand corner. In an instant, the out-of-control racecar careered across the now-very-narrow piece of tarmac and slammed into the barrier protecting the sea wall.

"Stirling Speed has crashed. He has crashed, and… Yes… yes, I think I can see, there is a lot of smoke and steam and what looks like a small fire breaking out. But, yes, I can see Stirling moving and, yes, he is jumping out of the car. We can only hope that he is okay. He is over the barrier and… And, well, he is running down the seafront with his helmet still on. A marshal has tried to stop him, but Stirling has pushed him way and has continued running away, down towards the beaches, away from the circuit. I really don't know… yes, okay, okay. Okay, folks, we are cutting away now. We will, of course, give you an update on Stirling's condition as soon as we know more. Let's go to Martin, who I believe is in the pit lane. Martin."

"Oh, Robert, is he okay? That was horrible," his wife said.

Robert looked at his shocked wife, then down at his wide-eyed children looking back up at him.

"Well, he is out and, well, running. So I'd say that has got be a good sign, I think."

Chapter 26

Stirling was up early and running. He faced a busy day, there were the numerous interviews, and he also had the demonstration of the P34 Tyrell. Before that, though, Peter Smith wanted a meeting. Stirling knew driving the Tyrell put him in a vulnerable position, and so it was a risk, but he also knew that he had to draw Troutman into the shallows, where he would be then easy bait. They had to get Troutman to react.

Stirling pushed hard as he climbed the foothills on the way out of Monte. Early morning running was like a lubricant for Stirling. Back at home, even in the winter months, Stirling would run the country tracks around Drayton House. The wildlife seeming to get used to this lone, often-bedraggled figure splashing through the muddy puddles. Since his retirement from the world of professional race driving, running, even cleaning and polishing his car, whilst listening to Radio 4, Classic FM, or one of his favorite tracks brought a contented pleasure that Stirling had missed for so many years. Running early woke Stirling's senses and got the blood pumping and the mind thinking. The Monza leg-shattering shunt had certainly made prolonged running an unnecessary challenge, but Stirling still felt the need to be out first thing, welcoming in another fine day, whatever the weather. When asked about his running, he had replied that it was either this or early morning dog walking.

Stirling's run up through the hills had been a thoughtful one. He had the feeling that the red lights were about to blink out on the overhead starting gantry and all hell was about to be let loose. Although a race driver tries to plan the start of a race, the reality is that every driver has to react to whatever is thrown at him on the chaotic run down to the first corner. In years gone by, drivers had tragically and, sometimes, fatally crashed within the first few seconds of a race through no fault of their own but because they ended up being the last link in a chain reaction of events. Stirling was beginning to realize that he was going to have to react to a chain of events that appeared to have started many years ago. When and where this chain had started, he knew not, but he did know that he had to break the chain before he ended up as one of its links.

"You have a nice suite, Stirling, and breakfast on your balcony certainly works for me," Peter Smith said and carefully arranged his napkin on his lap of his immaculate gray suit. He sipped his tea and took a bite of his croissant whilst allowing himself a moment to drink in the view of the glittering Mediterranean that stretched out before him.

Exactly on time, Peter Smith had glided through the main foyer doors of the hotel, unnoticed. Even the well-trained chambermaids failed to notice and make the compulsory greeting as this gray man presented himself at Stirling's door. Peter Smith made being part of the scenery look so easy.

He got down to business. "Stirling, we are certain that Luna knows my organization is involved."

"How can you be certain of that?"

"Because, we received a tip-off that Troutman's Tyrell P34 that you are to drive this afternoon has been tampered with. In fact, we were given details of exactly what had been tampered with, although we have not yet been able to verify the facts yet."

"Okay, yet again you seem to have a knack of getting my undivided attention, please go on."

"We were given details which show that small explosive devices that can be detonated remotely have been fitted inside the two top rocker arms on the left front suspension."

"Inside the rockers?"

"Yes, Stirling, inside. We presume they must have been fabricated that way, but that is not all. There is, as we suspected, an explosive device fitted in the fuel cell, either in the tank bag itself or at least in the tank housing the bag. If this is the case, it fits with previous techniques that have been used and will give us more solid evidence. The likely scenario we think will have been that the loaded left front suspension would have been made to fail as you reached high speed going through the sweeping right-hander in the tunnel under Fairmount Hotel. The crashed car would be hard to reach, and the ensuing petrol tank explosion, we think, would then put an end to our Mr. Speed."

"Wow, this man really does not like me. So, have you checked the car?"

"Not yet. We could not get authority in time to check the car, but we did manage to arrange for the officials to insist that the car be scrutineered, and because of its age, also insist that certain suspension parts be X-rayed to check for any signs of fatigue, because the team could not provide certificates to show that the parts had been crack-tested before this high-profile public display."

"But surely the team was not happy, because they would not normally have to scrutineer the car for such a demo run?"

"Exactly. The fact is that Troutman's supposed right-hand man Beechy did not complain. In fact, he even invited the scrutineers to take as long as they wanted, particularly when checking the front rockers! He wanted Troutman to be found out. Yes, Beechy, is the leak, but he would not have made the move unless instructed. We think that Luna are sending us a message to say that they want to work with us. Troutman is becoming a liability to them, and they want out, so they are trying to feed him to us."

Stirling stared at Peter Smith. "So you have evidence, now that the car has been checked?"

"Well, no, Stirling, we do not."

"Why not?"

"Troutman somehow found out. He apparently stormed out of a corporate meeting and demanded the car be loaded onto one of his transporters. When pressed, he insisted he had found out that an engine change he had asked for had not been carried out by his race engineers. One minute you saw it, the next minute it was gone."

Stirling suddenly noticed that he had been sitting forwards in his balcony seat. He sat back, taking his coffee cup with him. "No evidence and no race car for me to demonstrate. I must admit, I was a little worried that my last day on this planet would have been spent thrashing around the streets of Monte Carlo. Hey, thinking about it, that may not be the worst way to go!"

"The transporter carrying the Tyrell will be stopped at Dunkirk and impounded. Customs have had a tip-off that the car is hiding substances in it. It isn't, but as soon as the car is impounded, we can then get our hands on it."

Stirling found himself sitting forward again. "Why do I feel that there is more to come, Peter Smith?"

"Well, I sincerely hope that this is not your last day thrashing around the Monte Carlo streets, but Troutman had his other P34 transported down, through the night."

"Oh, excellent. So now I get to drive Troutman's other booby-trapped car. I am so looking forward to that. Call me soft, but one big shunt in any driver's lifetime, I think, is plenty. Seriously, given what we now know for certain, I am bit unsure about jumping in a 170 mph Troutman special. There is not a lot of space out there to play with, you know, when things go wrong."

Peter Smith paused to take a swig of his neglected freshly squeezed orange juice. He had been doing a lot of talking. "The car will still need to be scrutineered and X-rayed. In fact, I think it is being done first thing this morning. I am willing to bet that Troutman will not put up any objections, so I am also sure nothing will be found out of place within the car. We are then figuring that Beechy will ensure that the car is not tampered with between then and the time you drive it."

There was another pause, and Stirling knew for certain what was coming next. "Stirling, I can offer no guarantees, we think the car will be safe. But Troutman is getting desperate. You are deeply involved, but I cannot and will not force you to get into that car. Troutman is just outside the shallows. When he is finally drawn into them, we will have him hooked. We still need to link him directly to the deaths. I really think all the elements are in place, we just need a catalyst to create the reaction that will explode the Lawrence-Troutman façade."

Stirling replaced his coffee cup on the table, then linked his hands together, stretched his arms over his head, and then as far back as possible, behind his head.

"Okay, let's do this. Trust me, I have jumped in race cars with lower odds, I am sure."

Peter Smith only paused in reply and then took a deep breath. The strain and pressure he was under was starting to creep out into the open via his face. The fresh, clean morning sea air seemed to cleanse his lungs, and the vast view of the rich

Mediterranean-filled bay seemed to rest his eyes. For a moment, Peter Smith's thoughts wandered away from murder and death. Subconsciously, he allowed himself a comforting thought, *One day, I might retire here.*

Stirling watched the thoughtful Peter Smith. "Perhaps, this is a place for Peter Smith to retire to one day?

"Very good, Stirling, your observation skills are good, no doubt honed from years of keeping yourself in one piece around the circuits of the world and no doubt a skill that is keeping you out of the clutches of Troutman. Yes, you are right, retirement did wander across my mind, without invitation. You have a skill, Stirling that is hard to teach, never take it for granted."

"Oh, I have just been a nut that holds the steering wheel."

"Over the years, Stirling, I have seen many in my organization who have come, been trained, and then gone, but you are different. You see things, compute what you have seen, then react to them so much faster than us mere mortals. You just don't realize how good you are. We could make good use of you."

Stirling wanted to inquire of the last statement, but Peter Smith was quick to continue, "To answer your question, yes, maybe one day, retirement will be on the agenda."

"And when will that day be?"

"That day will arrive when I am struggling to shower off some of the disgusting stenches of this world. I joined this organization and rose up the ranks because I have never been able to tolerate injustice, even as a child. But, once this ugly underworld I find I have to operate in starts to leave its mark, its stain on me, then it will be time to stop and leave the fight to someone else."

Peter Smith stood and actually smiled at Stirling. "Well, to coin your phrase, Stirling, 'Let's do this!'"

Peter Smith's turn to go coincided with a knock on the hotel door, but it was Stirling who had stunted his exit. "Okay, try for this size," he said. Peter Smith reversed his turn.

"Last night, on Troutman's Yacht, I saw a reaction from Troutman, only slight. In fact, if you were a gambling man, you would probably call it a 'tell', and I definitely saw it."

"And what triggered this 'tell', Stirling?"

"I am certain it was Sian who triggered the reaction. When we were introduced to him, there was a sudden snap oversteer moment that he had to catch."

"Please, Stirling, what are you trying to tell me?"

"I think he had to quickly conceal the fact that he had recognized Sian and did not like what he saw."

The pressure began to seep through Peter Smith's face again. "Please, please, be careful, Stirling, Sian must also be in great danger."

Another more determined knock rapped on the door, followed by a cheeky French accent. "Mr. Speed, I hope you are not still in bed."

Peter Smith opened the door to see the back of a shoe-holding Sian.

"You see, Stirling, a girl never lets go of her new shoes!" Sian said. Sian swung around with a beaming smile on her face—her silky hair slightly delaying, then rushing around in a shining swoop to catch up. Blowing some of the hair away that had finished its swoop on Sian's face, her beaming smile turned into a slightly sheepish one.

"Oops, sorry, I really did not realize that Stirling had company, sorry."

"Oh, just leaving, my dear Sian, just yet another member of the press fraternity carrying out yet another interview. Thank you, Mr. Speed, for your valuable time." Peter Smith exited the room and clicked the door closed behind him.

"Come in, Trouble." Stirling gestured for Sian to take the seat exited by the 'journalist'.

"Okay, Stirling, let me tell something about that man who just went out."

"You have the stage, girl, go for it."

"Well, I can tell you that he is not a very good journalist, because he clearly has not done his research."

"And, may I ask in what area this man has dropped below your clearly high journalistic standards, Sian?"

"He called you Mr. Speed, and you hate that. If he had done his research, he would have called you Stirling. There you go, a rubbish journalist. There is not a lot that I miss. You stick close to me, Stirling, and you'll be fine!"

"Very observant, Sian. Top of the class, I think, for you, young girl." Stirling chose to ignore the fact that Sian had failed to notice that a gray total stranger had just called her by her name.

Chapter 27

With his soft under helmet now on, Stirling pulled on his familiar race helmet and felt a strange, somehow comforting feeling. It was a feeling he would struggle to describe to anyone else. Maybe, it was a feeling of satisfaction. It was hard to say what he felt, but he knew that he always felt it when he pulled his helmet on. Overdramatic sports writers who are not too familiar with matter-of-fact race drivers would liken the ceremony of putting on a race helmet to a gladiator preparing for battle. For Stirling, putting his helmet on was like a seal from the chaotic world around him, a seal that secured him into his natural environment.

Stirling raised his thumb whilst being aware of the vague-but-familiar nausea haunting his stomach, not as a result of nervousness, but the result of adrenaline surging through the body in preparation of the onslaught of a Formula One racecar.

An 'okay' was given with a replying 'thumbs up', so Stirling reached behind the simple leather steering wheel and pressed the obscured starter button. Eight empty cylinders eagerly gasped the intoxicating mixture of air and fuel and then the catalyst of a spark started a carefully timed sequence that resulted in the glorious sound of a Cosworth V8 DFV barking into life. Stirling stabbed at the throttle keeping the V8 clear and clean. A mechanic placed his hands on the back wheel and rocked the car slightly as Stirling attempted to select the reluctant first gear. With a clunk, it engaged. Stirling checked his small mirrors to ensure that the helpful mechanic had cleared, then built a crescendo of revs to coincide with the pit lane's traffic light turning from red to green. Holding onto the crescendo of revs, Stirling stepped off the heavy, depressed clutch pedal.

In an instant, the cartoon-like huge rear tires were ignited and buried in acrid smoke as they left two long, licorice-like lines on the pit lane's tarmac. The car lazily squirreled away from its rest with Stirling correcting the wayward drifts with varying degrees of opposite lock whilst purposely squeezing the throttle more than necessary to keep the rear tires asking for traction.

Stirling smiled from within his sealed environment. *That'll give the TV producer and commentator something to talk about, plenty of smoke and plenty of noise, if not much in the way of actual acceleration!* Stirling kept in mind that this old girl could still bite, especially on cold tires, and made a nice early lift and squeeze onto the brake pedal to be on the safe side. The still-cold brakes felt lifeless and lacking bite.

Exiting Casino Square on the out lap, Stirling squeezed the throttle and made sure not to use the full width of the road on the exit to allow for the bump that would throw the laterally loaded car towards the unforgiving, solid barrier. Now, after another nice early lift and gentle brake whilst feeling the downward gear changes on the approach to the sharp-right Mirabeau, the glorious Cosworth crackled through its exhausts on over-run. The 1976 Tyrell felt heavy as the cold-but-warming tires coped well within their grip limit. *Come on, Stirling, keep it relaxed and calm on this out lap, give the old girl time to wake up.*

A press on the brake with a rock of the foot onto the accelerator at the same time ensured that the engine revolutions matched those of the gearbox and helped with the selection of a good, deliberate change into first gear. Stirling took a good handful of all the available steering locks to make sure that the Tyrell made it around the tightest hairpin on the Grand Prix circuit.

Stirling craned his head to the left to look through towards the exit of Loews hairpin. *Don't forget the promised wave, Stirling boy.* Stirling waved at the invisible spectators high up, out of eyesight that lined the balconies and swimming pool area of the Fairmont Hotel, which surrounded the hairpin. He hoped that Emily and her smiling family were waving back. The Tyrell was starting to wake from its slumber.

Now, pushing hard through Casino Square, a brief lift of the accelerator and a moment's roll of right steering lock, then quickly off, as Stirling applied the throttle again. As suspected, the rear of the car broke free over the bump. Now, a quick roll on of opposite lock attempts to change the direction of the front of the car to open up the corner and the lurid oversteering slide is negated.

Mirabeau was now rushing up and demanded a hard press on the brakes. They were alive and grabbed hold of this pure racing-bred beast and reigned in its head-long flight. Instinctively, Stirling punched down the gearbox and rolled the steering lock slightly early to allow for anticipated understeer, the front tires still not matching the back for temperature and effectiveness. The car had spirit and fought against Stirling's steering requests as he hurled it into Mirabeau. *Come on, girl, let's get hooked up, I'm waiting.* Stirling held on to the right-hand lock and waited for the front of the car to respond. As the speed dropped, the front tires finally started to grip and pull the car into the corner. Stirling sensed it more than he felt it and was instantly on the power.

Now, it was time for the rear tires to ask for grip as they tried to cope with the 450-brake horsepower being sent through them. The now-slightly-oversteering car negated the understeer and the car pivoted into the corner. A blast of throttle did not last long as Stirling changed his attention to pressing the brake pedal hard for the incredibly tight Loews hairpin.

Make sure you get this first gear, my man, and wait, wait. Man, I am struggling to get temp into these fronts. Stirling trailed the brakes into the corner to load more weight onto the front tires to help them discover their grip. A balancing act was performed as Stirling pinched off Peter to pay Paul and gradually reduced his braking pressure as he rolled on more steering lock. The grip that had been used to brake was now gradually being transferred to the grip required laterally for turning.

Okay, girl, power on, let's go. And watch for that snap oversteering when it comes. As the back of the car tried to step out, Stirling was the match of it and flicked on the opposite lock instantaneously as he accelerated hard down the short shoot to the next 90-degree-right-hander that led on to an even smaller, tiny straight that led to the next right-hander, Portier. Then, it was onto the seafront and the run into the famous Monte Carlo tunnel.

For most people, the violence of the acceleration, the face-distorting cornering G-force, and the gut-wrenching braking forces would cause life and vision to become a blur. Every sense focused on reacting to whatever this unruly beast was trying to throw at, but not for Stirling. With everything coming up to temperature, Stirling was now predicting the car's every move.

With the beast firmly under control, Stirling had more time to observe when in this state of mind—it was as though he could slow time down. He could see the changing colors of his tires as they wore down; he could see grids and manhole covers. He could detect movements and even faces in the crowd. Once, whilst leading a Grand Prix, he approached a blind corner on the second lap of the race. His keen observation picked up first on the rapid movement of a marshal as she grabbed for her yellow caution flag to wave. Next, Stirling observed that the crowd looked a different color. Quick assimilation of this fact made him arrive at the conclusion that Stirling was looking at the backs of people's heads, instead of the pinks of their faces. Instantly, Stirling slowed and crept around the corner to find the track partially blocked with a shunt that had just occurred. Stirling had, in a millisecond, reasoned that there was something more interesting around that corner than a world champion leading the opening laps of a Grand Prix, so it must have been a big shunt. Stirling had not joined in with the shunt.

Even on the short straight towards Portier, on the seafront, Stirling was able to pick out the smiling face of Sian and her waving hands as she stood on the outside of the corner, amongst the orange-suited marshals in a restricted area! *How did she work that one?*

Stirling unleashed the Cosworth and nailed the throttle to its stops, away from Portier corner, down into the tunnel, feeding the hungry Cosworth more and more gears. Stirling tried to focus on the unfolding circuit ahead, but his mind dangerously wandered. The scene he had just seen with Sian in the middle of it was somehow wrong—what had his eyes seen that his busy brain had not registered? The moment of fuzzy concentration caused Stirling to miss his braking point to arrest his 160-mph projectile for the chicane that was approaching without delay. *Come on, Stirling, get a grip. Brake hard, now!*

The front tires, now overloaded with the weight of the car and diminishing assistance from the air pressing on the rudimentary front aero—generated by the Tyrell's nose cone—broke traction and locked. Stirling sensed them locking then confirmed this from smoke whiffs off the top of the protesting four tires. In an effort to get the tires to do their job again, Stirling eased the pressure on the brake pedal and the tires recommenced their rotation.

A split-second decision was made not to continue straight on down the escape road but attempt the turn into the chicane. The apex and ideal line into the corner were history, but Stirling was not against the stopwatch today and would be happy if the car responded to his admittedly erratic inputs. Releasing the brake completely, Stirling rolled on an extra-steering lock and allowed the understeering scrub from the front tires to bleed off the remaining excess speed, enabling the car to finally respond to the change of direction. Now, starting from a slightly slower corner speed than ideal, Stirling took a chunk of accelerator, caught the oversteer, and accelerated away from the chicane, onto the harbor front.

Mind wanderings began again. Sian stood in the restricted, no-public-allowed area, surrounded by orange-clad marshals. Stood in a restricted area, so all Stirling should have been seeing in this image were orange-overall-wearing marshals. Stirling eased his onslaught through the complicated swimming pool area on the circuit to give over more capacity to his wandering mind. Finally, the mind was able to sort the tsunami of visual information and Stirling saw the blot on the image. Behind Sian, behind the orange brigade, were two distinctly sinister, dark figures watching not the circuit display, but Sian. Two dark figures who just should not be in that image.

Stirling braked hard and deep into the right-hand Mirabeau corner, his racing instincts knowing that time was made up on the entry of this corner and not the exit. The quartet of front tires scrubbed slightly then responded in obedience as Stirling input steering instruction.

That's better. We seem to have both ends of the car wanting to play. Now for a bit more showboating, I think. Stirling resisted the temptation to instantly roll the steering angle off on the exit of the Loews hairpin and took a big bite of throttle. The fat rear tires already loaded to their limit with lateral corner forces instantly gave up grip as they were now asked for forward rotational grip, which they did not have. The back of the car made a break for the outside of the corner and certain oblivion with the barrier. The perpetrator of this spectacular Formula One drift was already there to catch the car as he flicked on an opposite lock. The six-wheel P34 Tyrell responded with pleasure and drifted beautifully out of the hairpin, the engine howling in rhythm to Stirling's stabbing throttle foot.

How can the time-consuming sin of drifting an F1 car feel so good? Amongst the chaotic environment, Stirling's mind recaptured the image of Sian the lap before, stood amongst the marshals with the two men standing at the back of the off-limits compound. Stirling negotiated the next right-hander, instinctively feeling the grip, and squeezed the throttle whilst searching for Sian in the picture now in front of him and fixated on where she was standing on the outside of Portier corner. He was expecting to see her waving again, but all he saw was an emptiness between the concentration of marshals. Portier corner, unaware of Stirling's distraction, continued to rush towards the Tyrell.

Racing drivers do not have the time to look at what is directly in front of them—they always look where they want to be, not where they are. They will always look through the corner, and even when they cannot see the exit with their physical eye, they will search for it with their mental eye. That way, they remain in a predictive state and not in a crash-risking reactive state. Stirling's eyes were not looking through the corner but were now focused on the back of the marshals' post, where at first, he picked up on aggravated movement. Looking past the attentive faces of the marshals, the aggravated movement now formed an image. Sian was being manhandled by the two dark figures and was clearly being dragged away against her fighting will.

Left unmanaged, the Tyrell ignored the importance of the corner rushing up. Stirling flicked his vision to the corner and resigned himself to the inevitable crash. The brake and turning point had been reached and were now well past. In an attempt to minimize the inevitable, he breathed on the brake pedal, resisting the temptation to jump on them and slide head-on into the outside barriers roughly where the interesting marshal post was positioned. He cut the corner shallower to try compensate for the excess speed that he was carrying there but failed to beat the laws of physics and hit the inside curb at the early apex. Instantly, the inside front wheels were bounced in the air and Stirling lost any hope of them offering grip. The outside wheels had nowhere enough grip available to them to maintain the change of direction, and the out of control car now careered across the circuit and hit the outside barrier hard, albeit at a three-quarter softer angle. Stirling let go of the steering wheel just before barrier contact was made and so protecting the bones in his hands from splintering. The steering spun wildly to the left as the front suspension and wheels were ripped and mangled. The grinding, sparking, steaming crashed racecar slid along the protective barrier until metal-on-metal and metal-on-tarmac friction brought the wreck to an abrupt stop.

As Stirling turned from driver to passenger, his thought instantly changed to thoughts of survival, and so he twisted the release buckle of his safety harness the moment the dead car grinded to a stop. Shards of torn aluminum tore at Stirling's race-overall-covered legs but Stirling felt no pain as they drew blood. He ripped himself out of the twisted wreck. *I can't let them take Sian, come on Stirling go, go, go!* He forced the fuzziness caused by the impact out of his head and stumbled over the barrier—smoke now surrounding him.

Trained fire-extinguisher-holding marshals had already responded to the accident and were pleased to see Stirling extracting himself as they dowsed the potential fuel-filled bomb in front of them. Other marshals arrived to assist Stirling but were shocked and surprised to have him brush them aside and then see him set off running away from the stunned circuit.

Think, Stirling, come on, think, where will they have taken her? Leaving a trail of race gloves, helmet, and under helmet, he continued his painful run down between the towering hotels, calling out Sian's name at the same time, oblivious to the few startled onlookers. It took a few high-pressure minutes to despondently stop and sit alone, so alone, on a low wall, drowning in the realization that Sian was gone, snatched before his helpless eyes.

Chapter 28

"Pardon, Monsieur."

Stirling was startled out of his trance, but still the question of what to do next ricocheted around his brain.

"Pardon, Monsieur?"

Stirling became aware that he was staring blankly at a young, may be mid-20s, man. The conservatively dressed man had been running, his skin glistening, chest still heaving.

"I'm sorry I… I, errm," was Stirling's best attempt at politeness. The heavily French-accented man stepped in with a reply.

"I have collected your belongings, your gloves, helmet, as you can see."

"Errm… well… thank you." Stirling reached for an explanation for his strange post-crash actions. "I had to catch up with a friend."

"It's okay, Mr. Speed, I know. Are you okay? That was a big shunt."

"I'm fine. Thanks."

"You are bleeding."

The young man pointed to Stirling's torn race suit.

"No, I am fine, nothing a hot shower won't solve. I have had worst. Listen, thanks, I think I owe you."

"No problem, Mr. Speed. I'll leave you to your thoughts. Oh, before I forget, I have put your watch in your helmet, under your gloves and under helmet."

The man went to leave, seemed to have a thought pop into his mind, and then turned back. "It might be an idea to hit those back streets on the way back to your hotel, Mr. Speed. There are quite a lot of people looking for you after your exit from the crash."

"That's a very good point. Thank you again."

It was during this statement that Stirling noticed something odd about this conservative Samaritan. As he turned, Stirling noticed that he had a very discreet earpiece in his ear, or had he imagined it? Was it just a hearing aid? Stirling remained sat and watched the disappearing young man. Then, he did it, Stirling just knew that he would. The man raised his left hand to his ear just like the secret agents in TV do. He had just radioed in his latest actions. Stirling stood up quickly but then had to steady himself. The shunt, the running, and the body-shattering Monza shunt suddenly all came together, making his body take a moment to recalibrate. A stumbling run, backed up with a shout, only ensured that the distant man would deviate to the right and disappear.

Stirling halted his stumbling run and found himself in a quiet backroad with private garages running down on one side. He placed his helmet and contents on the top of a large closed plastic bin. He was now aware of his superficial leg injuries and for a moment looked down at his stinging legs, then grabbed his left wrist with his right hand. He was wearing his watch! In fact, he was wearing one of his favorite watches—a 1969 Autavia Tag Heuer that was actually worn by the tragic F1 driver Jo Siffert, Seppi, to his friends. Yet another fine driver who had unnecessarily perished, this time in a fiery accident at Brand Hatch in 1971.

Stirling refocused. His overworked and probably dehydrated brain was struggling to stay on point. *Okay, I have my watch on, so why did the guy say he'd put my watch in my helmet?* He emptied his helmet's contents onto the top of the bin and in place of the mystery watch found a folded piece of paper. The note had clearly been written in a rush, perhaps even whilst the writer was on the move.

Return to your room. Do not speak to anyone! Stay in your room. Switch your phone off, stay off the computer, keep the TV off. Sian's life is in your hands! You will be contacted shortly.

Chapter 29

The knock on Stirling's door definitely caused a slight increase in his heart rate, having spent a very restless night and morning. *Where was Peter Smith when you really wanted him?*

Everything was now a dream, or perhaps it was better to say, nightmare-like. He had taken one call from the hotel management asking, one, if was he okay, and two, what were their instructions. To their initial worry, the request for a first aid kit had seemed odd, but Stirling had managed to put their minds at ease and ensured them that all was fine. He then asked to be left alone and in total privacy. They were used to the celebrity world and certainly knew how to maintain privacy when Stirling had informed them he did not want to be disturbed. Stirling's room had now become a no-go zone for anyone.

Stirling's cast-iron resolve to do nothing until contacted was at crumbling point though, so the knock on the door was actually a relief that something was happening. He decided to take precautions though, when opening the door. He stood to the hinged side of the door, so leaving the visitor to be greeted by an empty doorway.

"Who is it?" Stirling inquired from behind the door.

"Fortunately, not an attacker, who would by now have already weighed up where you are stood and slammed the door in your face. But, as you are inquiring, it is Peter Smith."

"Where have you been? What use are you and your organization when you disappear and turn up when you like? I needed you. Do you know what I have been through? Do you?" The knock on the door had raised Stirling's adrenalin levels to the point where it was difficult to hide the anger in his voice. Peter Smith walked over to the table in the center of the hotel suite, sat down, and reached into the bag he had carried in to remove a number of newspapers.

"Stirling, perhaps you should have a look at these first, then let's do the talking."

The headline barked out, 'Ex-Formula One Race Driver Stirling Speed Crashes and Sees His Girlfriend Kidnapped'.

The article continued, 'Stirling was not available for comment but is said to be resting after his ordeal. It has been confirmed that he has cuts and bruises but no serious injuries. Police have interviewed a spokesman for Mr. Speed and are appealing to witnesses and have confirmed that they do not have clear CCTV footage of the whole incident.'

Most of the media world had gone with the picture of Sian and Stirling arriving at Lawrence Troutman's yacht for the function he had thrown. Some had a grainy shot of them pulling up at the hotel in Stirling's battleship-gray E-Type, accompanied with the classy headlines like, 'Speed's Weekend Romp with Young Mysterious Girl Comes Crashing Down'.

One paper ran with the inevitable Monza crash picture and then a smaller one showed the Tyrell in the barriers at Portier corner. 'Speed Crashes at Speed and Sees His Wife-To-Be Kidnapped'.

'Speed remains in hiding fearing for his own safety but close friends say that he is inconsolable!'

Stirling held one of the papers up to Peter Smith to make his point, rather than to actually let him read it. "Have you seen this? I think we can safely say that my cover is blown. Sian is in great danger, and now even more so that you have turned up for all to see. I am supposed to talk to no one until they are in contact with me. I will not have Sian's safety compromised. I will ensure that they get whatever they are asking for.

"This has really now gone too far. And who is speaking to the press on my behalf? I have messages on my phone from concerned friends and family. And where has all this 'girlfriend and future wife' come from? I am worried sick about Sian, and you are supposed to be the expert. This is all careering out of control and is escalating fast. We need action, now! If you are onboard, then fine, if not, I go it alone. Enough is enough. The girl has been kidnapped, do you understand? And you sit there mute!" Stirling stopped and went to sit down, then changed his mind and flung another paper at the staring Peter Smith.

"Find out who has been speaking on my behalf, 'inconsolable'... And what have you been doing all morning, having a lie-in whilst dreaming of your retirement plans? It's 11 am and you finally decided to engage. Well, I need action." Stirling sat down and looked out to the sea and saw only despair.

Stirling had laid bare his frustration, but Peter Smith had been pleased to see that the frustration was not a display of uncontrolled rage but one of pent-up determination that needed an outlet. The greats in Formula one always seemed to have the ability to control themselves in moments of high stress and channel that into the most effective course of action. Juan Fangio, five times world champion, always seemed to be the perfect gentleman in any company, in any situation, even when many of his close friends were paying the ultimate price with their lives. David Coulthard was always the professional and always in control, even when the jet he and his girlfriend were flying in crashed tragically on final approach. The two pilots perished doing their job. Coulthard removed himself and his shocked girlfriend from the devastation, and after consultation with the brave families of the pilots, went on to race his Formula One McLaren that weekend. Top racing drivers have incredible machine-like self-control, which is why Peter Smith privately thought that Stirling would make a great operative in the future.

"Stirling..." Peter Smith started but was immediately interrupted.

"And this note that I was handed yesterday means that they could contact me here at any moment." Stirling heavily tapped the table through the note. After all his careful pre-conversation consideration, Peter Smith decided to change what he was going to say to respond to Stirling's eagerness for action.

"Stirling, we sent the note to you!" Immediately, Peter Smith held up his hand to prevent the inevitable interruption. "Stirling, we had to react fast to contain the situation, and we needed to put you on ice whilst we acted!"

Peter Smith's pause for breath was too long, and Stirling jumped into the gap. "Okay, let's start off with, why? Then, can we move onto what action?"

"Okay, Stirling, the why. We needed to use the situation with Sian."

"Situation, the situation? Do we not think the kidnapping of Sian and the peril she is now in are slightly more than a 'situation'?"

"Stirling, I know that you are out of your comfort zone and are operating in uncharted waters, but trust me, situations can be handled better without corruptive emotions that can cause mistakes. When you unexpectedly crashed, all hell broke loose."

"Tell me about it."

"The action. We needed to pick up Sian's trail before it went cold and to answer your next interruption, no, we have not got her back and are not sure where she is. We are certain that the organization Troutman works with, Luna, kidnapped her, but I have to say, Stirling, that this is all we have been able to establish yet. We have everyone working on this, Stirling, we all have to just keep calm and do our jobs well."

Stirling remained attentive; he could see concern and worry in Peter Smith's eyes. "Given the situation unfolded as it did, we decided to use the inevitable media frenzy that your name and crash would create to our advantage. We took the opportunity of your latest crash to form a catalyst that stimulated a reaction."

"Well, I would say it was more of a shunt than a crash. And 'my latest crash?' I really do not make a habit of crashing, you know."

"Exactly, Stirling, you don't, but because I put that catalyst in the sentence, the word latest, it created a reaction from you. I knew it would."

Stirling sensed a confidence in Peter Smith and decided to allow the story to unfold without further interruption. "Stirling, we used the situation and got a result! We hit every media agency outlet in the world and launched the story of Sian, your girlfriend, being kidnapped. In the last 12 hours, your picture, your story, and more importantly, Sian's picture have appeared in one form or another in nearly every household throughout the world."

Peter Smith paused, then said, "At ten o'clock last night, our agency was informed of a person claiming to know Sian entering a police station in a small Italian village. The individual claimed to have important knowledge about Sian's kidnapper and who was behind it all."

143

Peter Smith paused again—not to build tension, like in a game show, but simply to take a breath. He did not want to hesitate, to prevent further interruption, but yet again he found himself in a high-risk, high-pressure situation that was all part of the territory in his unusual line of work.

Stirling filled the gap, "And?"

Peter Smith touched his ear and spoke to a remote listener, "Okay, could you please bring her in?"

Stirling turned to the door, his bristling body just a passenger on this wild ride. The door opened and in walked a slim, well-groomed, carefully dressed, beautiful lady whose age was very hard to read but a guess would put her at 60-plus. Stirling was now paralyzed, due to the fact that he recognized this lady instantly.

"Hello, Stirling, it is good to see you. I have followed your career so closely."

Stirling stood, so as his eyes could meet those of his long-lost auntie, the wife of the uncle who had perished in the fiery crash all those many years ago—eyes that Stirling had last seen as a child.

Stirling looked at Peter Smith in an effort to search for words on his face. Peter Smith smiled as the uncomfortable lady stood with her hands clasped in front of her and then stood up and took hold of one of her hands in a comforting gesture. Peter Smith maintained his smile as he turned back to Stirling. Peter Smith spoke next, "Stirling, I'd like to introduce you to Sian's real mother!"

Chapter 30

Another crisp knock sounded on the door and sliced through the silence.

"Well, this door is certainly proving quite exciting this morning. Who do you have lined up for me next? Please tell me it is Sian."

"Sadly not, Stirling, I took the liberty of having coffee, tea, and sandwiches sent up. I figured you might have one or two questions for Sian's mother."

Peter Smith confidently opened the door and a well-trained member of the hotel staff wheeled in a well-stocked silver trolley into the room. He looked straight ahead, and then, when he had to, looked straight through to Peter Smith, awaiting instructions. It was a clear act of trained discretion that the hotel was very good at. The hotel was there to provide a room and service for the rich and famous with never a question asked.

"Thank you. Just leave it there, we can sort the rest, no problem," Peter Smith said and held out his hand with a discreet, undisclosed tip. The young man resisted the temptation to look at the amount, thanked his benefactor sincerely but without fuss, and turned and left the room.

The room remained quiet, with all eyes focused for some reason on Peter Smith as he carefully chose his sandwiches and prepared and poured his tea. Then, after opening the balcony windows, he carefully positioned his chair for his favorite Mediterranean view. The warm, refreshing late-morning air rushed into the stale room like the flooding moonlight appearing from behind a clouded sky. Stirling breathed in the fresh air and suddenly realized how hungry he, too, was feeling. He gestured at the trolley.

"Suzanne, please, do feel free to tuck in."

Sian's mother did seem slightly more at ease. "I think a black coffee and a glass of water will be fine for me, at the moment. I am afraid my appetite has gone by the wayside."

She smiled a warm smile at Stirling, then stood up to prepare her own beverages and prevented Stirling from serving her. It was as though each occupant in the room was taking a little timeout to regroup for the next stage of this fast-unfolding story.

A couple of times, Stirling noticed Peter Smith gently raise his hand to his discreet earpiece. There was clearly a lot of information being supplied to him. Stirling was now realizing the best way forward was to trust implicitly in this strange gray man just as he had trusted his chief race engineers. They knew what they were doing, and clearly Peter Smith knew what he was doing. Stirling settled in a seat that was at the back of Peter Smith's as he sat listening and surveying the harbor and bay. Suzanne settled on the brown leather sofa opposite Stirling, who was struggling to establish what the first question should be.

"Suzanne, you do look great, I am sorry that we meet in these horrible circumstances, but no one knew what happened to you. I am afraid that I really do not know where to start."

Sian's mother looked at Stirling. She was in control, but Stirling could see that her eyes were moist and she was riding close to the edge. "Thank you for the care of Sian. Mr. Smith has told me… well, everything. You are a good man."

"You do know that I am not her boyfriend?"

Suzanne smiled. "I know, I know, I was told the story was there to get the press revved up to, well, I suppose flush me out!"

"Suzanne, Sian believes you are dead." Stirling suddenly got a pit in his stomach as he remembered that Sian was not in her hotel room, waiting to be summoned.

Peter Smith sensed the moment and spoke from the back of his head. "Just keep focused, Stirling, it is the best anyone can do at the moment."

"Stirling," Suzanne said and sat forward on the sofa. "Stirling, Sian does not know me as her mother, but you are right, the lady whom Sian thought was her mother has passed away. She was a wonderful person who was taken away from us both. It was hard for both of us, Stirling, when she died."

"Why was it hard on you? Did you know her as well?"

"Oh, yes, Stirling, our lives became entwined together purely by chance. She was a very special lady, and I had the privilege of watching her bring up my little girl. Sian knew me only as a good friend of her mother's."

"You vanished off the face of the earth when my uncle died. I was too young to remember all of the details, but I do remember stories of nervous breakdowns, even that you had gone to prison. When I started to look into my uncle's death, I could find nothing about you, nothing. You simply had disappeared."

Stirling paused to give his mind half a chance to catch up. "Sian is my cousin, my uncle's daughter."

Now, it was Suzanne's moment of pause. "No, not quite. Stirling Sian is my daughter, but not the daughter of your uncle. Stirling, Sian is the daughter of…"

It was now very apparent that Suzanne was finding this statement hard to announce. "Sian is the daughter of Lawrence Troutman! I am terribly ashamed to say that, when your uncle died, I had an affair with Lawrence Troutman. When I fell pregnant by him, he made and paid for me to have a termination at a private clinic, then he paid for me to disappear. Stirling, I made the biggest mistake of my life getting involved with him. But he is an evil, evil man whom I—and from what I now know from what Peter Smith has told me—and many others have fell for. He threatened me that if I ever exposed him, he would, to use his phrase, 'have me removed from the planet'."

"And you believed that he was capable of carrying out his threat?"

"Stirling, you have to believe me, Lawrence Troutman is not the loving family man all believe him to be, he is an animal."

Suzanne paused again, now clearly showing signs of distress and struggling to form her next words. "When he threatened me with my life, he told me what had happened to my husband, your uncle. He told me that he had done as King David in the Bible had done. King David arranged for Bathsheba's husband to be killed by putting him to the front of his attacking armies. Stirling, Troutman told me that he had your uncle murdered! I am sorry, Stirling, but it was my entire fault."

"But, how had he, how did he…?"

Peter Smith interjected to help both parties out. "We will get this guy, we will. He is thrashing around. It is only a matter of time before we land him."

"Troutman lured your uncle into a car that he was so excited to drive. Your uncle was convinced he had finally caught the eye of someone who was going to open doors for his future professional drives. I was unsure, but your uncle was sure that this was the break he had always been looking for. Troutman laughed when he told me. He said that he had seen slugs with more driving talent, then went on to tell me that he rigged the car to crash and explode and that he'd done it just so he could have me."

Suzanne turned to look blankly out of the window as tears cascaded down her cheeks. "How could I have been so stupid, stupid, stupid?"

Stirling lifted a serviette from the silver trolley, sat next to Suzanne, placed his arm loosely around her shoulder, and passed her the serviette.

"I was just fodder to feed his selfish, animalistic lust— stupid, stupid girl."

Peter Smith turned to face Suzanne, pained that she had to go through the story again with Stirling. "Suzanne, we all have made mistakes, and in most cases, we get away with it. But, you made a mistake when being circled by a predator that devoured you the moment it got its opportunity. You had no chance."

Silence fell on the room as regrouping took place again. Peter Smith turned back to his panoramic view. He had already heard the tragic story in the small hours of the morning. Upon hearing the report from the Italian police station, he'd made use of one Monte Carlo's many helicopters and flown out to pick up the mysterious stranger who turned out to be the missing piece in the jigsaw. Peter Smith had taken a while to demonstrate and legitimize his organization to her. Then, he had patiently told this stranger what they already knew about Troutman and Stirling's involvement and the fact that they there to stop Troutman. It was then that Sian's newly found mother realized that she had been found by the good guys and was beginning to wake up from her nightmare.

But now Sian was gone. Troutman had won again. When Suzanne had seen the horrific headlines, she knew that Troutman had pounced. It had always worried her that Sian was the exact image of herself when she was younger. Troutman would have recognized her instantly, and from that point, Sian was doomed. When they had arrived back at Monte Carlo, still in the early hours, Peter Smith had sat intently listening to the unravelling story and began putting the pieces into place.

Stirling broke the latest silence, "Forgive me, you are a beautiful woman, but to murder your husband to be with you…"

"This was many years ago, Stirling, but you have to realize that Troutman is obsessed with women. What he wants, he will take, even if it is not given. Do you understand what I am saying? Women are like a drug to him. He cannot live without them. Because of the situation he is in, women are like the forbidden fruit to him."

"But, he is and has been for many years very happily married."

"You are right, and he must maintain that veneer and hide his disgusting lust under it."

"Okay," Stirling continued, "I could understand him wanting to hide his dirty little habits. Trust me, there are a few in my world of Formula One who have some, let's say unsavory activities. But to murder on what is appearing to be a number of occasions…"

Suzanne seemed to have got through the worst of what she wanted to say, and after standing to get a coffee top-up, sat down again to continue, "Troutman had nothing to speak of, compared to the billions he has now. He was a car salesman, and not a very good one at that. What he did have were good looks, a quick wit, a magnetism that could turn girls' heads, and what made it worst was that he knew it. He did his research, then set his aim on one of the richest girls in the world—the granddaughter of the owner of Arias cosmetics. He turned her head okay, and much to the dismay of the grandmother, they were soon married."

"Surely not, Troutman could not have moved in the same circles at that point," Stirling stammered, amazed by the story that had unfolded behind his own.

"Trust me, it happens. Only a few years ago, a married heiress of one of the major car manufactures in the world fell for a gigolo who had targeted her to get what he could out of her. She chose humiliation and honesty to expose him."

"Sometimes, there is no rhyme or reason behind misplaced love. Troutman's new wife funded his every venture and created the wealthy and powerful person he is today. What he had not counted on, though, was that the family had suffered terribly in the past at the hands of men who took what they wanted. The grandmother had been left destitute and Troutman's wife's mother had tragically committed suicide due to the actions of a man. The grandmother vowed that such a thing would never happen again. If Troutman's affairs were ever exposed, he would lose everything, and I do mean everything. Before the marriage, Troutman was made to sign legal documents that not only protected the family's wealth but also included a clause that any future business developments or profits that would come about by the family's initial investment would be returned to them if Troutman was unfaithful or broke their trust. Trust is everything to that family, everything! If it ever came out that Troutman had broken that trust, he would literally be homeless."

Shocked and sickened, Stirling was eager for the veil of this underworld to be removed. How had he been so blinkered to have missed all of this?

"So, how do you know all of this, how did you and my uncle cross paths with Troutman's world, and where did Sian come into all of this?"

"One fateful night, I met the serene Kristianna Troutman, the heiress of the Arias fortune, but let me continue with how our lives crashed together." Suzanne took a drink of her now-cool coffee.

"Would you believe that it all started by chance and what some would call luck, but for us it turned out to be bad luck! As a possible surprise for Roger, I entered a competition, the prize being to spend a day as guest of a race team at Silverstone, a race team that turned out to be owned by Troutman. To enter the prize, you simply had to send in a picture of you and your partner watching a motor race with a funny caption underneath. I knew exactly the picture. Some friends had taken a picture of Roger and me on a really hot summer's day at Oulton Park. I ended up sunbathing with my bikini top on. The picture showed Roger avidly watching the race whilst I appear to have fallen fast asleep behind him whilst sunbathing. The caption read something like,

150

'Motor sport can be tough.' Of the thousands who entered the prize, I could that not believe that we had won."

"I was so excited, I planned a whole day that would lead up to me giving Roger the two tickets that I had won. I knew he would be ecstatic." The tears started to flow again. "He was so excited when I gave them to him…"

Stirling reached across and squeezed Suzanne's hand. No words could ever take her pain away. Peter Smith had gone out onto the balcony again and closed the doors behind him. His hands could be seen gesturing—clearly he was in deep conversation with someone.

"Stirling, I could have no idea that I was signing Roger's death warrant, no idea."

Peter Smith re-entered the room and quietly got on with making Suzanne a fresh cup of sweet tea whilst she blinked away her tears.

The fire in her eyes then seemed to evaporate the remaining moisture. "Troutman murdered your uncle, my husband, Stirling, and I was not going to let him murder my baby. Now, after all these years of sacrifice, pain, and worry, he has got my baby! If he touches a hair on her head, I'll will hunt him and he will die, Stirling. With my last breath, I will make sure that he will die and I can be at peace forever."

"We will get her back, Suzanne, Troutman will pay," Stirling said.

Suzanne looked down to the floor, which enabled Stirling to look past her into the eyes of Peter Smith, which resulted in an action that unsettled Stirling. Peter Smith instantly looked away! Stirling knew that Peter Smith was hiding something, and it did not look like good news.

Stirling continued, "Suzanne, you coming forward has changed the game for us. You are saving her life again."

Stirling could feel panic in the pit of stomach and desperately tried to subdue it there. He hoped that there was a life still to save.

Stirling could now clearly see the pressure etched on Peter Smith's face as he returned and spoke, "Perhaps we should break and have some food. Maybe try a little sleep. We need to keep at peak performance."

"No, please, I want to go on, I want Stirling to know everything."

Pent-up knowledge of many years was now cascading out, relieving the huge pressure Suzanne must have been under. "We went to Silverstone and soon met the young, apparently dashing Troutman. He was attractive, kind, and funny, but never would I have entered into a relationship with him, though it was soon very clear that he wanted me. Even on that day, he manufactured situations where we would be alone. He made polite but definite advances, but I blocked them straight away—you must believe me on that. I gave him no idea that I was interested in him that way."

Stirling smiled, "I know."

"Roger loved the day and really got on well with Troutman and the team—he talked and talked about it after. Then, to his absolute delight, we started getting invites to Troutman's functions. And for us it was a different world, and it was so hard not to be taken in by it all. We even got invited to a garden party at his house, which is where I first met his wife, Kristianna. She was very polite and empathetic. She could see that we were clearly out of our depth. I mentioned to her what a wonderful life she had. I remember she smiled then and said something quite strange, 'Remember, when you are in the shallows, you can always see the predator approach. But in the deep, they can attack you from any direction without you knowing.' She must have picked up on how Troutman looked at me. We really were living the high life in our minds, but we really were way out of our depth."

"You said, 'where I first met Troutman's wife', so you met her more than once?" Stirling asked.

"Yes, we met twice. First, on that occasion, on the second occasion she saved Sian's life."

Chapter 31

The conclusion of the last statement occurred whilst Stirling was taking a sip of strong coffee, and that was certainly what he needed at that point.

"Stirling, I know that you are having to take in so much. But, I must try keep it all in order, so as not to miss anything out."

"I know, Suzanne, trust me, I am fine, I know how hard it must be for you to go through all of this."

Peter Smith was now realizing that he had gotten an abridged version earlier—in fact, much earlier that morning.

"We were flattered to be associated with Troutman and his life. Roger's club racing was going well, and he won a few races, so, privately, we hoped that there might be a way to get into one of Troutman's racecars. But, Troutman made it politely quite clear that there would be no chance of this happening. He was always looking for the next bright young new star who was on the rocket ship to stardom."

"As time went on, Troutman's advances became more direct, more desperate, and even scary. I tried to make it clear that I was not interested, but at the same time I was not trying to rock the boat for Roger. Troutman, then, offered to put Roger in one of his cars if I would go away with him for the weekend. I was disgusted by the idea; I was not going to prostitute myself for anyone. If I am honest, though, I was flattered that this young rich young man found me so attractive. My rebuff did not go down well, and he went into a rage. Knowing what I know now, I wonder whether I should have just said yes to his offer and just grinned and bared it. At the time, though, I had no idea how desperate the sick man was."

"Then, out of the blue, I received a phone call whilst I was at work from a very excited Roger. He said that Troutman had set up a test for him in one of his prototype race cars at Trac Mon, the race circuit in Anglesey. I had decided, where possible, to keep my distance from Troutman, and so I decided not to go the test. The first I knew of the accident was when your dad turned up at where I worked. We were a shattered family. No one could have imagined that Roger would die in such a violent way."

Stirling had lost track of time and was struggling with the fact that all this had happened around his own life, yet this was the first he was hearing any of it. "And what happened with Troutman?"

"He appeared inconsolable. He was very, very considerate and took a personal interest in me and my well-being! He made it clear that I would never want for anything. A comforting arm around a vulnerable, hurting young lady developed into a passionate affair, which repulses me to think about it now. He was demanding and I was stupid. I thought that maybe I would become the woman of his exciting life. I was brought back to reality with a bang, though, when I announced to him that I was pregnant with his child. His rage was evil. He hit me and demanded a termination."

"Troutman demanded a termination, yet Sian turned up at my door?"

"Everything happened in a whirlwind. I was in a nightmare state. I was taken to a private clinic. The night before the termination, a nurse sat with me, as I was in such a state. She was kind and perceptive and knew that something was not right. Later, she told me that her instincts screamed at her that an injustice was taking place. I blurted everything out to her, and that included, of course, my involvement with Troutman."

Stirling turned to the listening Peter Smith. "So, someone else knows about this story and Troutman's involvement. We need to find her."

Stirling turned back to Suzanne. "Go on, please."

"The nurse had been a locum in a few private clinics and had, coincidently, gotten to know Kristianna Troutman quite well through one of the other clinics she regularly worked in. Unbeknownst to me, that nurse took the brave decision to contact Kristianna that very night and relate the story. Early the next morning, I was awoken by the nurse with Kristianna standing next to her. Although very business-like in her communication, there was empathy in her eyes. She quickly laid out her plan—

she was such a strong lady. I was embarrassed to cause her this pain but relieved to be guided by her. The termination was not to go ahead, but it was to be made like it had. Money can make anything happen. The arrangement was that I should disappear, as Lawrence Troutman had arranged. The young nurse would come with me, and when the baby was born, set up a new life with the baby in France, all financed by Kristianna. We all knew that if Troutman ever found out about my baby, my life and that of the nurse's would be extinguished. We knew that Troutman would keep tabs on me, so there was no way I could be seen with a baby, so Mary, the nurse, took the brave, heroic decision to effectively become Sian's mother. We named our little girl Sian, a Welsh name."

"And Roger was Welsh!" Stirling paused, then confirmed his new knowledge. "So, who Sian thought was her mother who, sadly, died was that nurse, Mary?"

"Yes."

"So, for Sian's safety, she had to be told this lie and also never find out who here real father was?"

"That's right, Stirling, there were times when it was so difficult to maintain the untruth."

"For such a desperate, depraved man, why not finish his wife off?"

"Because of money, Stirling! Troutman has none of his own. The money will always stay in the Arias family estate. The grandmother had made sure of that herself when her daughter and granddaughter ended up being cursed with evil, selfish men who could not be trusted."

"Why did Kristianna not hang Troutman out to dry?"

"Why did any of us fall for this man? She was in love with him. It is hard to put in words, but he was the dangerous sort of guy that your body screamed, 'stay away, stay away' and yet you found yourself in his arms. Kristianna was still young and knew the consequences for her husband if news ever got out. Maybe, she thought it was a one-off blip that would not happen again. Whatever the reason, she took the decision to let him off the hook."

"You seem to know so much about Kristianna, yet you only met her briefly twice."

"When things settled, I needed a lot of blanks filling in, and Mary…"

"The nurse?"

"Sorry, yes, Mary, the nurse who saved Sian's life and went on to raise her up as her own child. Mary had gotten to know Kristianna very well. Kristianna, as strong as she was, had been through so much herself. Mary had the ability to listen and not judge. She was so wonderful. Over time, Kristianna had befriended Mary, and after clinic appointments, they would go on walks together, and this is when Mary got to know Arias' tragic history. Who else could Kristianna trust?"

Chapter 32

Stirling could feel frustration starting to build. He stood and paced the room. Troutman had brought to ruin so many lives just so he could fulfil his own selfish desires.

"I am tired of sitting around doing nothing. I think I need to go to Troutman now."

Peter Smith remained seated, but there was resolve in his voice. "And say what to him exactly, Stirling? 'Oh, Mr. Troutman, give me back Sian. You murdered my uncle, and we think you murdered a few others.' At best, he would laugh in your face. At worst, he would bolt down the hatches and head for the deep waters where we have no chance of hooking him in. Stirling, Troutman knows that he left himself vulnerable, and when you started looking into your uncle's death, he smelt fear. Fear that you would uncover the truth. That gives us an edge, Stirling, and we need to use that edge."

Stirling now stood in front of and over Peter Smith, said, "I know we have no solid evidence yet, but we cannot sit back and do nothing. I have to get Sian back."

"We are doing something, Stirling. My team is in communication with Luna. It is part of their organization that has…" Peter Smith minutely hesitated enough for Stirling to notice that he was searching for the right word, "…taken." This was the result, but Stirling wondered whether 'murdered' was his first word of choice.

"Taken Sian under instruction of Troutman. But, it is not as easy as calling customer services and stating that you have a query. Luna is one of the world's most powerful criminal groups. They have a line of command. They will only help us if we can help them. We have to be careful not to help organized crime. Hopefully, we can help them solve a problem. We just have to hope that Troutman has become a big enough problem for them to want our help."

"Stirling, Suzanne, I have to say that, at this moment in time, we have no idea what has happened to Sian. But I can tell you that Luna are talking to us and, sadly, it is a cruel waiting game. The best thing we can do is to keep our heads, be patient, and then, when we have some more intelligence, plan our next move."

"Okay, but what if intelligence is not forthcoming? What is our fallback?"

"Then, Stirling, we create another catalyst and cause another reaction. Troutman is clearly in a volatile and agitated state. We will keep on prodding until he exposes himself in the open and we will be waiting."

Stirling stood, hands on hips, looking out to the sea.

"Stirling, my job is a difficult one. That is the whole reason my organization exists. We go get the difficult ones who have avoided justice. We get involved when the normal systems of law and order have run out of options. I always get my man, Stirling, always. Sometimes, it can takes years, sometimes hours, but I get them."

Stirling turned back to Peter Smith. "But at what cost?"

"Sadly, Stirling, I can only count the cost when our target is behind bars, but the cost always has to be balanced against what the cost would have been if we had allowed these monsters to carry on. Trust me, Stirling, let's sit tight and wait. I have been here many times before. It never gets any easier, in fact, it probably gets harder but I have to give my operatives who are in the field, as we speak, space for them to do their jobs. You have done what we have not been able to do, Stirling, you have drawn Troutman out."

Stirling put his hand up to Peter Smith, then retreated to sit back down. "Please, don't make me responsible for all of this. I am just a retired racing driver trying desperately to stay retired!"

Stirling looked back across to Susanne. Her face seemed somehow gray in pallor as she sat with her hands so tightly clasped on her lap that her knuckles appeared white. Peter Smith could see that, whilst he had been managing Stirling's impetuousness, Susanne was slowly reaching the point of panic.

He turned to her with a genuine, caring smile. Her glazed eyes looked back at him. "Susanne, tell us what happened next. It looks to me like all three of you saved Sian's life. What happened in France?"

Susanne continued on in what at first seemed like autopilot as Stirling sat back and concentrated on the next instalment.

"It was all such a blur, at first. Mary and I traveled to France that day and literally picked from a map a village in the French Alps that looked the most remote. We sent in letters of resignation to our jobs but left no forwarding addresses. At first, we stayed in a bed-and-breakfast using our money. Mary had a small case of clothes. I literally went with the clothes I went to the clinic in. Mary had brought me a bag with a few bits. I had been given a parcel at the clinic that, to be honest, we nearly left behind in all the commotion—our focus being to get as far away from Troutman as possible."

"Kristianna had said that she would have someone tie up all the loose ends for us both at home and it would take a few days for her to set up a bank account that we could access. After that, she did not want anything more to do with us—we were on our own. It was difficult for my mind to keep up with everything. I remember questioning her as to whether she would honor what she said. She took hold of my hand in both of hers and said, 'I will not allow you to be hurt by this man anymore. You will both be fine and you will have your baby. Now go, be safe, and trust me'."

"The following day, after Mary had come back from shopping, we were sitting on our beds, unpacking our case, when we remembered the parcel. We opened it to find £250,000 in various notes. Stirling, we sat there and laughed and laughed. Not out of joy, but had become hysterical, it was like being in a movie, but this was real. With everything, we had forgotten that Troutman was paying for me to disappear after the termination. Little did he know that his wife was taking care of it as well. 48 hours later, we went to the local bank and asked if an account had been set up in our names. £500,000 had been deposited in each of our accounts."

"There was a note in my account saying that I had to contact a named solicitor before being able to access my account. Upon contacting their office, I was simply given the combination for a deposit box in the Gare Du Nord Railway Station, Paris. We decided that, given my condition and situation, it was best if I kept as low a profile as possible, so Mary set off to the station. What she found there was my new identity. From then on, Susanne Speed was no more. That day, I became known as Hannah Peeds. It was all so surreal. When Sian was born, we knew it would be too dangerous for me to bring her up. We were certain that Troutman would check up on me, so Mary adopted Sian straight away and settled in the village. I moved just across the border, into Italy."

"At first, it was difficult and there were lots of tears. But, day by day it became easier, and then it just blended into the norm. I took up teaching, Mary took a job at the local clinic, and we both shared the joy of watching our wonderful little girl grow up. Sian knew me as her mom's best friend, Hannah, and we just did everything together."

Peter Smith and Stirling looked on, wide-eyed.

"Wow, and I thought my life turned out different," Stirling exclaimed.

Peter Smith shook his head in admiration. "You are both amazing people."

"Sadly, we were both 'amazing people', as you put it. Both Sian's and my life were dealt a crushing blow when Mary was diagnosed with her illness. I nursed her till the very last moment. One of the last things she said to me was that she would not have changed a thing but that she did become agitated that we had led a lie to keep Sian safe. She hated Troutman for that. She left a massive hole in our lives, and I could see Sian become very restless in her own skin."

"Sian told me that she was into her karting, and I have to say she can pedal a car." Stirling smiled.

"Oh, yes, she grew up obsessed with cars and racing, and we all followed your career closely. In fact, it was quite a while before the two monkeys let me know that Sian had been karting and was very good at it. We were devastated when you had your big crash. Sian cried!"

"So did I!" Stirling joked back.

"Of course, we never mentioned any involvement with you. We needed to keep Troutman well clear of our lives. If I dwell on it, I had found it difficult watching the meteoric rise of

Troutman and his portrayal of his perfect family life. But we had Sian, and that was all that mattered. I had Roger taken from me by him, aided by my stupidity, and I was determined that I would keep hold of what I had left."

Peter Smith spoke next, "And Kristianna?"

"We never heard from her again, and we kept our side of the deal. Occasionally, I would see pictures of her in the press. It always played on my mind that I never actually said thank you to her, but I just hoped she knew that we were. We had all ended up under the Troutman curse."

Susanne turned to Peter Smith, who had clearly just been listening to a voice on his discreet earpiece. He quickly gave his attention to back to Susanne.

"You say that Mary left Sian a note and a picture. I never knew about it. It is amazing that she was able to track Stirling down off of that. She would have had no idea about her link with Stirling."

Stirling looked at Peter Smith in an accusing way. Peter Smith looked up and caught Stirling's glare and then put up both of his hands in a mock gesture.

Peter said, "No, no, Stirling. That has nothing to do with us. We had no knowledge of Sian until she started following you. No, somehow, Sian saw the note, the picture, and tracked you down under her own steam. She is a special girl."

A chill not caused by a temperature change floated through the room, and all three of them felt it and knew what each one was thinking after the concluded statement of Peter Smith's last comment.

Susanne refocused on Stirling, "I know you must think, if only Susanne had not gotten involved with Troutman, our lives would be so different. But, that is in the past, I cannot change that, but I am not important, Sian is. We must get her back."

Stirling tried to hide the hideous, dark thought that there might be no Sian to bring back. Peter Smith had left quickly for the balcony area again, clearly receiving information, then relaying orders and instructions. He walked back into the room and into Stirling's question. "Have we got her?"

Peter Smith replied directly, "No."

"Is she safe?"

"We really do not have an answer for that yet."

"Do we have any news about Sian, whatsoever?"

"No."

"Then what has your organization been doing?"

"We are slowly, carefully prizing open communication with Luna. They are very wary of us, and we are very wary of them. We have to go high in their organization, and we need to get them to work with us. The wrong pressure at this point, and they will disappear underground again."

Peter Smith took a deep breath, which in a small way prepared Susanne and Stirling for what he had to say next. "Luna is a powerful, evil, and ruthless organization that will not allow itself to be compromised. Susanne, Stirling, we have to prepare ourselves for the worst possible news."

Susanne left the room for the bathroom, her shoulders heaving as she disappeared. Something then, at that moment, seemed to click with Stirling and he started to feel more comfortable. He was now getting into his territory. His racing instincts, his focus, and his self-control were finally realizing a new arena to operate in.

"Okay, Peter Smith, 'sir', where do you want me and what do you want me to do?"

Peter Smith actually managed a smile. "Welcome onboard, Stirling. I knew that if we could get the properties you drew on to become a world champion, my world will have gained a big asset in fighting the war of injustice. I need you out of Monte Carlo in the small hours. Then, lie low and wait, I am sure Troutman will make the next move. We will continue to stay in the background and work into Luna. Troutman is now so focused on you he will not see us behind him."

"And as for Susanne. She will be taken to a safe house and well looked after. Now, I suggest sleep, then sneak out in the early hours. Will you head up to your base in France where you always stay at?"

Stirling looked quizzically at Peter Smith. "Well, yes, I will. But how do you know about that place?"

"Stirling, we followed you there, you tried to take out one of my men with a branch, and then we met for coffee in the village the morning after you sat with me in my hotel after supposedly damaging my car!"

"Okay, okay. The shunt has affected my memory a bit, it will reset, honest!"

Stirling smiled and winked, a gesture that somehow provided Peter Smith with assurance that it was the right decision to involve Stirling Speed. "Maybe, we need a bit more time for some of those world-champion properties to bubble through yet," Stirling said.

Stirling suddenly felt a blast from the past, and he liked it. He suddenly felt part of a team again; ready to respond to whatever they asked him to do.

Chapter 33

The polished underground car park floor was littered with car exotica. Stirling's E-Type was being kept company by an orange, low-slung Lamborghini Miura. They sat apart like miniature cars when compared to the modern, wide, loud sports cars and luxury travel mobiles that surrounded them. A very discreet young man had followed Stirling down to his car carrying an old-but-refreshed hamper basket that had not been asked for but volunteered by the hotel. Stirling opened the rear tailgate, which fooled the helpful young man for a moment as it opened sideways into him. He negotiated around it and put the hamper carefully into the rear of the sleek Jaguar.

"Nice car, Stirling."

Stirling smiled, the hotel trained their staff well. They knew to pick up on detail. "Thank you. I have had it a long time; it's like part of the family."

Stirling hesitated as he placed his well-worn hold-all next to the hamper. "In fact, it is my family!"

The smell of the leather came wafting out of the open boot.

"I hope I can have a car like this one day," the man said.

Stirling turned and handed over a generous tip to his helper. "Well, take another tip from me, you aim for the stars, you never know you might actually get to them, but if not, at least you will have missed the trees!"

"Thank you, have a good trip and don't worry about the press. If they ask me, I will say you are staying in your room and do not want visitors."

Stirling replied with, "Well done, and thank you again. Hopefully, we will cross paths again."

With that he was gone, and Stirling was left alone in the cool, quiet, deserted night-time garage. Stirling ran his fingers over the slender, shapely body of the eager E-Type as he walked around checking for any obvious sign of any tampering. He had asked Peter Smith if he could have one of his guys give the Jag a quick check-over. It had been standing for a couple of days now, alone in the garage, available for anyone who had the mind to booby-trap it.

The world that Stirling now frequented was like any racetrack he had been around over the years. They had to be respected; you had to be alert to their hidden dangers. Any drivers who became complacent, arrogant, or careless usually ended up paying for the error with pain, or worse.

A masked satisfaction permeated through Stirling's body as he pulled shut the long door, placed the old, jangly keys into the center-mounted ignition, and turned over the straight six. Oil was instantly awakened from its slumber and became agitated as it was forced around the oil galleries of this classic, long-serving engine to assist in maintaining its reputation for being silky smooth. Within two revolutions, the fuel mixture ignited, and after a little spitting and coughing protest from the carburation department, the multi-cylinder engine soon settled into a harmonious rhythm. Holding the warming engine just above tick over, Stirling pressed the slightly squeaky clutch pedal and gently worked the gears through all five of the modified gearbox and selected reverse for good measure to ensure, in Stirling's mind, that all the shafts and rotating gears had a quick dose of thick, sticky oil. The barking semi-tuned engine seemed fiercer and noisier than normal as its sound waves reverberated around the concrete-clad car park, perhaps exaggerated by the deadness of the night.

Stirling eased the long bonnet out of it parking space, flicked on the lights, and headed for the dark square that marked the exit of the car park. Stirling turned right out of the car park, still under the cover of the tunnel that lined the seafront. He resisted the temptation to squeeze the throttle to get the Jaguar howling. Quietly slipping out of Monte in the shadows of the night was the order of the day. Peter Smith had put a statement out that Stirling was to make his statement the following day at 10 am in the foyer of the Fairmont hotel and that seemed to dissipate the camping press. At 10 am the next morning the hotel management would know nothing of the arrangement? They would be only able to confirm that Stirling Speed had left their establishment.

By 10 am Stirling would be sat on a veranda deep in France overlooking carefully tended vineyards no doubt being fussed by a lady called Rosa and sympathized by a man called Thomas, away from all the fuss just like in the years gone by. The difference this time though was Stirling was not on the way to or from anywhere he was there to just wait.

Chapter 34

The shower was as hot as could be tolerated, the soap massaged into the glistening skin, cleansed, soothed, and refreshed. Victoria's long, jet-black wet hair felt heavy as it cascaded down over her white toweling robe. Soon, it was flying in all directions as Victoria blasted it with the hot hair from the dryer. It had been a long, hard night, so she just needed it dry so she could sleep.

She stiffly walked over to the blinds and dropped them to 'vanish' the bright sunlight that penetrated her third-floor apartment. Then at last, she climbed into her wonderful bed, home at last. She was sore, but that was part of the territory, sometimes, in her line of work.

And, Victoria earned good money and was a good saver. She'd already been able to put a sizeable deposit down on a small seafront restaurant that needed complete renovating. The little, quiet fishing village of Haraki, on Rhodes Island, off mainland Greece, was the perfect place for her to retire too. She nearly had enough to finish buying it, then another 12 months' hard work would mean she would have enough for the renovations and a small-but-adequate working capital. That time could not come soon enough. Victoria worked hard for her money and was pleased that she could earn so much, but she hated her job. Even though tiredness careered through her veins, Victoria lay awake for a short while as her confused body tried to forget that it was 8 a.m.

She'd come a long way from her horrendous childhood. A drug-ridden mother and abusive, drunk father gave her two good reasons to run away from her London home at 15. By 16, Victoria Blake was recovering in a hospital from an overdose, but it was then that her life changed. An older lady in the bed next to her took her under her wing, and when they both left the hospital, she offered her a place to live and work. As in any job, the first few weeks were horrible, but she got through them, just. She apparently was a natural and her poor pay soon started to increase.

When she told the kind lady who had befriended her that she had decided to set up on her own, she was greeted with encouragement to aim for the very top. Victoria had often thought it would be good for her savior to see her now, in her tidy third-floor Monte Carlo apartment. She had very much made it to the top. *Maybe when I retire to Haraki, I might be able to locate her and bring her across for a holiday. Maybe I could try find...* Victoria's conscious thoughts drifted away as sleep took over her body and began to heal Victoria's bruises.

Not far away, Peter Smith stood on the harbor front. It was busy. Monte Carlo was not a big place throw in a motor race and its supporters, and it became positively congested. Peter Smith liked busy though, he could blend easier into crowds, which was a good thing if you were following someone.

Today's target sat at a round metal table, a beer gently warming in the heating morning sun. Peter Smith took a picture of something in the harbor with his phone, then pretended to view the image whilst looking over his phone at the target, who was in the process of answering his phone. The call was short, just long enough for the man to write a telephone number down on a disheveled napkin.

Before he had finished writing it, a voice spoke into Peter Smith's ear through his earpiece, "We have made the call. He has your number. Expect a call imminently."

Peter Smith watched his target dial the number, then looked down at his own phone to await the connection. A caller with no ID started buzzing.

"Hello, Peter Smith."

"Hello, we need to meet."

"Okay, so who is this calling? It is John Beechy—we have mutual business. When and where can we meet?"

"Now, and stay where you are, I'll come to you."

"You know where I am?"

"Yes, I do, Mr. Beechy, I am stood about 20 feet away from you, to your right."

Beechy looked around to see Peter Smith 'doff' his imaginary hat. Beechy summoned a waiter and ordered another beer and water as Peter Smith walked over, pulled a chair from an empty table, and sat down without a greeting. It was not the time for small talk. Nothing was said as they awaited the return of the waiter, and so both looked out to the harbor.

"One beer and water, *Monsieur*."

Beechy took the beer and gestured towards Peter Smith for the water. "You look like a man who likes to keep a clear head, I think."

"Thank you. You have something for me?"

"Yes."

"Sian?"

"Who?"

Peter Smith changed tack. "Troutman, do you have his head on a platter for me?"

"Maybe, you do not know how much I would like to give you his literal head on a plate. But no, I have a name."

"Okay."

"Victoria Blake, she was with him last night. That's a picture of her, that's her address, and that is a café near her apartment she often frequents."

"She is acquainted with Troutman?"

"No, she's a hooker."

"Is that not a bit risky for Troutman?"

"She is high-class, and I mean high class. Charges 5K a night. Troutman gets me to check them out first. The big-league prostitutes hit on high-profile clients, charge big money, but keep their mouths shut. They soon build up a clientele that appreciates discretion. You want to blow Troutman's fantasy, a happy family world, then she could be your girl."

"What makes you think she will spill with me?"

"Word is, she is ready for an out. She has bought herself some retirement home somewhere and is just a few shags short of retirement."

"Thank you. I am sorry, but I must ask again, do you know anything about what's happened to Sian?"

John Beechy put down his empty beer bottle, turned, and looked at Peter Smith for the first time during the conversation.

"Listen, I agreed to do this because Lawrence Troutman is an out of control animal and it has come from the very top of my world that I speak to you. I have given you a name, and that is it. You get me?"

"I get you. Thanks for this. I'll have a wander over now and see if I can have a chat with this Victoria Blake."

John Beechy had resumed his staring look out to the harbor as Peter Smith slid his chair out and stood up to leave. "I'd leave the girl for a couple of hours if I were you, let her get herself together a bit. Troutman gave her a rough time last night and made sure he got his money's worth. Nobody deserves treating like that. He is scum."

Beechy raised his arm and gestured for another beer. Peter Smith left him to it.

Chapter 35

Troutman sat on the rear deck of the Serene Lady, surrounded by an entourage. The camera crew had been allowed on early to set up but had then been kept waiting because Mr. Troutman had apparently been up all night, having been at urgent meetings about the future of the Italian Grand Prix being held at Monza or so the story went. He had finally emerged and was clearly showing signs of a stressful night.

Makeup had gotten to work to ready him for an interview with one of the leading pretty lights of the broadcasting world. She was feeling confident going into the interview as she had been personally chosen by Lawrence Troutman over her more illustrious ex-F1 driver co-presenter. She was not going to miss this opportunity to shine. Interviewing the most powerful man in world motorsport was always going to be a scoop.

"Mr. Troutman, if the Italian Grand Prix is taken away from Monza, surely that would be like ripping a book out of the Bible."

"Suzy, everyone seems to be blaming me for Monza's failings."

"It's you who 'calls the shots', Mr. Troutman."

"Suzy, don't forget I am Formula One's biggest fan. My very own race team, which I used to own, has history at Monza. Drivers have paid with their pain, guts, and lives at this circuit, all in the name of Formula One. If the organizers want to make it happen, I will make sure that it happens. Let me ask you, did you place your pretty head on a nice pillar last night, Suzy?"

"I certainly did." She turned to the camera cheekily and winked. The producer loved the free-styling she could pull off.

"Being a TV presenter in Monte Carlo is such hard work." She turned back to Troutman, who was doing a professional job hiding his anger at being upstaged by a silly little girl having the last interview she was ever going to have with him.

"Well, Suzy, whilst you dreamed, I worked all night on a deal to bring Monza back to the calendar. I want it but do the organizers want it enough?"

Pleased that she had pushed him on that controversial current topic, she eased her attack and took a moment to look at her iPad to search for her next prepared point. Troutman raised his left arm in front of him and drew his cuff back with his right hand to look at his glittering diamond-studded gold watch. The camera clearly seeing the 'I am bored of this interview statement' which now irritated Suzy, who was just doing her professional job of keeping the millions of TV-viewing public entertained.

"So Mr. Troutman, we have brought this interview forward and are recording it, as I am told that right after this you board your helicopter to fly straight back home."

"Well, I have a helicopter that is transferring me to Nice, where my jet awaits, which will fly me into Heathrow where my helicopter is waiting to fly me to my home, to my family."

"So, this is the first Monte Carlo Grand Prix that you have missed in…"

"27 years, Suzy, but as you may know, there was a tragic accident at my private test track where a young journalist lost control of one my cars that she was driving and died. We are all devastated. She had been staying with us and had a lovely time with my wife Kristianna. I need to be back at home to support her during this terrible time. On top of that, we have had Stirling Speed's accident in one of my cars and the unbelievable kidnapping of one his close friends. It's all been so difficult to take. So, I think it is the right thing to fly home to my family as soon as possible."

"Lawrence Troutman, you are a busy man, and I'd like to thank you for your time. And, I would like to take this moment to say—on behalf, I am sure, of so many—our thoughts are with you, your family, and I think we should include Stirling Speed, a true champion too."

Suzy turned directly into the camera which responded by closing right down onto her face, cutting Lawrence Troutman out of the shot.

"Stirling, if you are out there looking in, best wishes, our thoughts are with you in this difficult time."

Suzy smiled at the camera until the producer shouted cut and turned back to Troutman, who was already stood up, ripping his microphones off.

"Thanks, Lawrence, that was great."

"Don't ever make jokes in my interviews again. And also, let's not cloud the issue here, it's my family and I who are suffering, Speed should take more care of his little tarts."

At that, Troutman turned to enter the bowels of his yacht and barked at one of his numerous assistants, "Please, get my yacht tidied up, which means I want this lot off now. And where's Beechy when I want him? Get him here now."

Chapter 36

Beechy sat in the private lounge area of Troutman's cabin and waited. He mused at the artwork that hung around. Bright splashes of color shockingly and indiscriminately applied to awaiting blank canvasses, no doubt depicting the artists' innermost feelings at that moment of time. For John Beechy, he found the pieces annoying—everything about them. The money they cost, the person who bought them, and the waste of paint and effort that had gone into making these masterpieces.

One picture, though, stood out from the rest of the daubs for a number of reasons. It was slightly smaller, at one-meter square, and was an actual photograph, so it had defined representations on it. You could actually recognize what was on it. The picture showed a laughing Lawrence Troutman knelt on a white, sandy tropical beach, wearing loose-fitting, no doubt cooling, white linen trousers and shirt. His two young children stood upright on both sides of him, each with one of their arms around his neck, their heads slightly crooked to one side and they were giggling too. The beautiful, slim Kristianna stood behind, her white, thin dress and her long, dark hair clearly just catching the warm sea breeze. Kristianna's hands had reached down and her fingers were attempting to mess up Troutman's slightly-too-long wavy hair. The perfect use of a camera as it caught the snapshot of a happy family. Beechy shook his head, clearly Kristianna frequented the yacht named after her by Troutman.

John Beechy was irritable and was not looking forward to his approaching abuse. He was tired physically, mentally, and was now slightly drunk. It had been a long night waiting for Troutman to finish with his purchase, then instead of bed, he had been instructed by his bosses to make contact with a strange gray man. It was becoming increasingly clear that his bosses at Luna were growing tired of Troutman's demands. The advantages of the discreet money laundering services that Troutman's huge sporting empire provided were now being shadowed by the volatile and increasingly erratic behavior he was now displaying. It was made clear to Beechy that they wanted Troutman fed to the apparent predators that were circling and did not want to end up being taken down with him. He had been told to feed another message to Troutman, although he had no idea what the foundation behind the message was.

Troutman walked out from his bathroom, followed by a wisp of steam from the shower. A tied white towel clung on under his white, bulging belly. He walked straight over to his drinks cabinet without acknowledging Beechy's presence and poured himself a large scotch. He raised it to his lips, then hesitated. "You sorted the girl?"

"Yes, Mr. Troutman, I paid her and made sure she discreetly left the yacht. She made her own way from there."

Troutman put his untouched scotch back on top of the polished wood cabinet and then looked up to the ceiling of his cabin in apparent despair. He controlled his anger by speaking slowly and softly, "Not the trash from last night, the girl I told you to discreetly dispose of, yet her face greets me on every form of media I can shake a stick at."

"Yes, she is gone. Speed's crash was just bad luck for us, but I have no idea how the media got hold of the story so quickly. We are looking into that, but she is gone, she is history and, soon, will be old news."

Beechy continued to look at Troutman's large, misshapen, fat bare back and could not help thinking how much this guy had let himself go—a man gorged on excesses like an ancient Roman emperor.

Troutman raised the glass to his lips once more. "There have been no errors this time, she is gone from existence?"

"Yes, Mr. Troutman, we…"

Troutman put one hand into the air for Beechy to see the back of. "Spare me the details. You got me the medical reports I asked you to get?"

"Yes, we got them, a girl called Suzanne Speed, she had a termination. It cost a lot of money to get them. They are on your desk. Can I ask why…"

Troutman did not want to hear more. "Now, go and keep where I expect you to be."

Troutman finally tilted the glass, its whole contents burned their way down his throat in one go and immediately started their job of dulling his senses. He put the glass back on top of the cabinet with ill-concealed force, then, with a spreading of his hands, leaned against it whilst looking down onto its top.

"Mr. Troutman."

"You are still here, why?"

"Mr. Troutman, I have been told to pass to you a message from my bosses."

Troutman looked up, this was out of the norm, he turned to face Beechy, now placing his hands on his hips almost defiantly, and flicked his head upwards slightly in a beckoning way. "What?"

"Speed. He is definitely onto something and is becoming a worry, and the records you wanted were for a Susanne Spe…"

"Well, give me some new news. That's probably why we have been trying to kill him for the last few years."

"With due respect, it appears to be more than just your women he is interested in."

Troutman boiled inside at the last statement, it made his whole being seem insignificant, petty even, and deep down Troutman knew that to be the case. He had risked everything; he had murdered and ruined lives just for the sake of 'his women'.

"Go on."

"Speed seems to have linked with another organization that is dangerous to our operation, and they have the power, backing, and resources to bring down individuals and large organizations. We think it is only a matter of time before he links you and Luna. This cannot happen. Speed will be fired up, now that we have done away with his girl. He is out for blood, and I don't think he is that bothered about his own. He clearly is a very resourceful guy, and Luna is not comfortable with the situation."

"Sounds like the bad guys are getting scared, you pathetic people. Leave it to me, I'll personally finish Speed off, then we can all be happy families again. Is that okay? Now get out."

Beechy turned to exit the cabin, but Troutman stopped him in his tracks. "To think I allow scum like you to talk to me like that on my yacht."

John Beechy pivoted, held onto the open door, and allowed maybe the tiredness and slight drunkenness to get the better of him.

"Listen to me, Mr. Lawrence Troutman, I don't like you. I tolerate you because I am told to, but remember, the moment I am off my leash, I'm coming for you. I'll blow your sordid little world to the world's press, and then I will use all my years of experience and skill to make sure you have a painful, slow accident. And trust me when I tell you that I can feel my owner slackening the grip on my leash. Don't ever call me scum again."

Not allowing Troutman the right to reply, Beechy continued his journey through the open door and left it to close itself. Never before had he spoken out of turn with one of Luna's clients, but what did they expect from a professional assassin? A puppy dog that barked when instructed and was then rewarded with a treat?

Beechy had a slight smile, some would say smirk, of satisfaction, though. *He took the bait, hook, line, and sinker, as they say. He'll go for Speed. I think, Beechy my son, your assignment is due to wind down, then maybe it's time for you to institute your retirement plan.* Luna had taken him from petty crime to serious crime to professional crime, and it had made him a moderately wealthy man. The trick was to be able to get out of the underworld, alive!

Chapter 37

Victoria took her time dressing after her short but, deep, well-deserved sleep. She put her hair up haphazardly, which had the effect of highlighting her high, defined-but-soft cheekbones that helped form her pretty heart-shaped face.

Her smiling emerald-green eyes blinked back at her in the mirror. *Make up or no makeup? Is the world ready for the naked face of Victoria Blake?* she smiled to herself. *I think the sun is out, so I think my Gucci sunnies and no makeup, girl. It's a Victoria day today, so I can do whatever I want!* Victoria was always sure to book a 'Victoria day' after she had worked with a client. It was a day to do whatever she liked, dress in whatever she liked, a day to recover.

She walked over to her drawers, on top of which sat a picture of a family. A young child lay on his front on the grass, his smiling head supported by his elbows, arms, and hands. The child's legs bent at the knees as his feet kicked in the air, and the adoring hand-holding adults glinted perfect smiles and looked straight down the camera lens of the professional photographer. Victoria had no idea who the perfect family was, but she focused on the fact that, one day, she would have a photo taken like that—a photo of her perfect family—on a day that would be far removed from the days she had lived in the past.

She opened her drawers and took out the underwear that she wanted to wear, something comfortable and pretty. Then, opening her wardrobe, she took out her favorite long, white flowing cotton dress that she loved the feel of as it dropped loosely over her body when she put it on.

She enjoyed these days; her work could be demanding, sometimes physically demanding, like the night before. Although, it had been a long time since she had been that badly treated—even her scalp was sore. She made a note to give that

178

client a wide berth if another request came through. Sometimes, it was mentally demanding. Some of Victoria's high-rolling clients just wanted some beautiful girl to be seen on their arm for various reasons. A top game show host and TV mogul liked the press to photograph him with as many different beautiful girls on his arm to deflect any suggestion that he actually did not like woman and preferred his own gender.

The same had gone for a huge Hollywood star Victoria had worked for. The media had followed them to a secluded, exclusive hotel where she had spent a night of passion with the star and been paid double the money for her night. The reality was the hotel got great publicity, the star proved he was a stud, and Victoria had proved to herself that she could watch two Star Wars movies back-to-back and enjoy being by herself in a secluded, exclusive hotel. Her only work for the evening and morning were: 1. To be seen hugging and kisses said star on the way into the hotel. 2. Show her bare, naked back at one of the bedroom windows and cover her face as she exited via the back of the hotel the following morning. And for her troubles, she would be paid 10,000 pounds, thank you very much!

Her favorite clients, though, were the rich, high-profile guys who were trapped in hideous marriages. One in particular she felt bad about was a politician who lived his life how others wanted him to live it. Victoria would sit with him in a private, quiet hotel room. She would make him cups of tea and listen to his life. Their closest physical contact was when she once brushed a fallen hair from his face. He liked just to talk about family and work and life just like a man and a wife do but for some reason couldn't with his high-powered barrister wife.

Unfortunately, that all came to a hideous end when one of their usually perfectly planned secret meetings attracted the attention of a clever, hungry journalist. Victoria had suggested that she come clean and explain that really nothing had gone on, but the politician insisted that this would make him seem mentally bereft, so he allowed the press to devour him. Victoria vowed that she would never allow her husband, when she found one, to get to the point where he had to pay a hooker 5000 pounds just to talk! It was weird that, even though they had no way of knowing they had been rumbled at their last meeting, Victoria had insisted that she take no payment for the night of... talk. It always made her smile that if she were a man and did what she did, she would been known as a fun-loving gigolo, but because she was a girl, a beautiful one at that, she was known as a hooker, albeit a high-class one!

Soft brown leather bag slung over her shoulder, Gucci sunglasses pushed up and into shining black hair, Victoria pushed through the foyer doors of her apartment block and smiled at the warm afternoon sun. First stop, lunch at her favorite corner café where she could sit outside and watch the world go by.

A strong French accent rang out, "Vikki, 'ello, you bring even more sun to my café, your usual?"

"You flatter, Maurice. But yes, thank you, my usual."

"And may I buy you that usual?"

Victoria turned and peered over her sunglasses at the gray man standing at her side. "And you are?"

"Well, I know this is your day off, so let me say that I am not a potential customer."

"So, that narrows the field to either a copper, a private investigator, or the press, either way it is my day off, so kindly and politely make it one. You got nothing on me and I certainly have nothing to say, no matter what threats or money you have to offer."

Victoria slipped her sunnies back up her nose and resumed her day off. Peter Smith slid a chair back and sat down. "I know the owner of this café very well, and he is a big guy, so if you need any assistance leaving, it can be arranged."

Peter Smith reached inside of his pocket and took out a picture of a beautiful, smiling young girl and laid it on the table for Victoria to see. "This girl was about your age, with a promising career as a reporter in front of her."

"Don't tell me she took an overdose because her boyfriend or husband is supposed to have had a fling with me. Save it, I have heard it all before. I have nothing to say. Please, do not let me have to create a scene."

"No, Victoria…"

"Oh, you are clever, you know my name."

Peter Smith continued, "No, Victoria, she did not commit suicide. She was murdered."

"And that concerns me why?"

"Because, Victoria, she was murdered by the man you were with last night."

Victoria did not come back with a reply

"I know how badly he treated you last night, and I know that you know he has the ability to murder."

"So, you are the police?"

"No, I am not. I am part of an organization that steps in when people who are above the law decide to break it. Victoria, I am not here to ruin your life. In fact, I have the resources to give you the life you have always wanted."

"Like you know what I want out of life. You are like all the rest of the people I have to work with—you are a user. You want to use me to get what you want. Well, I have my own plans, thank you. Now, go away."

"I can make sure that you get your café in Haraki and that it is fully refurbished. No more late working nights for you, Victoria."

Victoria rounded on Peter Smith like a cornered cat, hissing, "How do you know about that? How? Don't you dare go near that. I have worked hard and long to make a life for me. Don't you dare intrude on my private life!"

"I am not here to take anything away. I just want to help. Maybe we can help find your family. You have had a rough time, Victoria, just let me help."

How did this man know so much?

A concerned Maurice appeared at Victoria's shoulder. "Vikki, you need some 'elp with the trash?"

Peter Smith thought it better not to look into the eyes of Maurice but, instead, appealed to Victoria, "I am one of the good guys, Victoria, and you have not had many of those in your life. Trust me, I am the break you have always deserved."

Victoria decided to retract her claws, for now at least. "He is a friend, Maurice, thank you. Oh, and he will be paying my bill." Maurice glared at Peter Smith, then pasted his smile back and returned to bustling around his other customers.

"Okay, Mr. Gray Man, you have just got a dinner receipt for your expenses. But, I have gotten to know in my life that there are no free dinners, so what do want from me that is different from what men usually want, which, incidentally, would cost you 5grand if you are thinking of stepping into the marketplace."

"I'll come straight to the point, Victoria, then leave you to enjoy the rest of your well-deserved day off. I need you to blow the lid off Lawrence Troutman's world. I need you to testify about the true character and secret life of him. In return, my organization will offer protection for as long as you deem necessary. We will buy your café, refurbish it and set you up for life."

Peter Smith slid a white card over to Victoria with just a mobile number printed on it. "Ring me if you want to. If not you will never here from me again."

"So, you really think it is that easy? I testify about this man I have supposedly been with and we all live happily ever after? I am sorry, Mr. Gray Man, I'm afraid in my world it's not like that. I spill on one client, then trust me, I have a catalogue of other big, big fish that suddenly start thinking when it's going to be their turn for me to cash in on. The moment I play your game, I can assure you that it will be only a matter of days before I am found looking down at the harbor's bottom."

Before Peter Smith could answer, a barrage of wailing sirens came past and his attention and that of Victoria's was distracted as a commotion broke out in the harbor. Maurice had come out of his café and looked as well. Victoria looked up at him enquiringly.

"It is not good, Vikki. A body has been found floating in the harbor. Not good at all," he said.

Victoria broke her gaze and looked at Peter Smith. "Well, how's that for a coincidence? But, I am sure that you will agree that it does illustrate my point, Mr. Gray."

"I know that you have survived by your instincts, but we can change things for you, we will protect you and follow through with the deal. This man has murdered many times before and he will again. We know it, but we need to build a case, and you could be a very important brick for building that case."

"Why do you do what you do, Mr. Gray? Why not find a nice, respectable job looking after accounts or something?"

"Because, like you Victoria, I have a history as well, and maybe, I saw one injustice too many. But, I know that at some point it will be time for me to stop, time for me to wash the stench of my world off me. Maybe, this is the time for you to stop too."

Victoria went to complete the comment that she had started with her question, but then she saw the sadness in Peter Smith's eyes. In her profession, it paid to try and read what men were really thinking. "You have had sadness, Mr. Gray."

"Hah, yeah, you could say that. Although my sadness cannot be changed now, I can help change the sadness of others—just like you can."

"Don't try to shame me into anything. Trust me, I know how to compartmentalize my life. So, trust me, that approach won't work."

"You're a strong girl, Victoria, I would not try to undermine you."

"Okay, Mr. Gray, here's the deal. Pay for my dinner and I'll think about it. Only think about it. If I did this, I would need to find a way of protecting myself, because in my experience, relying on someone else does not seem to end well. Now, can I get back to my day off?"

"Thank you, Victoria."

"Hey, and guess what, Mr. Gray, if you are ever in the marketplace, you get discount rates."

That last comment dug deep into Peter Smith and he yearned to scream out, 'You stupid girl, can you hear what you are saying?' Instead, he dug deep into his suit jacket pocket and set towards the café's till. As he did, his phone rang.

"Hi... No, that's really not the news I wanted... So that was the commotion in the harbor... Have they established a time of death... Okay, so the body had been in the water a very short time, no more than an hour... And the cause of death... Okay. Do we know who is behind the death for certain and why the hit was carried out? This case is going from bad to worse... Okay, thanks. Keep me informed of any more developments."

Peter Smith turned back from the quiet corner he had migrated to and resumed his journey to the till. He wondered if he should tell Victoria the devastating latest news, then realized she wouldn't know the significance of this now-dead person.

"'Ello, 'Ello?"

Peter Smith became aware of Maurice waving a small cash receipt in front of his nose.

"You are a troubled man, I think. *Merci.* Vikki, she is a special girl, she is good inside. You do not harm her."

Peter Smith managed a smile. "I will not harm her, Maurice, it is good that you look out for her. No, keep the change."

He set off to walk as two men stood by a car, following his every move. One spoke into his discreet microphone, "Where now, sir?"

Peter Smith replied to them, "You go back to the hotel and await further instructions."

"And you, sir, are you okay on your own?"

"Yes, you head back. I need a walk and some time to think. Any problems, I will call you."

Back at Nice airport, a Monte Carlo helicopter had just deposited Mr. Lawrence Troutman and he was now being led by a very efficient member of airport staff to the private VIP lounge, where he would then be transferred to his private jet, which stood completing its final checks and awaiting its VIP passenger. As the entourage transited the airport, it was suddenly and apparently expectedly brought to a sudden halt.

"Mr. Troutman, please, may I have your autograph. Please, sir. I have never met anyone important before."

Troutman looked down and beamed at the little boy looking up at him. Security instantly responded, but Troutman dropped to his knee as the flashing cameras of the press caught the moment.

"Of course you can, young man. Otherwise, I think we might have a security alert on our hands."

The entourage rippled with laughter. With a quick rub of the little boy's hair, Troutman was up and continued on his brisk walk to his awaiting plane. The beaming boy turned to the camera and held up his little scrap of paper with the autograph on and camera lights flashed again. Lawrence Troutman's press agent stepped up to the boy and led him back to his proud and ever-so-slightly-richer parents.

"Thank you ever so much for the loan of your wonderful boy. He was perfect, and I hope you spend some of our little gift we gave you on him."

The overworked, underpaid press agent turned and instantly dropped his smile. Mr. Troutman's little outburst on the yacht after the interview had not gone down well at all. And so now, he was having to, yet again, flood the press with good, happy, and loving Mr. Troutman's pictures and stories. He passed his bag to his assistant who was nearly breaking into a run to keep up.

"Man, it is hard work with this guy. We seem to take one step forward, then ten back! With the launch of his new, stupid supercar coming up, we need good press and plenty of it," the agent said.

The hurrying assistant replied, "We do need to hurry, as the last call for our flight back to London has gone out."

"Then why are we dawdling? Come on, let's go!"

Chapter 38

An occasional rise in the noise level of the early morning bird song chorus could be heard above his breathing, above the rushing of blood in his ears. Mainly, though, Stirling's ears were full of changing sounds when his running feet struck the various ground surfaces he covered. A rhythmic sound, sometimes soft, as Stirling eased more pressure onto his toes as a rising surface demanded a change in posture to attack the climb. The sound could then become sharper, the posture more upright, as descent commanded a control of acceleration. The rhythmic crunching of running on a gravel road or path always reminded Stirling of someone crunching through a bowl of Rice Krispies.

Stirling liked running in the morning. He felt it decongested his body from its slowed-down sleeping state. He enjoyed feeling the elements of the morning on his face, be they rain or shine. He enjoyed the aromas he ran through, the dampness of a wet field, the wondrous scent of blooming flowers, or even a waft from a cooking breakfast.

The run on this particular morning was labored, though. Stirling felt tired, caused by a restless, mainly sleepless, night. Stirling had spent most of the night looking up at the white bedroom ceiling, listening to the gentle rustle of summer leaves outside the open windows. He had watched the dark be beaten back by the light of the day. His mind raced through all the scenarios that lay in front of him. Scenarios that always had two constant elements in them—Troutman and Sian. What was the fate of Sian? The waiting, though, and the feeling of uselessness were the main thieves that robbed Stirling of his sleep.

He had no choice but to put his full trust in Peter Smith and his strange secret organization. Peter had said to sit and wait to see what move Troutman made next, but what if that move never came? What if Troutman had already headed off into the cowering deep water?

The cooking breakfast waft that graced Stirling's nostrils was now the waft of his own breakfast being made by the bustling Rosa. He entered through the heavy, green front door of the pretty French villa and was met by the heavy French accent of Rosa. "Breakfast in 15, Stirling, do not delay. Both the dog and Thomas are looking hungry this morning!"

"Okay, Rosa, I will shower and be down. Don't let either near my plate."

Stirling sharpened his cutthroat razor on his leather strop, agitated the creamy lather on his face, and with careful skill shaved whilst still wearing his running gear. Then, he stripped and purposely stood directly under the big chrome showerhead as he turned it on, his body spiking with stimulation as the sharp, cold water exploded on his warm, clammy body. Gradually, the warm water made its way through the pipework and massaged the raging coldness away from Stirling's now-glistening body. A rigorous rub down with an absorbent-but-slightly-coarse, aging towel ensured that his body was now fully awake, fully switched on, fully prepared for whatever scenario today was to bring.

Stirling padded over to his bed and sat down, draping his damp towel over his lap. He was not handling this situation well. He was allowing the uncontrollable circumstances he found himself in to burn into his psyche. He knew that wayward slide could only end in one way—disaster.

In years gone by, he found occasion when the team, despite their best efforts, would provide him with a poor, underperforming racecar. His inexperienced approach was to allow the car's underperformance to out-psych him. He would lose confidence in his own proven ability, then in response would overdrive the car and eventually make the mistake that would fling him off the circuit. Often, as he climbed out of the smoldering wreck, he had the feeling that the car was laughing at him.

In later years, he knew to do the opposite with a poor car; to back off until the team could reestablish a baseline set up, then gradually build on that. Stirling knew that was what he needed to do now, to back off and wait for a baseline to be established again, so as he could get a confident, sure footing to launch himself at Troutman. He realized the last thing he wanted to do was make a mistake that would see Troutman laughing at him from a distance. Yes, instead of pining for Peter Smith to establish contact with news for him to go, go, go, he would use this lull in time to prepare himself physically and mentally, to the best of his ability, to be ready for the inevitable onslaught. *Peter Smith, I will see you when I see you, but when I do, I will be ready.*

Stirling walked over to the big lightwood chest of drawers that contained his clothes. From the left top drawer, he selected a pair of black cotton boxers and black cotton socks. They were all black and all the same make. Stirling liked his clothes and went to great lengths to have everything made just as he required. But when it came to his boxers and socks, he kept all exactly the same, to the point that even the people he stayed with—his housekeeper in the UK, Rosa, and even some hotels he frequented—knew exactly what to order in for him. The morning run had given evidence that today was going to be a nice, warm French summer's day, so a pair of khaki combat shorts and a crisp, simple white t-shirt was selected, finished off with a pair of soft leather loafers.

"Stirling, Stirling, your breakfast is in jeopardy, come quickly!"

"Okay Rosa, defend it with your life, I am on my way."

Stirling leapt into action and chased down the stairs following the wonderful aromas that were sneaking out of the kitchen. He felt good that he had given himself a talking-to and felt a little more in-charge as he banged open the kitchen door.

"Right, you two, stand back from the food. Stirling needs to…" Stirling was halted mid-sentence.

"Peter, you're here."

Chapter 39

Peter Smith was in the process of stemming the stack of bacon appearing on his plate, courtesy of Rosa the cook.

"Thank you, Rosa, that really is plenty for me. No, honest, it is... Well, okay, maybe one more piece. Stirling, hi, how are you?"

Peter looked worryingly and pleadingly at the clearly surprised Stirling. "Rosa, Peter will need hospitalization if he is able to consume the amount of breakfast you are presenting," Stirling joked.

The rotund figure of Thomas proved that his body had adapted well to his wife's cooking excesses, and so he stepped in to save the moment by forking across some of the pile from Peter's plate to his own, a balance now apparently achieved.

The breakfast pantomime was carried out with uneasiness in the air, and it was Stirling who broke it without any further wasteful chat. "Sian? Do we have any news about Sian, Peter? It is so difficult doing nothing."

Peter Smith looked around the slightly smoky, bright kitchen and all knew from his look that the news was not good.

"No, we have no news that we can give you as far as Sian is concerned, I'm afraid."

Stirling looked out of the open kitchen door into the dusty, sunlit courtyard feeling a sickly pit in his stomach. Peter Smith continued, "We are still hopeful. Really, we are. In this case, no news is good news..."

"How can that be? That beautiful young girl," Rosa injected.

"We have found nothing, and well, something would have turned up by now," Peter said.

There was a moment's silence, and then Stirling grasped the nettle. "You mean, you would have her body by now?"

"Well, yes, we would have some sort of news to tell you. But at this time, I can only tell you to be hopeful."

Stirling sat at the big wooden farmhouse table, his plate of one rasher of bacon, a single bright yellow-and-white egg, some lightly fried mushrooms, and a good helping of beans cooling in front of him.

"Do eat, Stirling, you need strength."

"I know, Rosa, thank you."

Thomas took this as his cue and attacked his mountain but then hesitated as his bacon-filled fork reached his lips. The hesitation being caused by a stony, withering look from Rosa.

"What? You said to eat, we need to keep our strength up," Thomas protested.

"I said Stirling needs to eat, you fat oaf. You could miss eating for a year and still be living off your reserves."

"Oh, shut up, you silly woman, a working man needs to eat. Especially one who has to work around you." Thomas loaded his mouth and chewed whilst looking defiantly at Rosa, who sat down to her own well-stacked plate.

"Fat oaf."

"Silly mare."

Stirling looked at Peter Smith, who looked back at Stirling and offered a bit of a smile. "I think Rosa has a point, Stirling, let's eat first, then maybe we can walk and talk after. Although I do not have news of Sian, I do have other news."

The yet another occurrence of a Rosa-and-Thomas spat had broken the tension, and all got down to busying themselves with the morning banquet. As Stirling ate, he watched Peter Smith make polite conversation with, first, Thomas, then equally with Rosa. Although Stirling could not put his finger on it, he somehow took confidence in the fact that Peter Smith seemed slightly more relaxed, slightly more in control. When Stirling had left Monte Carlo, he had a left a clearly stressed, under-pressure, and worried Peter Smith. Yet now, he seemed to be back to his old self, efficiently going about doing what he did.

Stirling had long since controlled Rosa's cooking excesses and so cleared his less-stacked plate first and found himself waiting for Peter Smith to work through his. At last, Peter Smith stood up with a look of achievement, having beaten the plateful Rosa had settled on. He took a final swig of the cool, strong tea from his blue-and-white striped mug and gestured to Stirling to make a break for the open door before Rosa could find anything else for him to eat.

Outside, they headed across the courtyard towards a path that didn't follow the road but found its own way to the little local village. Leaving the courtyard, the sound of raised French voices and the slamming of doors could be clearly heard. Stirling turned to Peter Smith and smiled a comment, "Trust me, I have known them a long time. They were made for each other!"

Chapter 40

"Stirling, we have movement from Troutman. But first, I want to bring you up to speed with we what we now know—the jigsaw is really coming together. I have just come back from a two-day meeting with Luna in Italy. It took careful negotiation to arrange the meeting and get them to open up about Troutman."

"So, we have Luna on our side?"

"Don't be fooled, Stirling. Luna is a murderous, worldwide criminal group that has fingers in business, politics, and many walks of life that we are in contact with every day. The only reason we have been able to speak to them is because they want Troutman off their books. He has become a liability. They want to feed him to us on a plate, but we need to get him legally, and that is where the difficulty lies."

"Were they involved with Sian's disappearance?"

"Stirling, I just do not know. But, if there is a slim chance that she is still alive, the last thing we want to do is spook Luna. Sadly, they know they have all the cards, and we have to play their game. Let me run through everything with you, some of which you already know."

"The Troutman fortune, power, and his whole empire is reliant on him being faithful to his wife, Kristianna. As you know, the Arias family had suffered dreadfully from bad men, and they put legal blocks in place to prevent this ever happening again. Unfortunately for him, and human society, Troutman is a serial woman abuser. The despicable being thrives on abuse and control of women. He takes mainly two routes. Sometimes, he has his victims or anyone getting near the truth murdered. The other route is slightly more obscure and not initially obvious. When he sees a woman he wants, he will arrange to have their husbands and boyfriends killed so as he can step in as the caring, supporting, grieving team owner. It's a form of grooming that ends up with him satisfying his despicable wants. Often, he wants the glamorous girlfriends of racing drivers, and so he can use his method of murder in a racecar. In the early days, he sullied his own hands with the deeds, but in later years, he came to an arrangement with Luna. They murder when he orders. Murder is their day-to-day job. But, what a criminal organization of Luna's size struggles with is how to launder its illegally earned money. Troutman's worldwide, fast-moving empire provides the perfect vehicle to launder their money. Both their requirements fitted together well. Troutman could feed his despicable desires, Luna would cover his tracks under his instruction, and Luna had their own personal banker."

"So, how come I ended up in his sights?"

"The murder of your Uncle Roger was the first time he had committed such a drastic deed, and he knew that he had never covered his tracks properly in it. He knew he was vulnerable, and then to make matters worse, you decided to become a multi-F1 world champion! Every time he saw you in a pit lane, on a TV screen, or in a magazine, you reminded him of just how vulnerable he was. Things escalated to serious-mode when you started looking into your uncle's death, even to the point of hiring a private detective. He knew it would only be a matter time till you uncovered something. The more you dug, the more you became an irritant. The more of an irritant you became, the more he became more irrational. Luna started to get concerned. They certainly did not want your high-profile blood on their hands, so they were careful to bungle their attempts to kill you."

"Well, thank you, Luna!"

"Then, you turned up with Sian, who Troutman instantly, to his horror, recognized as Suzanne's daughter, and so his daughter, as he knew Suzanne never had another child, because he'd had Luna keep an eye on her. His fear was then confirmed when you introduced Sian as your young cousin. Troutman straight away thought that you knew more than you were letting on and were taunting him. In recent weeks, Troutman had been operating on his own and yet demanding Luna support him. Troutman has a number of personnel that work for him that belong to Luna. When they found out we were involved in trying to hook Troutman, they decided they wanted out and eventually made contact with us. The last thing they want is my organization digging around in their affairs. They got one of their operators, Troutman's right-hand man, John Beechy, to communicate that Luna was unhappy with your and our investigations. They also allowed Beechy to feed us one Troutman's prostitutes."

"When we drag Troutman through the courts, we will need to break the worldwide perception of this wonderful, kind family man and also need to prove his murderous actions."

"So, have we made contact with the prostitute?"

"Yes."

"And?"

"Well, it's a work in progress. Remember, these people operate in a dangerous world and they survive because they see nothing, hear nothing, but more importantly, say nothing! I am hoping she will trust me and decide to speak out. We can provide an escape for her life; we can help her realize her dreams. But the ball has to be in her court."

"Okay, I get that, and I get that Luna will never come out of the shadows. But what about Beechy? He must have so much on Troutman. Can we not make him squeal, as they say?"

"Beechy will not be doing any squealing of any sort. The day I met him, I went on to meet the prostitute he'd given us. By the time I had finished meeting with her, Beechy was already face-down in the glittering Monte Carlo harbor."

"Wow… Why? How?"

"The police said his body was full of booze and drugs and that he had banged his head and fell overboard. Our investigations have shown that he was knocked unconscious, had his alcohol level topped up, pumped full of drugs, and then tossed overboard. We don't know the full facts, but we do know it was a Luna hit."

"Why would they hit one of their own?"

"Stirling, trust me, this is not an uncommon occurrence for them. It appears that he did have a run-in with Troutman and spoke out of turn. Also, he did indeed have a lot of dangerous knowledge that they knew we would try to extract. Luna have to be seen to be rock-solid when it comes to protecting their clients. If they were seen to be helping convict one of their own clients, their world would turn on them."

"And why is it that they did not snub out Troutman themselves?"

"I am sorry to say that I think we saved Troutman's life. By the time they were getting tired of Troutman, they realized that we were already involved and would want to know how and why he was snubbed, as you said."

Stirling and Peter Smith had made their way down to the edge of the village and now hesitated before they entered amongst the buildings.

"So, where are we up to then, Peter?"

"Thanks to Luna, Troutman has now been fed information that you definitely have something on him, and so he is after you. And, we are sure he is about to set a trap for you. He has privately hired the exclusive use of the Nürburgring, Nordschleife circuit, to test his new Centar sports car and is going to use you as the test driver. The world's press has been invited, and he will be allowing a number of the motoring press to drive the Centar. He wants you to demonstrate just how quick this car is, and a new lap record around the Ring will be just the ticket."

"So, I presume he is using such a high-profile event to prove that all is above board when he gives me the chop. It's nice to know that I will make instant headlines when I crash!"

"Yes, exactly. Also, as you know, the Ring cannot be marshalled conventionally, due to the layout of the track and the length, so Troutman will be using two traveling marshals. Both will be Luna men and, no doubt, will be briefed to make sure that they are in the wrong place when Troutman stages your accident. Luna has a new inside man who is prepping the car for the test. We will know Troutman's every move. It's going to be dangerous, but this is likely to be our only chance, Stirling. I have to ask you, Stirling, are you up for this? I really don't want any more deaths on this case, but I am sure you realize that Troutman is thrashing around and battling for his life."

Stirling looked Peter Smith in the eyes. "Trust me, Peter, when I say that I have never been more ready for anything in my life. Let's land this guy, once and for all. Life is full of firsts, and I can honestly say that I am experiencing a lot of them at the moment. I have never gotten into a racecar with the knowledge that it was definitely going to crash! Wow, maybe it's not a good idea to think about it too much. In fact, I think I will make sure I don't think about that at all! Let's think about you buying me a coffee and let's get back to what I seem to be getting a lot of practice doing at the moment—waiting!"

"I am confident, Stirling, that Troutman's people will be contacting you imminently regarding your Centar test drive!"

Chapter 41

The crowded, chattering, darkened room was suddenly hushed with the slow, sultry tones of *Money for Nothing*, by Dire Straits. Suddenly, there was a quick flash of a moving image that was the Nordschleife often described as the 'green hell' on the huge screen in front of the gathered journalist, many of which had already made full use of the complementary alcohol and were now facing a tough ride around that green hell on the following day.

A circuit that prided itself on its twists, turns, jumps, and bumps; a circuit that could easily turn the most solid of stomachs to jelly! The flash of images kept time with the building music. The next image flashed and showed a silhouetted outline of a muscular supercar, the camera slowly, almost sensually, following its carefully crafted lines. The music quickened in pace as the next image from a low-mounted, forward-facing camera exaggerated the speed of its carrying vehicle as it hurled itself at the never-ending bends of this infamous circuit known to all as simply the Ring! The jump between the images now increasing in speed as the music built to a crescendo. More moving images showed off the lines of the Centar supercar, then back to the blind bends and jumps of the Ring, then the huge low-profile tires that kept the Centar anchored. Then, the closeness of the barriers holding back the green hell off this majestic ribbon of tarmac; then again, back to images of the fire-breathing V12 engine that powered the beast that was here to do battle with the beast of all race tracks—the Nordschleife.

Finally, the music reached its crescendo and a guitar ripped through the speakers to coincide with a screenful of the Centar, leaping from corner to corner. The infamous natural mountain track trying to trick the new supercar into oblivion whilst the contained technology of this new kid on the block proving it could match anything thrown at it.

Suddenly, the screen went blank, the music was gone, and the room was plunged into darkness. The chatter of the journalists did not recommence. All in the room were held in a suspended state of animation—all expectant for what they did not know. The stage was pitch, inky black.

The acute of hearing could pick up on it first. Then slowly, all in the room started to hear the very low pulsing noise that was starting to permeate the room. The noise seemed to come from all directions, and some in the room actually felt unnerved by it. The warrior tribe of the Zulus would use this technique to make their surrounded enemies panic—a sound created by them banging their spears on their shields in unison. A noise that sounded like a single steam train approaching in the distance, at first, but then built into a sound like 1,000 locomotives coming to devour your very soul. Again, the speakers bled noise as the pulsing, chanting-like cry peaked and caused some residents of the room to start thinking about looking for the exit doors. At this instant, a hot V12 engine fired up and immediately hits its rev limiter. As the throttle pedal relented, flames of unburnt fuel ignited the blackness of the stage as they fired out of the exhaust, and at the exact moment spotlights ignited and the gleaming black, panther-like two-million-pound supercar was displayed for all to stare upon.

A human voice bellowed from the overworked speakers, "Distinguished ladies and gentleman, may we present the Centar!"

Stirling stood in the wings, awaiting his cue for his grand entrance. Sadly, he'd had to be at all the rehearsals and had also spent a full day filming on the circuit with the Centar. It was an impressive supercar. 900 BHP, reactive aero, and like the Typhoon fighter plane that could not fly, without considerable computer input, so the Centar relied heavily on computer programmed decisions. For a road car, even Stirling had to admit it had stunning performance, backed up with 'to die for' looks that had school kids buzzing and adults drooling.

Lawrence Troutman was now being interviewed, and he was showing the supposed drawings on the large projection behind him that he'd made as a child, drawings of the supercar of his dreams. The enthralled interviewer listened to how he had held onto the child sketches all his life.

"One day, I knew that I would bring those drawings to life, and today sees the realization of that dream!"

Two images appeared on the screen; one of Troutman's expert child drawing, and one of the profile of the Centar. The match was amazing. Stirling could not help thinking that either Troutman had a crystal ball as a child or had a very advanced knowledge of car aerodynamics at a young, tender age!

The alcohol-lubricated launch was clearly going well, judging by the rapturous applause after the dramatic unveiling. And yet again, the applause rolled around the packed room as Troutman stood, smiled, waved, and even took a bow to his blinded public.

The energetic interviewer bounded back onto the stage, clapping along as he appeared. "Ladies and gentlemen, I give you Mr. Lawrence Troutman. Wow, what a guy. Talk about childhood dreams coming true. Come on, Gents, admit it. Isn't there a little bit inside of us all that wants to be Lawrence Troutman? He has everything, doesn't he? Just everything!" The crowd was on a roll, and yet again a peel of applause rang out!

"Okay, phew, let's catch our breath for a moment. Mr. Troutman has indeed built a stunning car for us all. But, ladies and gentleman, you all know why we are at this track of all tracks, don't you? He did not want just a pretty posers' car to be photographed in. No, he wanted a thoroughbred race car made for the road, and the only way of proving that's exactly what Mr. Troutman has achieved is by putting it in the hands of a thoroughbred race car driver. A racing driver who knows how to put a car through its paces. Ladies and gentleman, put your hands together for three times world Formula One champion, Mr. Stirling Speed."

Stirling was relieved that the mood for clapping had not died away, and the crowd responded on cue. Two seats were put down on their marks on the platform and Stirling gave a wave as the crowd settled into silence to await the interview.

"So, Stirling Speed, I must start off by asking, are you okay? That Monte shunt looked pretty nasty."

"Thank you for asking, but I am really fine. Trust me, I have had a lot worse."

There was a small ripple of laughter.

"Did something break, or dare I say, did you make a mistake?"

"Oh, I think I was trying to wave at a pretty girl in the crowd and effectively got slapped in my face for the cheek."

Again, a ripple permeated around the room.

"Now, Stirling, since your official retirement, you have been well off the scene. What have been up to? Catching up on your sleep?

"Sleeping? What's that? It has been nice to take my blinkers off and look around and see that life actually goes on outside of motorsport. It has been good taking time to just observe things. I have kept involved by doing some private testing for various teams and manufacturers and have really enjoyed doing some driver coaching. I have also had time to look back more at some of my family history, particularly that of my late uncle, who died in a race car at Trac Mon, the race circuit in Anglesey. Some might have possible heard of him. Roger Speed? In fact, any one driving the Anglesey Trac Mon circuit will be familiar with the rise in the track before the Rocket corner complex. It was renamed a few years ago, Speed Rise. Well, that is named after my uncle, Roger Speed. Over the years, I have taken time to look into what he drove, etc. Sadly, he died in a fiery, rather unexplained testing accident at that very beautiful, picturesque circuit. Coincidentally, he was driving one of Mr. Troutman's cars when he perished. I don't want to worry anyone, but I do hope someone has checked that Centar over well for tomorrow?"

The audience laughed and the interviewer joined in with a forced nervous laugh. He did not like his guest going off-piste when they were on his ski slope. Stirling noticed a sharp movement at the edge of the stage and just caught the back of Troutman's receding figure. Stirling smiled to himself inside. *Come on, you little runt. Come and get me if you dare.*

Clearly rattled, the interviewer flicked through the pages on his iPad.

"So, Mr. Speed, you have been drafted in at the last minute to drive this car, and you have actually pushed out the current world champion, who was scheduled to drive. Were you asked or did you ask for the drive?"

"Well, I was asked. And, well, at first, I did wonder why Mr. Troutman had especially asked for me, but then I thought, 'Hey, people would die to drive this car, so I thought, well, why the hell not?' So, I canceled my dinner arrangements for tomorrow night and contacted my insurance brokers to give them heads up to dust off my life policies."

The crowd crackled, but with Troutman now out of earshot, Stirling decided to sit back and let his sweating interviewer bring his interview back under control.

Chapter 42

Stirling could not help but smile to himself as he guided is E-Type the short distance from the hotel to the entrance car parks of the Nordschleife. After settling his bill and signing a rather large photograph of himself for the hotelier, Stirling had walked out, travel bag in one hand and kit bag in the other, to find that his car had been washed and polished without his request. Except for a little residue polish around the chrome E-Type badge on the back of the car, someone had done quite a good job. It was a nice gesture, but Stirling somehow felt uncomfortable that someone had been handling his car—a car he always washed and cleaned himself and always used the same wax on. Stirling would always spot if one extra stone chip had occurred What made Stirling smile was that he felt more disturbed about the phantom washer then the fact that he was about to drive a 200 mph super car that had been booby trapped to kill him!

Stirling slicked the purring E-Type down to second as he approached the roundabout, then timed a slow change into first as he noticed the surprisingly large group that had gathered at the entrance. An official-looking person pointed at Stirling and gestured for him to keep moving and turn into the right-hand car park that had been sectioned off from the general public. Stirling stopped, though, wound down his window, and reached out to sign a couple of autographs. The crowd started to gather, but with a blip of the throttle, a slight ease forward, and with the help of the official, a path was reformed to the segregated car park.

This side of the car park was dominated by one of Troutman's bright-red, 45-foot tri-axle race transporters, pulled by a totally unnecessary but still impressive 730-bhp Scania.

Center stage in the car park sat two glinting, black Centars with girl pseudo-race mechanics dressed in very impractical overalls that seemed not to be able to fasten at the front! The girls busied themselves pretending to check over the cars whilst press photographers snapped away. Stirling could not help feeling what a negative image this was for the many talented female race engineers, technicians, team managers, and owners who fought their way to the very top in this male-dominated world.

Under a large awning, fastened to the race transporter and shaded from the hot sun, sat the almost-sinister-looking Centar that was Stirling's steed for the day. A steed that Stirling knew would try to kill him at some point during the day!

Stirling eased his Jaguar to a halt behind the transporter and lifted his kit bag out of the boot. As he walked away and around the end of the transporter, he gave his car a quick look back and hoped that he would still be in enough pieces to be the one driving it out of the car park at the end of the day. Stirling took time to stop at his black steed and shake hands with the genuine race engineers tending to its every need. He checked to make sure that it had been communicated to the guys that his high-speed runs later in the day would be done on scrubbed tires. He'd found that, even during the high-speed filming runs, the high-performance road tires, as good as they were, failed to live up to Stirling's requirements when pushed hard for the duration of a Nordschleife lap. The treaded tires moved even when kept within their traction limit, heated quickly, and lost performance to the point where both Stirling and the car were waiting for them to catch up. Slick tires and a change of suspension geometry would cure the problem. But at the end of the day, this was a road car. By using scrubbed tires with a slightly lower tread depth, Stirling could at least attempt to manage the temperature build-up.

Stirling headed up the stairs within the transporter knowing that he was about to have probably one of the most important private meetings of his life, with Lawrence Troutman's new team manager, put there by Luna!

"Okay, Mr. Speed. Let's…"

"Please, Stirling, just Stirling."

Stirling hesitated and stared at the man in front of him. "I recognize you. Haven't you worked on my cars in the past? Did you use to work in F1?"

"Let's say I have been around, Stirling. Anyway, back to the point, I have checked the car early this morning, thoroughly. I followed Troutman last night, and he spent two hours tinkering with the car on his own. I can confirm that he has booby-trapped the car. I marked all the wishbones beforehand, and I know for certain that he has changed the top front-left wishbone. We know from the investigations your guys did on the first P34 that was impounded on its way back to the UK from Monte Carlo that the wishbones had been remanufactured with a small incendiary device inside. I, then, scoped the fuel tank in the Centar you are to drive. The other Centars have an explosion-safe foam within them. Your Centar does not. I soon spotted another explosive device that has been dropped in the tank of your car. These are simple devices that are set off manually by something as simple as a key fob that you would use to lock your car."

Mr. Luna Man paused for a Stirling comment, to which Stirling could only reply, "Nice!"

"The weather is good all day, and it's going to be hot, so you are scheduled to do three demo runs this morning with a journalist onboard. Just before lunch, there will be another filming run. After lunch, the journalists will be driving the other Centars with race instructors onboard with them. At three, we expect the track temperature to start to drop, and the circuit will be cleared for you to start your solo high-speed run to see if you can break the track record. That is when we think the fireworks will start."

"Well, thanks for the graphic description. Why do we not think we will have fireworks this morning?"

"Well, because of instructions that Troutman has issued. This morning, the traveling marshals can circulate as normal and as required. But, when you start your high-speed run, only one traveling marshal car is to be used, and it also must start at least five minutes after you have set off. This is when we think Troutman will carry out the hit."

"On me!"

"I am sorry."

"The hit will be on me. You seem to mention it a bit casually for my liking."

"Well, yes, on you. Which, at the end of the day, is why we are all here, Stirling!"

Stirling sat back in his chair. "Yes, that is a point. At the end of the day, indeed all are here for Troutman to try and dismiss me off this pretty planet earth!"

Luna Man shoveled his papers together like it was just another day at the office. "Try to be as normal as possible around everyone, Stirling. If I need to have a private word with you, or vice versa, then I or you will just say, 'I have a query over the tires' pressure.' That will be our code. Now, it is time for you to get ready to start your demo runs. I'll leave in peace."

"Please watch what you say, that sounded far too close to rest in peace."

Luna Man turned and actually smiled. "Trust me, you will be fine. If we had wanted you dead, you would have been. In fact, Monza would have been the last circuit you ever saw. I know, because it should have been my hit."

Stirling couldn't quite believe his ears. "You were my hitman? Do you know how smashed up I was after Monza?"

"Yes, that was unfortunate, and Troutman very nearly got you there, which, to be honest, would not have been good for us. I was due to pop you at Monza, but my bosses made me stage a breakdown of my car on the way there, so that I would miss the opportunity. Unfortunately, I allowed Troutman to get wind of my staged breakdown and he set up his own hit. Luckily for you, his kit malfunctioned and you ended up with a bad case of traction in the hospital. But, at least you still had your balls to play with! I got took off the gig for that and John Beechy got put in."

Stirling sat, aware that his mouth was open but unable to respond to his desire to shut it. "You talk about it like it's your day-to-day job!"

Luna Man went to leave, then turned back to face Stirling. "It is my day-to-day job. And trust me, if I am told to kill you tonight whilst you sleep, then I would. And, if you ever breathe a word of anything I have just told you to anyone, I will not need any instructions, you will be history. Oh, and when all this is sorted, maybe we can have a drink together and I will tell you about all the other times I have been told to bungle a hit on you. The last time being on the way down here as you pulled away from the tollbooths on the M6!"

Stirling was completely dumbstruck as Luna Man smiled, winked, and left the room. People would say that living the life of a Formula One Star was like living in a movie, and perhaps they are not far off the truth with that thought, but at this moment

Stirling really did feel like he was in a movie. Had he really just been talking to a man whose job it was to murder? Indeed, a man who could have murdered him. He was really having to use all of his focusing skills to keep his mind on the job in hand to stop himself totally losing it when thoughts of Sian cascaded through his head. Peter seemed to waver between positive about Sian and then negative. Clearly, he had no solid news or control over the situation.

Stirling stood up and looked out of the transporter's window. The small car park-cum-paddock bustled with press and people, lots of them. A little bit of him wanted to lock the door and stay hidden in the cool air-conditioned trailer, but what racing driver didn't feel like that at some point? He was here to drive, and that is what he had done all of his working life. Peter Smith and his crazy world would have to take a step back. He grabbed his helmet and checked his freshly polished visor, then he grabbed his gloves and under helmet and stuffed them inside his helmet.

Come on, Stirling my boy, let's go do some driving.

He walked down the steel-clad stairs and opened the door. The fast warming heat of the day hit him and mocked his triple-layer race overalls.

"Stirling, your thoughts on the Centar? It looks the part, but has Lawrence Troutman bitten off more than he can chew this time?" Stirling looked straight at the reporter with his camera crew sat on his shoulder.

"It's a good car, but I really can't comment as to whether or not Mr. Troutman is out of his depth. He has just asked me to come along and drive his cars, and that's what I will do—hopefully without crashing them."

The pretty reporter giggled a little too enthusiastically. Stirling continued on his walk towards his awaiting Centar, which was now surrounded by a gaggle of people.

"Now, who wants to come for a ride with me around the Ring?"

Some who had not been aware of Stirling's approach swung round suddenly. One guy stepped forward, a respected motoring journalist whom Stirling recognized.

"I'll go for a ride with you, that's provided you don't put me in the scenery or in the wall!"

Stirling smiled back. "Steve, grab yourself a helmet, sir, and we'll see what we can do about keeping it on the black stuff!"

Stirling really wanted to say, 'Well, actually, Steve, provided the left-front suspension does not explode, we will be fine', but thought better of it.

Chapter 43

"You got away from the circuit, okay?" Peter Smith inquired, to which Stirling replied, with a mock surprised look on his face.

"Well, if you count getting away from it not in an ambulance, still able to walk and talk, then yes, you could say I got away okay."

"We are certain, Stirling that the fireworks will start this afternoon, when you go for your record-breaking high-speed run."

"Well, I have three statements about your last comment, Peter. One, would you people stop using the firework description? Two, we actually don't know if it is going to be a record-breaking run. And three, I worked out myself that Mr. Troutman would be thoughtful enough not to crash one of his nice, tame journalists who are writing good things about his new creation. He'd rather write off a big bad racing driver who decided to look into his racing uncle's crash."

As lunch silenced the circuit, Stirling made his excuses about wanting a shower and a fresh race suit and left to go back to his hotel room, where he covertly met Peter Smith.

"How did your runs go this morning with the press?" he inquired.

"Well, once I had gotten my head around the various bombs fitted around my car, all went well, with the exception of having to stop at one point for a press boy to throw up. Apparently, a night of booze and a hot lap around the Ring do not go well."

"Ah, yes, that did cause a moment of concern when we saw from the tracker that your car had stopped. We scrambled our helicopter, only to abort when the report came back from one of the traveling marshals that it was just a 'sicky' stop. We, then, had to circulate a story that the helicopter was there for filming."

"And Troutman? Is he skulking around anywhere?"

"He has kept a low profile around here, so no one has seen him, but our guys have been discreetly trailing him. He has been wandering around various corners and watching you come by very carefully."

"What's he wearing?" Stirling inquired.

"What's he wearing? Sorry, Stirling, I am not sure, but I will find out if you want. Surely, at the speeds you are doing, you can't spot people in the crowd."

"Peter, now you are in my world. Let me decide what can and can't be done. Can you please get me the color of his top. Just maybe I can spot him, so at least I get some sort of warning where I am about to crash!"

"Not long after the helicopter had been scrambled and then brought back down, the team received a call from Troutman. He wanted it made clear that there would be no aerial filming this afternoon. He also wanted to know who had okay-ed the helicopter in the first place. And also, he decided that he wants no traveling marshals on track whilst you are doing your solo high-speed runs."

"Well, that is comforting to know! So, I am right in saying that it is a totally private test session this afternoon, no press, no spectators, just Troutman's staff?"

"Yes, Stirling, that is right. The press and guests are being taken on another boozy presentation whilst you get down to beating the track record, or attempting to, with the Centar. So, really the only person you should see out there is Troutman himself."

"Where are we up to with the car?" Stirling put his hands together in a mock prayer stance. "Peter, I don't suppose I could take one of the other Centars instead?"

"If only I could agree to that. Stirling, I hate to say it, but we really need you to have the crash. My men will be there to jump on Troutman straight away, and we will have him caught red-handed, as they say. Regarding the car, the guys have carried out the adjustments on the car you requested and fitted the scrubbed tires that you have chosen. What you will be pleased to know, is that the Luna man has discreetly removed the incendiary device from fuel tank."

Stirling put his hand up with a stretched-out index finger. "Why wait till lunch to remove it?"

"That was my decision, Stirling. We had no way of knowing that Troutman would not check the car, so we left the device in the fuel tank for as long as possible."

"Well, that is a relief! If I survive the exploding front suspension, then all should be good. All I have to do is be comfortable on left-handers but watch the right-handers, boy, when the left front suspension is loaded, because there could be a good chance we are going in at that point. And of course, the Ring is well known for its lack of corners, not!"

Stirling shook his head in utter disbelief. "How did I get so deep into this? On top of it all this, the guy who is watching out for me at this moment is a professional assassin who has been told in the past to kill me. But fortunately, his bosses did not want my messy high-profile body to clean up. Can it get any more crazy? I seem to remember my retirement was sitting in my local country pub, drinking my favorite ale, and watching a bee busy itself!"

Peter Smith knew this was not the time to reply. In the past, when he had introduced people from everyday life into his underworld, they all took time to adjust and take it all in. Some never were able to deal with it, but Peter Smith knew that Stirling would recalibrate and be a major asset to his organization.

Eventually, the silence urged Stirling to speak again, "I tell you now, if I do come out of this alive and Sian has not, I will finish Troutman myself and your organization can protect me or throw me to the authorities. But that scumbag will not take up any more space on this earth, trust me on that one!"

Peter Smith sat forward on his seat and stared at Stirling earnestly. "Stirling, leave Troutman to us, you do what you are good at. Remove emotion, focus, concentrate, and go out and drive. When Troutman pulls the pin, you will handle it like you have always handled the unexpected in the past; your natural instincts will kick in and you will deal with it. I have never put any of my operatives into such a position before, but I know you can take the pressure and deliver. That is what made you a three-time world champion. When Troutman makes his move, we will have him."

Stirling appreciated the vote of confidence. "Well, let's hope that I am still around to see you guys get him."

Chapter 44

Stirling arrived back to a much quieter circuit. After the hustle and bustle of the morning, the quietness seemed to add to the foreboding atmosphere Stirling was desperately trying to dispel. After years of top-line Formula One, Stirling had a system for controlling pressure and taking emotion out from his driving. Although, he had to admit to himself that he had never knowingly gotten into a racecar that was actually certainly going to crash, but he had a job to do, and do it he would.

Freshly race-suited up, Stirling walked up to each race engineer working on his car, as he always did, and greeted them again as a way of checking in with them to see if they had anything to report. He, then, caught the eye of the man from Luna and knew what was coming next.

"Stirling, could I just run through your tire pressures with you?"

At which he disappeared into the transporter and up the stairs. Stirling tried desperately to follow as casually as possible.

Luna Man was still stood up when Stirling caught up.

"Call it assassin's intuition, but…"

Stirling jumped straight in, "You have got to be joking with me, 'assassin's intuition!'"

"Well, call it what you want, but it could possibly have just saved your neck! I decided, for some strange reason, to check the remote-locking mechanisms on your Centar's doors. The lock actuator on the driver's door has been changed and is visibly different to the other doors and other cars. I am not sure whether it is just a coincidence or not, but just in case, I have disconnected the one on your door. It will not lock or unlock with a remote control; it can only be opened manually."

Stirling conceded the point. "Okay, my friend, we will go with the 'assassin's intuition' on this occasion."

When Stirling walked out into the bright sunlight, his car had been moved into the pit lane, ready for its run. It sat gleaming in the sun with both of its gullwing doors gapping. A race engineer knelt next to the driver's seat. Stirling acknowledged him, passed his helmet to another waiting engineer, and slipped into the heavily bucketed seat and settled himself in by reaching out and gripping the steering wheel with both hands. He, then, gave the knelt engineer the nod, which was a sign that said, 'I am ready to be strapped in.' Stirling always breathed in when his belts were being tightened, so the outbreath always provided slightly more reassuring belt pressure. For reasons he never quite worked out, he always had his left strap tightened a little more. Next, he asked for the excess dangling belts to be tucked in. Maybe that was a single-seater-driver thing. He hated his belts flapping around. Finally, he gestured for his helmet to be passed to him. Before taking it, he took out his gloves and under helmet, which he then pulled on, making sure no errant annoying hair could dangle in front of his eyes. He squeezed his helmet on next and secured its fastening before pulling on his gloves. Stirling allowed himself a little smile privately. He was ready to conquer the Ring, a circuit that did not take prisoners. But unfortunately, there was the small matter of a crash that had to be dealt with!

The knelt race engineer was replaced by a knelt Luna Man. "Okay, Stirling, you know the score. When you go from here, your timed lap won't start till the old start line, so you have time to get temperature into the car. But, don't push the tires hard, or you will lose them before the end of the lap. We are just waiting for confirmation that the track is clear, then I will close your doors and you can go in your own time."

Stirling looked up at the now standing man from his strapped position and caught a genuine look in the potential assassin's eyes.

"Go easy out there, Stirling, the world could do with not losing guys like you."

Stirling replied with a wink that said, 'I've got this.'

Stirling felt the snugness of the cockpit squeeze in on him as his door closed shut. He, then, pressed his foot on the brake pedal, lifted up the red flip-up covering that hid the start button, and pressed it. The Centar responded eagerly and blindly with a V12 roar. Stirling blipped the glorious-sounding multi-cylinder

Audi-developed engine to ensure that its natural rhythm had been established. He pressed the corsa button on the center consul and felt the car hunker down on its expensive suspension. He saw the rear aero foil rise, and he heard the exhaust note increase in growl. Stirling and the car were becoming one to the point where he could almost feel each individual explosion in each of the twelve busy cylinders.

Luna Man walked around the front of the car and reached up to bring down the passenger gullwing door. Stirling looked across in anticipation. The door started its journey downward but then hesitated. Stirling blipped the throttle—he was ready to do this. He looked forward up the pit lane to the awaiting circuit. The solitary track-blocking orange-and-white cone had been moved to one side—the Ring awaited its next contestant.

Stirling looked back to the still open door and was surprised to see a race-suited leg stretching into the empty passenger footwell, followed by a rotund figure squeezing into the slightly more forgiving passenger seat. Stirling had asked for a snug full race seat to be put in for him, but it would have cried out surrender for the figure presently loading. The helmeted head was the last bit of the body to enter the confines of the Centar. The helmeted head then turned to its high-speed chauffeur.

"Hello, Mr. Speed. I thought I would keep you company to see what all this fuss is about regarding your prowess behind the wheel and make sure that you create some big headlines for my new car."

"Welcome onboard, Lawrence. You know what they say, any press is good press! So, let's go make some headlines!"

Luna Man reached across Troutman's stretched race suit, searched for one of the safety belts, and gave Stirling a discreet look that clearly said, 'I have no idea what is going on.'

Chapter 45

The passenger door clicked shut. Stirling held his foot on the brake and pulled the first gear with the right-hand paddle attached to the steering wheel. Corsa mode ensured the gear went in with an instantaneous clunk and a slight lurch that gave the impression the V12 was being held on a tight leash. Stirling flicked off the small electronic hand brake switch and squeezed the throttle pedal. The Centar needed no more invitation and leapt forward. Stirling continued to squeeze the throttle whilst pulling short gears with his right hand.

Even though Stirling knew that he had his genuine assassin next to him, he stuck to his usual drive and warm-up mode. He rested his left foot gently on the brake pedal to build heat through the system and also let some of the heat bleed through the wheel hub, through the tires, and to their surface. But, he was careful not to work the tires too heavily with erratic steering input.

Troutman remained mute, his left hand rested on his left thigh, his right clenched and resting on his right thigh. Stirling pulled for the lower gears with his left hand as he braked through the Tiergarten section of track. He slowed the car and rolled the steering hard to the right. The Centar responded with grace and ate the sharp corner. Exit in sight, Stirling rolled the steering off and squeezed the throttle hard—the Centar howling with delight. The slight throttle blast was followed by an early brake for the first slightly downhill left-hander, which he exited with a nice, positive camber—Stirling being careful not to give the Centar an excuse for the lack of instantaneous steering response. A good squeeze of throttle awakened the rear of the car, the low speed ensuring that no aero grip could assist the mechanical and electronic grip produced.

Stirling settled the Centar into the ensuing combination of medium-speed right-left sweeps, taking more curbing on the right than the left. The sweeps culminated in a compromised right-hander, so as to be in a good position for the next left-hander that led onto an exciting, undulating pseudo-straight. Stirling took command of the throttle early and launched the Centar out onto the straight on the limit, causing Troutman to visibly tense and look for something to hold onto with his left hand. The Centar gobbled the straight as Stirling put his total trust in the aerodynamics, forcing the car down as he took the first jump flat. Then, much to Troutman's dismay, he took the second jump flat, before squeezing the brake hard to scrub the crazy speed off in preparation for next medium-speed right-hander.

By rolling on the right-hand lock, Stirling was only too aware that he was heavily loading the vulnerable left-front suspension and so used all the senses in his fingertips to feel for any changes in the expected response. Troutman's head leaned into the corner as the g-force loaded up and Stirling exercised the throttle again—the Centar now appearing light on the exit of the corner, as it had almost skipped along. The V12 Centar was now breathing deeply as Stirling planted the throttle and allowed his mount to skip at high speed across the undulating track, gently introducing steering input as required.

145, 150, and 160 mph. The Centar was alive through Schwedenruez. And, Stirling was only too aware that his mount would have loved to continue at this speed and preferably in a straight line, but there was the small matter of the Aremberg right-hand fourth-gear corner coming up, and so he prepared to ease out of the throttle. It was at this precise moment when Stirling's hyper-alert eyes detect a movement within his cockpit domain. Troutman's clenched right hand relaxed slightly and exposed something black, plastic, maybe just slightly larger than a remote-control car key fob. Instantly, Stirling's brain recognized this as Troutman's weapon of death, which he was now holding tight to his stomach.

As Stirling's synapses dealt with the bucking high-speed car, the rest of his considerable mental capacity started to deal with what was about to happen. They were approaching the Aremberg right-hand corner that would load the explosive left-front suspension. Aremberg had a safety gravel trap on its outside to catch errant, out-of-control racecars before they obliterated themselves on the unforgiving retaining barrier.

Of course, that was why Troutman had risked his soul in the car. None would ever suspect him of crashing a car he was a passenger in, especially at such a potentially dangerous circuit as the Ring. But, if he fired Stirling into the gravel here, he could get out of the car and then have his little firework display with Stirling trapped in the locked car whilst no doubt desperately pretending to save the burning life of three-time world champion Stirling Speed. His car would make world headlines, and he would be a hero.

Stirling's thoughts crystallized within the blink of an eye and he snapped the throttle closed. The slightly laterally loaded, unsuspecting car wobbled in surprise as the back of the car went light and the onboard computers complexly input a stability control to stun the imminent potential lift of oversteer. The erratic throttle management was followed by an erratic stamp on the huge carbon-fiber disc brakes. The car sensed straight away that all was not well with its usually silky-smooth driver and the onboard computers conferred again to deal with a potentially out of control supercar as Stirling flicked down the gears.

Aremberg innocently arrived, and Stirling had no choice but to input the right-hand steering lock and start the sequence that he knew would lead to the crash. He almost sensed rather than saw Troutman press the upper button on his little black box, and Stirling was almost reacting to the exploding suspension before it ignited.

The description, 'all hell breaking loose' was an apt one. The explosion caused the heavily loaded wheel-holding wishbone to fail instantly. The grip of the expensive tire now took command for a brief moment until the whole wheel's assembly was slammed and smashed backwards into the carbon-fiber tub that was the backbone of the Centar. The errant wheel, now jammed at 45 degrees to the direction of the travel, caused the still-functioning right-hand wheel to overload its grip levels, and this in turn totally overloaded the front of the car, causing it to break traction. Stirling and Troutman were high-speed passengers—last stop, the Aremberg gravel trap.

The noise of expensive steel, aluminum, magnesium, and carbon-fiber dragging across an unforgiving tarmac surface at

100 mph was horrific. To a racing driver it would be terrifying; it would be their biggest fear, as they'd realize that something had broken and they were now no longer in control. Over the tragic years of motorsport, this would have been the last thing some drivers ever heard.

Instinct put Stirling into one of two modes during such violent moments. The first mode was one of control; to try and control the situation as best as possible. The final phase of control was trying to minimize the accident. Stirling kept his foot jammed on the brake, this now being the only working input he had over the car. Even that control was compromised, as now only the rear brakes responded to his request, causing the car to half-spin into the gravel. The second mode was self-preservation, and it was arrived at when the first mode, that of control, would have been exhausted. Stirling's hands left their place on the steering wheel and grabbed hold of the safety harness running down over his chest. He attempted to bring his knees up towards himself as much as possible, so distancing his feet from the potentially-bone-shattering pedals and wayward suspension parts. He inclined his head forward to take up the slack on the straps of his lifesaving head restraint; then finally, he closed his eyes. There was nothing more to do or see but wait for the outcome.

The outcome, the end, mentally took minutes, five to ten minutes. *Why so long? Why is this accident still happening?* In reality, the whole violent moment, which started with an explosion and ended with a sudden stop, lasted less the four seconds. Stirling opened his eyes, a gravel dust storm raged outside of the car. Some dust somehow had entered the car and was looking for a place to settle. He fought his survival instinct and stopped himself from hitting his harness-release buckle and punching out of the car. He somehow sat and waited for the next scene.

He turned to Troutman. Troutman was breathing heavily and his wide eyes were surrounded in his helmet opening by white, clammy skin. At first, Troutman seemed to not know where he was, then appeared to quickly regain mental control.

"Don't try getting out of the car, Speed, I have control of the locking mechanism in your door." Troutman showed Stirling his small box of tricks.

"The top button, well, that sets off the explosive device on the suspension. The bottom one, that controls the said locking mechanism. That's a new feature."

Troutman took a moment to grin at Stirling. "Now, I can see you are wondering what the big middle one does. Well, that sets off the explosive device in the fuel tank situated just, I would say, behind your kidneys. It's a tried-and-tested method that I use, Stirling, this being the latest development. I did get a bit too clever at one point and tried to use a phone signal to set off the devices. But, fortunately for you, at Monza, phone signals can be a bit unreliable. The first device was actually used on your uncle. It worked really well, but that system was done with timers, a bit crude, if I am honest, but one has to start somewhere. Anyway, talking of time, I have a world champion to save, oops, slight slip there, try to save. When I get out, I am sure that you will undo your belts and try to scramble across here and try to open the passenger door. But, by this time I will be stood over there and pressing the center button I told you about. Goodbye, Mr. Speed."

Troutman released his belts and prepared to support his weight to clamber from the now-quiet, sad-looking, wrecked Centar.

"Why, Troutman? Why?"

Troutman hesitated, then released the pressure on his hands. "Okay, I will tell you why. Only because, well, well, to be fair, some of the fault rests with me, Stirling, I admit it. When things did not work out for me with that slut of an auntie of yours, well, to be honest, I left loose ends. I know, I know it was stupid of me. But, hey, I was young. Then, you decided you wanted to be a silly racing driver like Uncle Roger, and sadly, you turned out to be quite good. And then, you decided to start sticking your nose into history and being the sort of stupid little terrier you are. I figured you would not stop digging for your little bone until you found something. Sadly, my, shall we say, 'personal interests' do need to be hidden, otherwise, I lose everything— and I do mean everything."

Troutman positioned to exit again. "Sian, what have you done with Sian?"

Troutman continued his stumbling exit and finally stood up, before then turning back to the car. Troutman stooped back down to look Stirling in the eyes. "Sian, you mean the abortion that never happened? The illegitimate daughter of the slag who disobeyed me? I finished what should have been done in the clinic, Mr. Speed."

"You are lying, Troutman, that was your daughter."

"Why do I have to lie to a dead man? Oh, Stirling, have you been hoping that she is locked up somewhere. Oh, dear, I am sorry, she was dead before you even got back to your hotel room the day you crashed my racecar. The people I work with, Stirling, kill their own without a moment's hesitation when I click my fingers. That 'being' should never have seen the light of day. She should have been aborted, and I have merely righted a wrong. I believe her slutty mother died of cancer, so that does save me a job. Now, I am sure there is concern back in the paddock, and I really do need to stage a fiery rescue attempt. So, if you don't mind, goodbye, Mr. Speed, and say hi from me if you meet your Uncle Roger."

Troutman slammed the gullwing door shut and started his short trudge to a place of safety at the end of the barrier. Stirling had acted quickly when Troutman had been concentrating on heaving his heavy frame out of the smoldering Centar. After clicking the safety belts undone, he'd left them in place, so as to look still fastened, and he'd also gently clicked the door open but left it closed up. He had to admit to himself that he was relieved when the door had actually clicked open.

Now, though, the thought that he had failed Sian, that after all these years and the sacrifices her mother had made to keep her beautiful daughter alive, away from Troutman, Stirling had allowed her to be taken from the world, was unbearable. Stirling launched himself out of the car. Troutman rounded and could not register what he was seeing, then held the little black box up like a TV control and pointed it at the car, frantically pressing the center button, which responded dutifully by sending out its destructive command message. But sadly, there was nothing to receive it.

Troutman threw the box and ran towards the end of the barrier. Stirling covered the distance in a quarter of the time it had taken the lumbering Troutman and hurled himself at the flailing bulk in front of him. Troutman hit that ground hard, half on the gravel and now half on the grass that lay behind the barrier. For the first time ever in his life, Stirling was truly out of control as rage, anger, frustration, and hate formed a lethal cocktail that cascaded through his body. He stood up. His raging eyes looking for a death implement to bludgeon Troutman and his hands immediately found a large, red metal fire extinguisher. Something put there to save a life but, actually, was about to be used to extinguish one. Troutman had taken to trying to crawl away, putting distance between himself and his captor, his executioner. Stirling halted his pitiful crawl and waited for Troutman to half roll and look up at the towering Speed, who held the extinguisher in position, ready for the first debilitating blow. The following out of control blows would be fatal ones.

Suddenly, the gravel dust storm awakened and all vision around Stirling blanked out so all he could see was Troutman's pleading face in front of him. A face he was about to destroy. Stirling could not hear himself think as noise blasted through his ears, filling his head with a pulsing that hurt. Stirling screamed through the noise that threatened to overwhelm him.

"Troutman, you are scum, and just in case you were worrying, I have friends who will make sure that I am not charged for dispatching this scum with a click of their fingers. Goodbye, Mr. Troutman."

"No, please…" was all Stirling heard as he used every sinew in his every muscle to bring down the extinguisher towards Troutman's screwed-up face!

The pulsing noise seemed to begin to fade and voices now screamed through his head. "Stirling, no, no!"

Next, Stirling felt a sharp pain in his left side, caused by a force so strong that it threw him to the side of Troutman, the extinguisher flying out of his hands and impacting the soft grass next to Troutman's ear. The voices continued screaming, more voices now, and the pain in his side was replaced by a weight that had landed across his chest as he found himself scrabbling on the floor. He turned to see Troutman re-establish his distancing crawl. Stirling threw the weight from his chest.

"Scum, you are scum. I will kill you…"

Stirling rolled onto his front and set off in a pursuit crawl but now his legs felt tied together and again a weight stunned them.

"Stirling, no, please, no. Listen to me, Stirling!"

Stirling's mind desperately tried to get control of what was happening. Is this what a fatal crash was like, noise, voices, struggling to get free? Then, Stirling realized the weight he was trying to kick off his legs was shouting at him. Another voice now separated from the screaming voices in his head had arrived at his ear.

"Stirling, leave it, leave it. We have him, Stirling, we have him, Stirling. It's Peter. Peter Smith!"

Stirling stopped his struggle. The voice and face still seemed muffled and unclear. "It's Peter, Stirling!"

The weight across his legs disappeared and Stirling pulled himself up onto knees and remained focused on the blurry face in front of him and the voice that babbled information at him. Stirling's body relaxed, and he could feel hands fumbling at his throat. Then, fresh air, light, vision, and voices became clear when someone lifted Stirling's dust-covered helmet and under helmet off.

Stirling stared at Peter Smith, who had a weak smile and a huge look of relief across face.

"Stirling, I think you need to apologize to someone and probably thank them as well."

Stirling blinked at Peter Smith. "Who...?" Stirling stammered out.

A French accent rang out from behind. "To me, you clumsy oaf. You so owe me at least a day's appointment with your credit card."

Stirling turned around to see Sian sat on her bottom, her stretched legs out front. The white gravel dust covering her face and once-shiny black hair contrasted sharply with a little crimson-red stream of blood that originated at her bottom lip and traveled down her chin.

"You bust my lip, you big animal. Boy you take some taking down."

Stirling sat and surveyed the scene around him. A helicopter sat on the track next to the crashed Centar—its once-pulsing blades just gently rotating in the afternoon breeze. Two men on both sides had a bloodied-but-still-alive Troutman to his feet, and a woman was walking from the helicopter straight towards the shell-shocked Troutman. Troutman recognized her instantly and almost subconsciously muttered her name, "Suzanne, I thought…" Troutman's voice trailed off.

Suzanne Speed stopped in front of him and just stared at first. It was a fleeting moment that appeared as an age. Then, with the force that only a wronged woman could conjure up, she swiped Troutman across his face with the flat of her hand, causing him and his captors to stumble back. The woman reestablished her position in front of him again. Peter Smith stood up to stop the next assault, but the staring, in-control woman simply put her hand up to him, which stopped him in his tracks.

Troutman prepared his sore, bruised face for another slapping and squeezed his eyes closed. The pain never came. He wanted to scream his hatred for her, but nothing would form in his mouth. Only his eyes could convey his hatred for this woman. *A woman, how dare a woman even think of raising a hand to him!* The woman closed in on Troutman again, not once taking her eyes of his. She got close to the point where she could taste his acrid breath and he could feel hers on his skin. Then, she spoke in a slow, low, vibrating voice that caused a tremor in his resolve. Nose to nose; eyes boring into each other's eyes; Suzanne Speed faced the evil of her life, "Don't you ever, come near my daughter again, ever!"

She saw the rage in his eyes crumble. He broke her gaze and turned to his captors, captures

"What you are you going to do let this woman continue to abuse me… What you going to do hey? Let her castrate me? Well I don't know yet who you all are but you have no idea the connections I have, I will see you all in court. Now, get me away from this mad woman."

Stirling watched the scene, then turned back to the now standing Peter Smith. He needed to say nothing. "I know, Stirling. I think we need to give you some explanations."

Stirling turned to the still-sitting-down Sian, who, much to her relief, had stemmed the bleeding from her now swelling lip. She smiled a dusty smile back at Stirling. "Well, that's going to take more lipstick than normal to cover. And guess what, you'll be getting the bill for that as well."

Stirling felt it as a slight itch, at first, in one eye, then felt the itch in both eyes. The itches started to travel down his cheeks. Then, when a route had been established through the dust on his face, the tears cascaded down his cheeks. Sian shuffled up to him and pulled him tight to her, his shoulders heaving as he sobbed.

The years of tension, pressure, and focus to make Formula One, to race in Formula One, to come back from his Monza shunt, and to come through this journey and now find Sian still alive finally released as Stirling sobbed. Never before in his life's journey had Stirling allowed his emotions to overtake him. Peter Smith stood looking down at the two crumpled bodies sitting in the dusty gravel. Shame crept through his body. Never, ever would he push someone this hard again!

Chapter 46

Stirling needed space, he needed time. He needed to just drive. Peter Smith had reassured worried faces.

"Just let him go, he'll recalibrate in his own way."

Stirling had asked for a fresh hamper to be made up, which he loaded into his freshly washed E-Type. He had pulled on a fresh white polo shirt, a pair of crisp chinos, and his Bogatta driving shoes. Then, he pointed the nose of the Jaguar out of the hotel car park and drove.

His first day of driving had been troubled. Yes, he had been through a lot mentally, a true roller coaster ride. He realized that his life would never quite be the same again, because he had now experienced the vile underworld that surrounded everyone, every day. He had come to terms with the guilt he had felt over Sian, and then the elation of finding her still alive. Stirling had accepted that Peter Smith had used him and even accepted the fact that he had been kept in the dark whilst being used.

What troubled Stirling Speed so much was that he now realized that he had inside of him a terrible ability he never knew about. Stirling was appalled to find that lurking inside of his usually in-control body was the ability to kill another human being. He was in the process of killing Troutman when Sian had launched at him. He was not thinking about killing, or threatening to kill him, Stirling had already made the decision to kill him. Had that been what his whole career was built on? He drove faster, harder than anyone else, and was not bothered if other drivers were killed trying to match him. Was this inner killer instinct what made him different from the others? What made him the best? What made him a three-time world champion?

Stirling had refused explanations from Peter Smith. He needed space and had arranged to meet back in the UK in four days' time, so he decided to do what he did best and just go for a drive.

The first day's driving had ended sooner than Stirling had planned. Keeping off the auto routes, Stirling had found himself pulled up fueling his hungry Jaguar at a small petrol station in the middle of a picturesque French village, the name of which Stirling had not even registered. It had been a hot day's driving, and as the late afternoon threatened to turn into early evening, Stirling's eyes were full with the idyllic view of a number chaps playing boules in the village square. For the first time during the long day, Stirling's thoughts had strayed away from his painful worries. Whether it was the sleek lines of the E-Type or the fact that its refueling driver had been staring at them, he was not certain, but one of the boule-playing chaps had gestured for Stirling to go over and join them. Stirling eased the fed cat on to a dusty lay by next to the petrol station and switched off the silky 6 and pondered whether he should head down the road to look for a hotel or take break and join a game of boules. Pulling the clinking keys for the center of the machine finished dash Stirling opened the long door of the jag, carefully closed it with a clunk and wandered over to the laughing chaps that were about to start another game.

For a moment, Stirling forgot who he was. "Hi, never played, but I'm keen to learn if you have the inclination…"

All had now stopped talking and laughing and were staring at Stirling. It was the older chap who had originally gestured to Stirling who spoke first. "Ah, racing drivers make terrible boule players, but let's see what we can do."

For a brief moment, Stirling wondered how he knew that he was a racing driver but then came back into the moment. "You're probably right there, you know. We are only good at driving around in circles."

The older chap had a wonderful ability to smile with his eyes. He turned to his fellow players, muttered something in French, and all returned to their lighthearted banter.

The next hour of tuition and laughter blinked by as a beautiful warm evening developed.

"Are you staying for wine and cheese?"

Stirling looked up from yet another pitiful attempt to match his new mates at the man with the smiling eyes. "I would love to, but I really do need to find a hotel, so I must be pushing on."

The aging man smiled back. "No, no, please come with me."

He led Stirling out of the square, down the side of a house, and into a farmyard dominated by a dark wood barn. After pulling open the large barn doors, the duo walked through to the back of barn where, after opening another door, Stirling found a simple-but-clean little bedroom.

"Our, errm, how you say, 'part-time staff' stay here. Please, you stay here. I think you need it."

"Sorry?"

"Stirling, my gray hairs have seen many faces, and your face is a troubled face for a man who has had a charmed life."

Why Stirling chose to open up to this complete stranger was one of those questions with no answer. "I found something out about myself just recently, and it's pretty ugly."

The gray, smiling-eyed man closed his big barn doors and hesitated in his walk back to the village square. "Stirling, no matter what your beliefs are, we have all inherited sin somehow. We are all not perfect, even though I know you look at me and think otherwise."

Stirling smiled in reply. The man continued, "Stirling, a man is made up of good and bad, and some would say the ugly. We cannot get away from that fact. What you have to do is look at how much good and bad and ugly is in you. If you find that you have more good in you than bad or ugly, then build on the good and eventually the bad and ugly will be buried, hopefully forever. I am thinking that you are a good man, Stirling, so why don't you do some building on that?"

Stirling chose to say nothing verbally in reply but chose to reach and put his hand on the wise gent's shoulder and squeeze it. The gent replied and smiled with his eyes, "You are welcome, Mr. Speed, now let's get back into the village before all the wine and cheese is gone!"

The rest of the evening saw Stirling drink more than he had for many a year. There was much laughter, much chatter, even though not all who had gathered spoke English. And sadly, Stirling's French consisted of just four words: *oui, sorte, fromage,* and *froid,* the latter word be taught to him by a two-

and-half-years-old Anglo-French boy call Ilan. The randomness of happening to stop at this village, the good company, the gray-haired man's advice, and, perhaps, the wine produced a wonderful healing potion that helped Stirling to reset, recalibrate.

Stirling woke the next morning to the opening creak of the barn door, followed by the rattle of the latch to his small, wood-clad barn bedroom that he actually found quite cozy and restful. His kind boule-playing host appeared with a steaming mug of tea in one hand and a plate holding a slab of bacon sandwiches in the other.

After bidding his heartfelt goodbye, Stirling, now in a better place, gently warmed his E-Type. He knew that he'd be on a better road today and was looking forward to an altogether better driving day. Mentally, he had been battered around, but just like when he had battered his body in the past, it was a case of just allowing some time for the healing to take hold. He eased his Jaguar into first gear, looked through his bonnet-mounted chrome mirror, and pulled out of the lay-by onto the firm, smooth tarmac. It was time to run for the ferry and head back to the UK and a place called home.

Chapter 47

The recent months had seen the world's press ignite with the ferocity of an out of control bushfire. Lawrence Troutman had been removed from public life and the rumor mill spun out of control. The final rumor that had taken root was that Troutman was in court for huge financial irregularities, and the entire world watching was surprised how quickly the court hearing had been secured. When after the first two days of procedures it was established that Troutman—the family man, the charity man, the perfect husband—was being charged with counts of murder, the media rubbed their hands together in anticipation of the devouring about to take place.

Four days after the Nürburgring staged crash, Stirling had sat outside his favorite country pub in the idyllic village near Drayton House. A classic white Alfa Romeo GTA Junior, its boot loaded with a suitcase, its backseat loaded with another, sat in the car park. Stirling looked around the old wooden table and was pleased to see the faces of Peter Smith, Sian, and her mother, all together in the same place and all alive. Sian had put out on the table the letter from whom she thought had been her real mother and the picture of Suzanne, Roger, and young Stirling Speed.

Suzanne picked up the picture. "Who could have imagined what events and lives lay in front of us?"

Sian spoke next, "So, you did prove to be my shining David who slayed a Goliath."

Stirling smiled back, "Not sure about the shining bit, Sian, maybe a bit more of a dented and bashed-up David."

The table fell silent. All knew that they could only sit there together thanks to Peter Smith's organization and a good, large slice of luck.

Upon kidnapping Sian at Monte Carlo, Luna had, unusually, gone against Troutman's instructions to kill Sian immediately. They had instead contacted Peter Smith's organization, and over 24 hours of negotiations had taken place to hand over Sian. Luna demanded two things. 1. That Troutman would be brought down. They needed him off their books without the rest of the corrupt underworld knowing they had fed Troutman to Peter Smith. 2. They needed a cast-iron guarantee that no one would find out they had failed to kill Sian.

"Stirling, only four people in the world knew that Sian was still alive. We could take no chances. We had to keep it that way until we had Troutman. How I wanted to tell you all as you grieved. I so wanted to say that Sian was safe, but the risk was too high. Luna had the cards and I had to play their game. Stirling, we had to feed Troutman live bait to hook him. We could not risk spooking him or risk losing communication with Luna."

Peter Smith turned to look directly at Stirling. "The only thing that saved your life and that of Sian's was that you are a three-time world champion. Your high profile saved you. If you had been a 'joe bloggs nephew looking into his uncle's death, then Luna would have followed Troutman's instruction to the letter and you would be history. As soon as Sian had come into the scene, she too would have been sent the same way."

After an hour of intense explanations and questions, sitting outside in the gentle, cooling afternoon sun, the tense atmosphere had been broken by the sudden, erratic wafting actions of a bee on Peter Smith.

Sian's mother had taken charge of the situation, "Peter, sit still, then it will leave you alone."

Peter Smith had sat statue-like as his table guests laughed and watched the little yellow-and-black striped busy bee heading off to a more interesting and calmer flower.

Now, seven months later, Stirling sat with Peter Smith again, in a private room deep inside the huge sprawling court buildings. They were two weeks into the hearing and Troutman was thrashing around in the shallows, his astronomically expensive legal team ensuring that he was not about to be landed easily. Proceedings were not going well.

"I thought we had him, Peter, a slam dunk. He tried to kill me and admitted it."

"It's crazy. We never planned for Troutman getting in the car with you. We missed that possibility. If we had known, we could have switched the in-car camera on and recorded the confession. The idea was that our guys would have been standing behind him at the side of the track when he detonated the devices and we would have gotten him red-handed. Luna have handed us all the evidence about how it was done, but we need someone to actually link Troutman with the executions. We need someone totally trustworthy who has inside knowledge, inside solid evidence. His career and reputation are in tatters, and he is a ruined man, Victoria made sure of that, she buried him with her statement."

"Victoria?" Stirling questioned.

"Yes, the escort Troutman abused whilst he was in Monte Carlo. Because she came forward to testify, many others took courage to come forward and testify against him. Apparently, she had lobbied a good number of her colleagues to come forward and spill the beans on Troutman. I suppose she was working on the idea that she wanted to show the court, she wasn't just a one-off rogue spilling the beans. She wanted to demonstrate that this guy was out of control and needed stopping."

Stirling responded, "Strength in numbers, they say. I was disgusted the way Suzanne, Sian's mother, was treated under cross-examination. She was made out to be a liar who had fabricated her story."

"I know it was painful, but we needed to get her story out there. If we could have found a way of backing up her version of the account, I think that would have tipped the jury."

Stirling and Peter Smith fell silent. The room they sat in was dull, almost depressing, with high windows that did a good job of bringing daylight to the ceiling but left the rest of the room to rely on the power of electricity. Stirling checked his phone. Peter Smith's legal people had informed them that it looked like there was going to be a development, a late witness. But, they were in negotiations with the judge and defense team to get the witness to be allowed to testify.

"What will you do, Stirling, when all this is finished?"

Stirling looked up from his phone. "Oh, errm, well, actually, as crazy as it might seem, I have bought a big stupid American RV and a CCM Scrambles bike, and I am going traveling across Australia for two months. Just me, a steering wheel, and a toy! What more could a man ask for after that, well, errm…? I am not sure really, maybe my two-month drive about will give me the answer."

"Stirling, my organization can use someone like you. You can open doors, and you're a good guy, trust me, that's an unusual combination. Think about it."

"Peter, I know nothing about your strange organization."

"I'll take that as not a no, then? Trust me, if you work for me, then you'll know all you need to know, Stirling. Remember, there are a lot of wrongs in this world that need righting."

Stirling looked across the dark, scratched, aging surface of the table that separated them. "Let's leave it as a maybe then."

Silence fell again, and it was Stirling who eventually spoke next, "What will you do?"

Peter thought about listing all the cases he had on his desk at that moment in time but then decided to change tack. "I am off to Haraki, which is a small fishing village on the island of Rhodes, Greece. I made a deal with Victoria that I would arrange for her house and bar to be paid off and set up. I want to see that it is done, personally."

"Why the personal attention, Peter? I am sure you have minions to sort that for you."

"I do, you're right. But, you know, Stirling, there is a reason why I chose to join the organization I am now heading. When I met Victoria, I saw a young girl wronged, through no fault of her own, like the one that once devastated my life—a wrong that I could not put right. Victoria has finally got the break she has deserved, and that makes every troubled night's sleep, every moment of anguish, and every hard decision that I make worthwhile!"

Stirling felt guilty for stepping into Peter Smith's private thoughts and knew to ask no more.

The door of the small side room sprang open and a wig-wearing barrister bounded in. "We've got it, Mr. Smith, we have got the new witness' testimony accepted."

"And this is going to make the difference?" Stirling inquired.

"Yes, the witness can confirm Suzanne Speed's account and also has direct evidence linking Troutman to the murder of the journalist at his private test track."

An hour later, Peter Smith and Stirling sat in the gallery wide-eyed.

"I call, Your Honor, my next and final witness on behalf of the prosecution. Your Honor, we call Mrs. Kristianna Troutman."

The murmurings and barely muffled gasps caused the judge to take control. "Order, please. Order, please, ladies and gentleman."

The shine on Troutman's moist face could be seen from the gallery, a face that slowly followed the image of this serene lady as she climbed the three steps to the witness box. Troutman felt the hook take a hold deep inside his quivering mouth and felt the fight ebb out of him. In one last flash of movement, he stood up, the officers by his side grabbing at his flailing arms. He screamed and almost sobbed across the court at his beloved wife.

"Kristianna, why, why? Think of the family, Kristianna, why?"

Kristianna turned calmly, serenely to the judge, who broke protocol and nodded an okay for Kristianna to reply. She turned to the sweating, struggling animal she once loved with all her mind and body. The courtroom fell silent and time seemed to freeze as Kristianna Troutman spoke with such a steely resolve that the whole court seemed to want to almost bow in her presence.

"I am thinking of my family as my grandmother thought of her family. A family devastated by disgusting, selfish men like you."

Kristianna removed her eyes from the pleading eyes of Lawrence Troutman and turned to address the court, "I stand here for you all to hear the truth about this man."

She pointed accusingly to the now-crumpled being, "A man whose life is finished because of..." Kristianna turned her head to follow her pointing finger, "The broken trust!"